MONEY BRINGS DRAMA

Published by:
Street Entertainment Writing Etc.
P.O. Box 182
Bellflower, CA 90707
Telephone: (310) 920-7991
website:www.streetentertainmentwriting.com

Distributed by:
Milligan Books, Inc.
1425 W. Manchester Ave., Suite C
Los Angeles, California 90047
Website: www.milliganbooks.com
Telephone: (323) 750-3592

Cover Design: Kevin Allen
Formatting: Milligan Books

First Printing, October 2009
10987654321

ISBN 978-0-9842669-0-6

Publisher's Note:

MONEY BRINGS DRAMA

Christopher Buchanan

STREET ENTERTAINMENT WRITING ETC

BELLFLOWER, CALIFORNIA

DEDICATION

Over the past few months, several people that were close to me suffered from major illnesses and from death. To Bridgette, I hope you get well. I know your children really miss you. We all do, so get well soon!!!!

And to all my family and friends who passed away in 2008, I dedicate this novel to you. To Doris Buchanan, my grandmother, whose birth date I was born on. To my aunt Linda, who passed two days after my grandmother's funeral. To Trulie, my daughter's grandmother. And to Khary, known by everyone as Bro-Bro. You all will be missed by those of us who love you. So I take this time now to say, I thank God for putting such lovely people in my life, and it has been a pleasure knowing all of you. You all left a piece of your life within me. And that is something I will never forget. Thank you for being part of "my" life, and may God rest your souls.

—CHRISTOPHER BUCHANAN

ACKNOWLEDGMENTS

I was asked to do an acknowledgment page and realized it would take several weeks, if not months, to try and think of everyone who encouraged me to keep writing after they read my first book, *Street Poison*. To those friends and family members, and even the foes as well, I want to really thank you all for helping me to keep keeping on when I wanted to give up on life itself. The fear I harbored I didn't know how to deal with—until a good person told me there were two things I could do with FEAR. (1) Forget everything and run, or (2) face everything and regroup. Because of all the positive encouragement from my people, I chose (2). No names need to be mentioned, because you already know who you are. Thank you all, and may God bless you as He has done to me!!!!

One more special thanks—to God Himself. Thank you for removing that procrastination block off my shoulders and letting me tell stories again. Thanks for finally humbling me and removing my cravings, as well as my addiction I had to the streets. So many didn't make it out of those mean streets, so thank you, Lord, for lending me Your helping hand to give me that extra hard push that I needed to better myself as well as my life. Just when I thought everyone and everything abandoned me, You gave me the faith to live life again, and for that, I am eternally grateful.

Sincerely yours,
The Once-Infamous Christopher Buchanan

chapter
1

THE INFINITY Q45 ON 20-INCH AME rims rolled smoothly, going west on 120th Street heading towards Normandie Blvd. Both occupants were longtime friends and were in a heated debate.

"Why do you even deal with these niggas?" the passenger asked, upset and pissed off. The passenger's name was Ricky, but he preferred to be called by his gang name, which was Scrappy, or Scrap, for short. He was solidly built with wide shoulders and a broad chest. Muscled arms bulged from many days of weight lifting. His skin tone was caramel-colored, his eyes were piercing black, and his hair was cut in a fashionable fade style.

Scrappy could be just like a dog at times—mean and stubborn. He turned his gaze to look out the window.

"What the fuck you mean, why do I deal with these niggas?" the driver repeated harshly. He was staring at Scrappy and trying to keep his eyes on the road. "I'd be a damn fool to answer such a silly question since you can't tell me when, why, and who I should spend my money on."

The driver's name was C-Note. The "C," he said, stood for "cash." His features were almost the same as the passenger's.

C-Note was built with a solid, muscular body, too, but instead of coal-black eyes, his were chestnut brown. A half-moon part in his haircut separated his hairstyle from Scrappy's. When they were together, people were always asking if the two were brothers. Their resemblance, they both figured, probably came from their twenty-one years of friendship. Both were now twenty-seven.

They reached Normandie, and C-Note made a right, going north. "Don't you think it's about time you put that gang-banging shit behind and start thinkin' and focusin' on business?" C-Note asked tartly.

Scrappy shifted uneasily in his seat. Still looking out his window, he unconsciously reached in his pants pocket and brought out a pack of Newport cigarettes. As he pushed in the lighter, C-Note clarified boldly before the lighter could pop back out, "Nigga, ain't no smokin' in my new shit!" This seemed to anger Scrap even more, but he said nothing as he put the cigarette pack back into his pocket.

After a few moments, Scrap said, "You know, you've really changed."

C-Note's eyebrows slightly went up. Scrap was now staring at him while he talked. "Years ago, you wouldn't even talk to niggas from the other side, let alone deal wit'em. Now it's like you don't even care."

There was an awkward silence. Scrappy was searching C-Note's face intently. C-Note could feel his stare as if heat were radiating from the depths of Scrappy's eyes. He finally turned his head to let his gaze rest on his friend.

"To be honest, dawg, I don't care," Scrappy snorted in disgust. The light was red at the corner of Imperial and Normandie. "I'm too old to be thinkin' about that bullshit. I'm out here, unlike you, chasin' this cheddar cheese. Money is green, and like the white man, I don't give a fuck who it comes from."

The light turned green, and C-Note thought, *How ironic.* As he stepped on the accelerator, Scrappy looked with an expression of such hatred at his best friend, so displeased as he was. He said nothing though. But inside, he boiled as he sat, wondering how F.B. could do the 'hood like that. He had even changed his longtime nickname, which used to be Fat-Boy, to C-Note, Scrappy reflected. But since he wasn't fat anymore and his money was steadily growing, he had taken on a new persona. Scrappy promised himself right then and there that if he ever got some real money, he wouldn't change, nor would he ever stop bangin' the 'hood.

C-Note turned the car left when he made it to the place. He wheeled the car to the end of the block and parked two houses from the corner. Then he killed the motor and hopped out. His cousin and several of his cousin's buddies were hanging out in front of his cousin's house. Scrappy hesitated to get out, but C-Note waved him to come on with his hand.

C-Note's cousin was a Crip gang member, and his friends, too. But they knew where C-Note used to be from, and no disrespect was involved. Scrappy was wearing black jeans, a black and red Atlanta Falcon's jersey, a red Falcon's hat, and black and red Jordan sneakers.

"I hope these niggas don't trip," Scrappy said, closing the door.

C-Note smiled slyly. "Man, we here fa' business. These niggas ain't gonna trip." Scrappy shot him a sidelong glance as if to say, "Yeah, riiight!"

They walked up to the porch where C-Note's cousin and his friends were posted up.

"What up?" his cousin asked, sticking his hand out for dap.

C-Note pounded fist. "Too much of nothin'," he stated. "Just tryin' to get this cash."

Scrappy stood there saying nothing. "You remember Scrap?" C-Note asked his cousin, pointing his head at Scrap. C-Note's cousin smiled. "Yeah, I remember 'em. He stays on the same street as Grandma stays on, right?" C-Note's cousin stuck his hand out, and Scrap pounded it in the same fashion C-Note had.

C-Note's cousin, whose nickname was "Sneaky Snake," reached into the top pocket of his Maurice Malone shirt and produced a blunt. He lighted it and instantly began choking.

"That's the bomb, huh?" C-Note asked as he received the blunt. He pulled one good time and passed it to his best friend.

Scrappy pulled several times and began coughing as well. "Dat shit is the bomb," he said in between coughs.

"Now maybe you'll loosen," C-Note cracked jokingly.

A smile played across Scrappy's lips as the weed took its effect. Everyone sat around, chatting idly as they puffed the weed. C-Note watched Scrappy relax more and more as the blunt floated around. Then C-Note slipped into the house briefly and was back out before it was his turn to hit the blunt. After he hit it, he passed it back to his cousin.

"You can come by whenever and pick up those ends," C-Note said to Sneaky Snake.

Snake checked his gold Rolex watch. "I'll be by there in a few hours."

C-Note tapped Scrap on the arm. "Let's roll." They both headed to the Infinity and got in. It was ten minutes after five—*the best time to be transporting dope, while everyone was getting off work*, C-Note thought to himself smartly.

∘⟞⟝∘

THE DOOR WAS opened by two youngsters, Two-Down and Little Poke. C-Note and Scrappy crossed through the heavily barred door and headed right for the kitchen. The trip from Sneaky Snake's house was smooth, and they only encountered one LAPD patrol car on the way. Two-Down and Little Poke were gang members from C-Note's old 'hood when he was gang bangin' in his day. Even though the two youngsters were barely twenty-one, both had already been to the penitentiary and held their own. That was the main reason C-Note liked the two—because they were courageous and loyal. That's why he chose them to run one of his most profitable dope houses.

Inside, the house was dim and smoky from indo weed and Black & Mild smoke. "Damn! Open up some windows and doors and air this muthafucka out!" Scrappy said irritably, opening the back door. "You can't even see in here. It's like a goddamn dungeon."

C-Note pondered his words briefly as Two-Down and Little Poke began to do his bidding. C-Note stared blindly at the two, his anger mounting. "Fuck, what he's talkin' about?" C-Note barked, and the two youngsters stopped and looked at C-Note questioningly. Scrappy shifted his eyes to C-Note's contorted face. "Whose dope spot is this?" C-Note asked heatedly, locking eyes with Scrappy.

"He ain't runnin' shit but his mouth! Close the place back up like it was," C-Note ordered.

The two youngsters quickly did as they were told, snickering openly as they went along closing the windows and the door Scrappy had opened. Scrappy tried his best to appear unruffled, but he was seething inside.

C-Note had had a special harness made that was similar to a shoulder harness for a gun. But this harness was used for storing dope. It had a pouch with a zipper and could hold up to a kilo of cocaine. C-Note wore the harness under a jacket or shirt so that if he were ever stopped by the police, he could break and run without worrying about the dope falling off him. Plus, the harness made it easy to stash once he got away from the police in case he had to run. Now C-Note pulled the dope out of the harness, and Scrappy's face first registered surprise, then shock.

"F.B., I just know you didn't have me ridin' around wit' all that shit in the car."

C-Note ignored his words. "Two-Down, look out for me and bring that scale outta the room."

Two-Down disappeared into one of the back rooms and came back with a Triple-Beam Scale in hand. He placed the scale on a wooden table in front of C-Note. The house was bare except for two sofas in the living room, a 27-inch color TV with a PlayStation 2, and a chipped cable box. A bucket of acid sat next to the door in case the law tried to make a quick entry. The kitchen had a stove and icebox, three chairs and the wooden table. The cabinet was empty except for the paraphernalia to cook dope: a glass 1,000 ml beaker, several boxes of fresh Arm&Hammer Baking Soda, a pot to boil water, and Ziploc baggies in various sizes.

C-Note went to a drawer that was used for silverware and took out a single-edged razor blade, knife, and spoon. Little Poke went to the cabinet and got out the gallon-sized

Ziplocs. Skillfully, C-Note cut the wrapper off the brick-sized kilo on the table. Two-Down was filling the pot up with water, while Scrappy stared at the dope on the table in amazement.

Little Poke spoke. "Can I cook up a few ounces to see if I can bring back the few extra grams like you were showin' us the last time you were teachin' us how to cook?"

C-Note thought for a minute. He could see the contempt in Scrappy's eyes. The two youngsters didn't see it, or didn't care one way or the other.

"You might as well let us try."

Two-Down added, "'Cause it'll save you time and let us make more money."

C-Note gave it a great deal of thought, then said, "I guess you two are right. Plus, it's about time y'all got a bonus."

Scrappy shifted uncomfortably from foot to foot. C-Note knew he was furious inside and wanted the tension out in the open.

"What's eatin' at you, Scrap?" C-Note looked him square in the eyes. Scrap averted his eyes before speaking. "Nigga, we been in cahoots way before they were from the 'hood."

Scrappy shook his head sadly. "Damn near probably before they were even born," he added for emphasis.

C-Note wasn't surprised to discover how Scrap had felt about him. The two youngsters just watched the small confrontation quietly. C-Note decided on the course of action needed to minimize the fuss. His hands were powdery white, and he was now putting chunks of the lumpy block on the scale. "It ain't like I didn't try an' show you the game," C-Note said, rubbing his hands together. He looked up from the scale. Scrappy's facial expression was a mixture of hurt and anger. C-Note rolled on.

"Scrap, you was the one who said you didn't have time to learn the game. All I was doin' was trying to put extra funds in your pocket."

This was something Scrappy didn't wanna hear it. "Fuck it!" he said grudgingly, waving a hand in the air. C-Note hunched his shoulder. *Fuck it*, he thought as well.

Two-Down grabbed the beaker and scooped the dope off the scale into it. Scrappy stomped out of the kitchen into the living room and began to play the PlayStation. C-Note mused to himself over how silly Scrappy was acting as he took a seat and watched the youngsters take turns as they cooked up the poison over the stove.

It was well past midnight by the time Two-Down and Little Poke had finished cooking the dope. Their spot had been jumping with clientele, but shop had been closed while business was being conducted. Scrappy snored loudly as he lay stretched across one of the sofas. C-Note had been watching *The Jerry Springer Show* until it went off and then began playing the video games the youngsters had hooked to the TV. It was late, and he had phoned his girlfriend to let her know he'd be on his way home soon.

Little Poke and Two-Down were in the kitchen chatting animatedly about how much extra money they would make in the next few days and what "broads," as they called them, would be gettin' hit when they rolled up on them in brand-new gold Daytons on their cars. C-Note stood and stretched like a cat. He woke Scrappy, than called the two youngsters in the living room. Scrappy was rubbing his eyes, trying to fully wake up.

"Wrap up half that bird and put it up for me. I'll come by an' pick it up tomorrow." C-Note turned off the TV and then asked, "How many extras did y'all get over?"

Two-Down's face lit up as Little Poke did the speaking. "A little over seven ounces."

C-Note saw Scrappy's head jerk up. Two-Down said, "Since it's all your work, we was hopin' to split the extras three ways." C-Note grinned ear to ear. The two were keeping it honest all the way.

"Just give me an ounce and split the rest between you two. Plus, each of you keep a quarter key apiece, as usual."

Scrappy was smokin' worse than a tailpipe on a car with a bad exhaust system. His anger spread from his eyes to his face. "I ain't sat here all night for nothin,'" Scrap steamed. "Why the hell can't I get my work tonight like them?"

C-Note didn't want the problem to be blown up and decided to nip it in the bud. "Listen, Scrap," he began smoothly, "it's way past midnight, and my car is too flashy to be ridin' around wit' dope this late."

Scrappy's face was set in lines of hard determination. "This is pure bullshit! Pure bullshit!" Scrappy tried his best to exploit the situation. He was the hardhead type, and C-Note didn't want things to get in a chaotic uproar.

"Tell you what," C-Note said, "we can ride dirty, but if we're stopped, the case is yours."

Scrappy took a second to absorb this. And C-Note gave him a warm, but devious smile. The youngsters again looked on quietly. Scrappy was in a curious position, his mind racing as he tried to decide what course he should take. Scrappy felt he'd be considered a punk if he didn't take the work and a punk if he did take the work. C-Note had left him in a no-win situation. At the same time, C-Note also felt bad about talking and treating his best friend this way. C-Note figured he'd change tactics, letting Scrappy feel he was getting the upper hand.

"It's my bad," C-Note said. "I just thought you were goin' home an' it's so late that you could wait until tomorrow. I don't want you hot at me 'cause you think I want you to miss out on some money.

"Two-Down, break my half down an' slide Scrap nine of those Zips."

Two-Down headed for the kitchen without a word. Now there was conflict on Scrappy's face. He suffered from a moment of doubt. "I was goin' home," Scrappy said feebly. "It wouldn't make sense to ride dirty this late, huh?"

C-Note shrugged his shoulders nonchalantly. "Hey, that's up to you, Scrap. I don't see why you can't come by early in the mornin' an' pick it up when everybody's on their way to work. Your chances are better then."

Scrappy smiled an expression of embarrassment. "Hey, Two-Down, don't trip! I'll come by in the mornin' an' pick that shit up."

Two-Down reappeared from the kitchen, smiling. Little Poke and Two-Down exchanged a knowing glance. C-Note and Scrap walked to the door. "I'll have Low-Bone come by as well to pick up the last nine," C-Note said as he and Scrap stepped into the fresh night air. They both walked to the car saying nothing. Two-Down was about to close the other door. "That extra zone left," C-Note yelled over the roof of the car, "give it to Scrap when he comes in the morning."

They got in the car and drove home, the best of friends again.

THE SUN CLIMBED in the sky and peeked through the blinds in C-Note's room. His mental alarm clock told him he had slept longer than usual, and his eyes shot right to the clock. It was a little past nine and the aroma of breakfast wafted throughout the house and filled his nostrils. He sat up in bed, clicked on the TV with the remote just as his girlfriend, Sheila, was coming through the bedroom door with a plate of food in hand. She handed him the plate.

"I hope it's enough," she started, "because Christian ate enough for all three of us combined." Christian was C-Note's four-year-old son, his heart and joy, and one of the main reasons why he was in the dope game. He wanted to give his son everything he never had, including a father that was there. C-Note told himself, just six more months the way things had been going and he was through—set for life—if he invested the money right. Sheila smiled a great deal, and C-Note loved her almost as much as his son.

"Did the little tyke get enough?" he asked, surveying the plate in his hand. The potatoes were piled high, and the eggs were scrambled just the way he like them. Butter dripped off the raisin bread, and a spoonful of jelly sat on top.

Sheila's face filled with pride and pleasure as she spoke about her son. "He's had enough 'cause I said so. I don't want no fat-ass son who wobbles when he walks by the time he's six."

At first, he gazed at her uncomprehendingly. He didn't feel combative, so he said, "I guess you're right. Just make damn sure he's not undernourished. He's a growin' kid, ya' know."

She playfully hit him on his arm that now held a fork. "Just eat your food, smart-ass." She stood there with a hand on her hip. "What would you like to drink? Orange juice or grape juice?"

C-Note pondered the question for a second. "Half-and-half. Mix 'em, please."

"Ughh," she said as she disappeared from the room and down the stairs. While he ate, he thought of the spectacular figure Sheila had, with a combination of beauty and sex appeal as well. They'd been together for six years and both knew each other like a book. C-Note's plan was to marry her, but he wanted to be out of the game before then.

First, he wanted a deeper commitment with her. But he also didn't want to put her through the many changes the game brought.

Sheila came through the door with glass in hand. Christian was on her heels. She handed C-Note the filled glass. "He asked if you were up when he saw me comin' upstairs with the glass."

Christian's eyes sparkled, and his lips curled into a smile when he saw his daddy sitting up in bed.

"Hey, little daddy," C-Note said as Christian climbed on the bed and tried diving in his lap. It all happened too quickly and unexpectedly. Food went flying over the bed and floor. And the juice spilled on C-Note and the mattress.

"Aww, shhhit—" C-Note caught himself instantly. Christian's smile turned to fear, his eyes big as saucers.

"Christian!" Sheila shrilled.

C-Note saw his son's fear and quickly grabbed him. "It's alright, little daddy," C-Note said while showering him with kisses. Then C-Note wrestled around with him, tickling and playing with his pride and joy while Sheila picked up food from off the bed and the floor.

"See, little man, that's what we got the mama for," he said jokingly, as he picked up a piece of potato and tossed it in his mouth. Sheila shot him a humorless smile. C-Note climbed out of bed, bringing Christian with him. "I guess your daddy is gonna have to eat cereal."

At the mention of cereal, Christian's eyes again sparkled. He hadn't mastered the sounds of certain words yet. Instead of "cer," he said "ther." "I want th-ome ther-eal, too."

Sheila's voice spoke with authority. "Boy, you just ate eggs and potatoes. You don't need no more to eat."

Christian stuck his lips out pouting.

"You heard what your mama said," C-Note said complacently as they moved to the stairs. "No more to eat." Halfway down the stairs and out of earshot, C-Note whispered in his son's ear, "She said you can't have no cereal, but you can help your daddy eat his cereal, can't you?"

⊙═⋖⊢

THE DAY BREEZED by like the wind from the Pacific Ocean. C-Note had taken his family shopping at Nordstrom, Foot Locker, Macy's, and Robinsons May, Toys 'R' Us, Kay-Bee toy store, and Kid's Foot Locker. Once they finished shopping, they stopped for a bite to eat at a Red Robin Restaurant. And from there, they went to see an animated movie by Walt Disney. The day had been perfect, and C-Note felt exuberant. It gave him great satisfaction spending time with his family. Christian had run around and played all day, and now, he was sound asleep. The night was Sheila's and his.

Alone, both had undressed. C-Note sipped on Cognac Sheila had bought earlier that day as he lay in bed watching her pin up her hair. In the mirror, her reflection threw him a lascivious wink. Her look made his loins stir as he looked on her naked body. Sheila had filled out while she had been pregnant, making her sexier than ever. A look of fondness came over his face. Sheila grinned knowingly.

"Why're you lookin' like that?" she asked, still watching him through the mirror.

His throat went dry as he stared at her voluptuous café-au-lait skin. He swallowed dryly. "After all these years, I find you sexier now than I did when I first met you."

She had a faint smile of pride on her face. "Nigga, that's the alcohol talking."

An injured look came over his face, so she quickly said jokingly, "You still ain't gettin' none." She tilted her head to one side, grinning.

"You can make excuses if you want, but I speak the truth. You are finer now." C-Note quenched his dry throat with the remains of the cognac in his glass, his head slightly spinning.

Sheila was astonished at his sudden display of tenderness. "Boy, you really need to stop drinkin', 'cause you damn sure can't lie worth shit."

C-Note nodded dumbly. "Fuck it, then!" he slurred, his black eyebrows drawing together. "If I'm accused of being a liar because to me you look better than you did in the past, then I need not say any more, 'cause if I do, then this will surely turn into an argument."

She gazed back at him wide-eyed. The alcohol warmed his body, and C-Note was ready now for a challenge. He straightened up, placing the empty glass next to the bed. She knew he was becoming drunker by the second, and she waited in anxious silence for him to begin his charades.

C-Note's expression toughened. "Sheila, just answer me one question, would you?" She held a silent expression. "Did you, or did you not notice how many men in the mall turn their heads to take a double look at you?"

The question threw her. She'd been aware of the men, and some women, too, who had been checking her out. Quickly, she collected her thoughts. "And? What's that got to do wit' it?"

C-Note sighed, shaking his head. "Sometimes, I think you make me out to be crazy, when all actuality, you're the one who's Koo-Koo for Coco Pops."

She couldn't resist the temptation to laugh. She had never met a man that she loved more. She climbed into bed. "I love you," she said, grabbing between his legs. "And I love hearin' your compliments to me." She reached over, placing her lips on his. Her tongue played around in his mouth, and C-Note became more excited. He gently laid her back on the pillow and flicked her nipples with his thumbs and forefingers of each hand. Her breasts were firm and rounded. C-Note leaned forward to kiss them, sucking her taut nipples in his mouth. Sheila moaned in pleasure. He moved down to her flat belly, licking her, sucking her, working her into a frenzy when his tongue touched her soft spot. She thrilled to the touch of his body, and he made love to her slowly until she gasped with pleasure from orgasm after orgasm. Afterwards, they lay in bed talking for hours until they both fell asleep in each other's arms.

THE PERSISTENT RINGING of the phone woke C-Note out of his deep sleep. It was his own private phone, used specifically for business, and Sheila wasn't allowed to answer it. She rolled over and put a pillow over her head, hoping to block out the persistent ringing noise.

"Answer that damn phone," she grumbled grouchily. Naked, he got out of the bed and lumbered to the dresser where the phone was. He admired his toned body in the dresser mirror as he picked up the phone.

"Hello."

It was Two-Down. "What's up, C-Note?"

C-Note's voice was clogged with sleep. "Fuck the formalities, Two-Down. What the hell you callin' me so early for?"

Two-Down knew C-Note had a fearsome temper and rushed on. "Sorry. There's a car parked down the street from the spot, and whoever it is, is watchin' the house with binoculars."

C-Note's anger evaporated. "You saw 'em watchin' the spot yourself?" C-Note asked.

Two-Down hesitated slightly. "No, but a loyal puff head client did. The smoker said he was comin' to the spot and walked right past a guy in a car lookin' through binoculars aimed toward the house. He was on his way here anyway."

C-Note always took the long view of things. "Did you clean out the place?" he asked as he sat on the edge of the bed, thinking.

"Didn't have to," Two-Down said. "We been dumpin' it, and Little Poke only got a few grams left."

C-Note thought for a second. "Did Scrap and Low-Bone come pick up that other thang?"

Again, Two-Down hesitated. "Low-Bone didn't come, but Scrap did. He said you said to just give it all to him."

C-Note was becoming teed off again, and Two-Down must've sensed it.

"He used your name, sayin' you said it was all good."

It was like Scrappy to think he was being clever. Lately, he'd been asking C-Note to front him more work for the spot he was working, claiming business was picking up. It was C-Note's dope house Scrappy was working, and C-Note knew how much money flowed through the spot and how much dope was being sold.

C-Note focused his thoughts on the present situation. "Did you get a look at the car the person was in?"

Two-Down was more than happy to change the subject. He was feeling he had done something wrong by giving Scrappy Low-Bone's share of the work. "Yeah." He quickly added, "It was a four-door Oldsmobile. I think a Cutlass Ciera."

C-Note was quiet briefly, thinking. After a few moments, he asked, "You ain't served nobody y'all didn't know, have you?"

"Not at all," Two-Down countered. "But that still don't mean one of the people we did serve didn't get busted and snitched." Two-Down had a good point. That's how the sheriff and other law agencies were doing it now, making the dope fiend tell.

"Once y'all get off those last few grams," C-Note continued, "close up shop until I give further notice. And don't even hang around the place. We gonna let the spot cool off for a while." C-Note hung up. He sat there on the edge of the bed wondering if his new spot had already become hot after only three weeks. If it had, then he'd just have to find another one.

That was the easy part, he reflected, finding a new dope spot. Where there's smoke, there's fire. And where there's dope, there's smokers. And where there's smokers, there's money. And money was C-Note's name, and where the money was, C-Note was, trying to fulfill his golden dreams.

Since he was up, C-Note decided to get an early start. A feeble sun was out, and the sky was clouded. He had a wary look on his face as the blood pounded his head. He could hardly distinguish what was going on with the spot and this new information about Scrappy. Scrappy was first priority, he told himself, since Scrappy had lied and tricked Little Poke and Two-Down out of the work for Low-Bone.

C-Note took a shower, shaved his head and face, and got dressed. He went down the stairs on cat's feet, trying not to wake Sheila, entered the kitchen, grabbed an orange and the last slice of honeydew melon, and headed for the door. Just as he was turning the doorknob, Sheila appeared on the bottom of the stairwell, tying her robe together.

"Trying to sneak off, aye?"

C-Note gave her a weak grin, then took a bite of the green melon. Sheila walked the short distance to him and kissed his sweet lips. He swallowed the melon. "Important call. So now I got to go holler at this nigga, Scrappy."

Sheila's face changed at the mention of Scrappy's name, C-Note observed. He studied her face, trying to read her mind. She had a faraway look in her eyes. "Be careful," she said, wrapping her arms around his waist, looking in his eyes. "There's something about that nigga I just don't trust." She paused a moment to let her thoughts sink in.

"You do remember how he tried to dirty mack you when he was tryin' to get at me on the under?"

The scene was still vivid in his mind. When C-Note had first met Sheila, C-Note had taken Scrappy with him to her apartment in Hawthorne. A few days after that, Scrappy had claimed that he had been in the vicinity visiting a friend of his and had accidentally left his car headlights on. Scrappy had asked her if he could use her phone to call for help, and since she had just met him through her new boyfriend, C-Note, she figured it was okay to let him in.

Scrappy had faked the call, and she had allowed him to wait until his help came because she knew he was a gang member and because he was C-Note's friend. She didn't want him to get hurt or shot up by members of a rival gang. It was then Scrappy secretly confided to her that she, Sheila, ought not to be fuckin' with a nigga like C-Note. Sheila was somewhat shaken by Scrappy's boldness and didn't say much out of fear that she might anger him. Scrappy had showed no love toward his best friend. Instead, he told her about all the women C-Note had all over town and how he was a coldhearted womanizer. Then he told her that he, Scrappy, was the man and C-Note worked for him.

Sheila had been unprepared for such news and decided not to say anything to C-Note at that time. She finally became alarmed when Scrappy had been sitting in her living room for over an hour and no sign of his ride had showed. She knew he wouldn't take rejection with good grace, plus, he seemed dangerous and unpredictable. Using her smarts, she quickly said, "I have to take my mother to an appointment, and I'm already late." She had said this, hoping she didn't sound too nervous. She hurriedly scribbled a fake home number and a pager number, and then shoved it into his hand.

"You can call me tomorrow," she said gathering her purse. "Or later tonight, that is, if you're not too busy." Then she walked him to the door, opened it, and left the house with him, leaving him with no time to think. She knew her voice sounded vulnerable and thin. "I do hope you call," she added as she went through the door to the garage, leaving him standing there in front of her apartment building. Sheila stayed away for hours, making sure he still wasn't lurking around.

C-Note came out of his reverie. "I will, big butt," he said pinching her buttocks with the orange in hand. "I grew up with Scrappy, and he's all bark. At least, to me, he is." C-Note kissed Sheila again. "You know how we men can be when women get involved. Ya dick can make you do some strange shit."

She gave him a sly look. "Yeah, I know," she retorted.

C-Note whispered a few endearing last words in her ear and then quickly left.

⚬═╤╾

C-Note pulled the car in Low-Bone's driveway. Just as he was opening his door to get out, Low-Bone stepped out of the house and made a beeline right to C-Note's car. Low-Bone was 5'8 and 175 pounds. His face was hard and lined from life on the hard streets. He had clear, eagle eyes that caught everything, and hands rough like asphalt. His thick lips broke into a smile.

"What's up, F.B.?" Low-Bone, too, had grown up with C-Note from the early days and was one of the last remaining of their generation who wasn't dead or locked up. He still called his friend F.B. instead of C-Note. Low-Bone walked to the other side of the car and got in.

"What's crackin', Low-Bone?" C-Note asked as they pounded fists. Low-Bone was about to light a Newport cigarette, but C-Note stopped him.

He looked at C-Note, still smiling. "I don't blame ya. These things'll kill ya dead befo' these triflin'-ass niggas will."

C-Note smiled back, thinking about the task at hand. "Why didn't you go by the spot earlier and pick up that medicine I had for you?"

Low-Bone looked at C-Note, puzzled. "Scrappy said you were gonna take care of me on the next go-round. He said you were runnin' short."

C-Note muttered a curse. Low-Bone was watching him closely.

"Why? Is there something wrong?"

C-Note thought it best not to say anything. He shook his head in the negative. "Naw, nothin's wrong," he said meekly. "But, it's gonna be later on today, or in the morning, before I have something else ready for you."

Now it was Low-Bone's turn to mutter a curse. "That's cool," he said after a minute. "I guess I'll just have to make those fools wait. I got their money anyway, so really, they ain't got no choice." Low-Bone opened the door.

"Soon as I get it crackin', I'll call you," C-Note said. "Jus' make sure you pick it up this time." They pounded fists one more time, and Low-Bone got out of the car.

C-Note backed the car out of the driveway, grim-faced, on his way to his and Scrappy's dope spot. He parked the car at the curb and got out. The grass in front of the house had been dead for a long time from the trample of feet constantly walking over it. The house was brick and barred. Looks just like a dope house, C-Note thought. A sheriff's car rolled by slowly, looking at C-Note as he walked to the door.

C-Note hoped they wouldn't stop and harass him. He had a key, but knocked roughly on the barred door instead, thinking maybe the sheriff would think of him as a visitor. Certainly he didn't look like a dope dealer or a smoker. He banged again on the door, this time harder. He waited in anxious silence. Finally, after a couple of moments, the locks could be heard turning.

Scrappy opened the door still sleepy-eyed and with stinking breath. "What's happenin'?" he said as C-Note stepped in the house past him. A quick glance over his shoulder showed that the same sheriff's car had turned around and was cruising slowly back by. Scrappy closed the door, locking it. He was astonished to see C-Note so early.

"What time is it?" Scrappy asked dryly, his voice cracking.

The house was semidark. C-Note held his watch up for elaborate scrutiny. "Few minutes til nine," he answered sternly. "Why the hell you got it so dark?"

He went to the windows and began to open the blinds while Scrap watched. Across the room, C-Note could make out a figure sleeping on the couch, a blanket covering the head. A pair of women's shoes sat next to the couch. Scrappy, following C-Note's eyes, quickly said, "That's my friend. She spent the night."

C-Note's tone was a little abrupt. "This ain't no fuckin' motel. It's a dope house."

Scrappy looked at him with an expression of hatred, but C-Note ignored his look. "You want to fuck? Take it somewhere else, because this house here is strictly for dope sellin'!"

Scrappy gave him a hostile stare. "Come to the back room and talk to me," Scrappy said hotly, heading through a door that led to the hallway and to the back room. C-Note followed him. Scrappy looked hurt, angry, and baffled, all in one. When they reached the back room, Scrappy went to the closet, still silent for a brief moment. In those seconds, C-Note's thoughts went wild. *What if he shoots me? What if he stabs me? What if he kills me?*

Scrappy came out of the closet with a brown paper bag and tossed it to C-Note. "It's gotta be the only reason you're here this early," he said with a sneer. "Other than that, I don't know what you're here for."

C-Note opened the bag.

"That's the money for everything I got from those little punks that you call workers," Scrappy added scornfully.

C-Note's brow furrowed in thought. He looked troubled but did not comment. His head buzzed with questions. *Why was Scrappy acting so spiteful? Why did he have so much animosity? Why had he called the young homies "punks"? Why?* That was the question bothering him.

C-Note began to count the money in the paper bag.

"It's all there," Scrappy snapped, then walked out of the room back into the living room. C-Note stayed, counting the money on top of the bed that was in the room. When he was done, he padded back into the living room. Scrappy was sitting on a smaller couch, across from where the female lay. C-Note's penetrating eyes met Scrappy's, and they locked stares.

After several seconds, C-Note spoke as he held the bag of loot. "This is only *half* of what I came for. The other half is that I came to talk. To get some questions answered."

The woman on the couch stirred, grumbled, and turned over. Her tangled hair fell from under the blanket. C-Note gave a quick mystified look. Had he seen the person under the blanket before?

Scrappy stood up, walking to the back room. C-Note stood, tried to steal another quick peek, then followed Scrappy. He just wanted to get this whole thing over with a minimum of fuss. Plus, he was in no mood to be argued with.

Once in the room, Scrappy turned to examine him with a cold, clear gaze. C-Note met his gaze with a devilish grin of his own. "You can pretend to be hard, but you're soft as Jell-O, nigga! I know you, grew up with you." His eyes never left Scrappy's. Scrappy laughed aloud, trying to hide the fact that he didn't know whether C-Note was serious or whether he was joking. It took him a moment to regain his composure.

"I want you to keep believing that, F.B.," he said, smiling wolfishly. "As long as your thinkin' is fucked-up like that, I have almost nothin' to worry about then."

C-Note knew he would have to use stronger measures. "Check this out. This is the deal of a lifetime, and I brought you along for the ride. I won't let this opportunity slip through my fingers. And I won't allow you, or anybody else, to fuck up what I got goin'." He paused to let his words hit home. "So if you ain't rollin' until the wheels fall off, then I suggest strongly you do your own thang, in your own spot, with your own shit! My program is too smooth to get too bumpy all of a sudden."

Scrappy said nothing, his face now expressionless.

"Because to have a problem means to eliminate a problem," C-Note said as an afterthought.

Scrappy's face looked blank for a moment, then it cleared as his greed outweighed his wisdom. "I suppose you're right," he said flatly. "It is yo' shit, you're right. But it won't be for too long."

C-Note frowned. "And what the fuck is that suppose to mean?"

Scrappy smiled deviously but didn't answer. He hunched his shoulders. "Take it how you wanna take it." He started for the door, but C-Note cut off his path, causing him to halt.

"I'm deliberately ignoring your rudeness, dawg. But if there's a conflict of interest, then I suggest we put it out in the open, for both our benefits, so no one gets the wrong impression, and so no one gets hurt."

Scrappy stood silently, watching C-Note's face. His black eyes looked deep and cold. C-Note wanted to take him by the neck and strangle him, but he knew it wouldn't be that easy. Desperately, C-Note searched for something to say. He figured Scrappy was just testing the water, trying to find the right buttons to push. But in all actuality, C-Note knew the rules of the game. And like the great naturalist said, "It is to seek one's own pleasures, no matter at whose expense."

Scrappy stood there, helpless with frustration.

"Now about this shit you told Two-Down and Little Poke about me sayin' to give you Low-Bone's work," C-Note said tonelessly, "what the fuck is up with that?"

Scrappy tried to stay outwardly cool, but his tone was guilty.

"I told'em I would take it to Low-Bone since he didn't come get it. While on my way to the spot, I got a call from Do-Wrong, saying he needed a quarter of a key. Since I already had it on me and I saw a way to make some extra money, I hooked him up. I went on and sold it to him."

C-Note's eyes went cold. "You know we don't deal wit' scandalous-ass Do-Wrong ever since he gave Two-Down those counterfeit hundreds and didn't wanna reimburse for the dummy cash."

The spitefulness in Scrappy's eyes flashed. "That was on Two-Down for bein' so gullible," he spit out.

Iciness ran through C-Note's blood. "I'll let that comment ride." Then he said, "Just don't let your cutthroat maneuvers get yo' ass in a sling."

Scrappy gave him a dirty look, which C-Note ignored. Then C-Note turned and left the room as a maniacal rage formed in his face. He reached the barred door, where he came through earlier, clenching his jaws, trying to bite back the rage he felt. "'Cause the next time you play wit' my cheese, as you've already done, it won't be taken so nicely." He opened the door. "So if you wanna chance your life, go on ahead and test my words. See if they're real or not." Then C-Note walked out the door into the crisp morning air.

Scrappy stood in the doorjamb with an ugly grin on his face. "Yeah, whatever," he smirked, not hiding the sarcasm in his words.

C-Note paused, and then decided to keep walking. He knew one day that he'd put Scrappy to the test to really see where his heart was at, and to see how tough he really was.

C-Note couldn't think properly and found himself in a distracted mood. The morning was still early, and he figured he might as well check on another of his dope spots not too far from where Scrappy's spot was. In the back of his mind, he'd been flirting with the possibility of doing something drastic to Scrappy. The thought crashed against his head like waves on rocks, then he had to check himself for his heinous thinking. He was debating himself and felt a moment's unease. He knew in his mind that to let someone get close to you, you were giving them the power to betray, wound, and irritate you.

His mind quickly altered as he turned onto a quiet residential street in a middle-class neighborhood. All the houses were old, but kept up, and most had been remodeled. C-Note pulled to the curb and parked in front of one of the remodeled houses. It was on the right-hand side of the street and at the east end of the block. The house he parked in front of was two-story and freshly stuccoed. The old, rectangle windows had been changed to a new modern style, and the trimming around the house was newly painted. In the driveway sat a fairly new Cadillac STS four-door Seville.

C-Note opened his car door and got out. On his way to the door, he was admiring the well-groomed lawn and the exotic flowers in their beds. He rang the doorbell once and glanced down the street to the other end of the block while he waited. He noticed several cars parked in front of the dope house at the end of the block.

The door opened. "What're you doin' on this side of town this early in the morning?" said the voice behind the white security door. Next, he heard the locks opening, then finally the door opened. Honey Bee was in a black silk robe. She stepped to the side, indicating for him to enter.

"I just came to see how things are going on your side of town," he said as he walked past her into the living room. She shut the door behind him.

"Things couldn't be better," she said, picking up a remote for the TV and turning down the volume. "Our spot at the end of the block is rollin'. But the neighbors are startin' to complain about the traffic." Honey Bee was in her late forties and had the body of a twenty-five year old. Her honey complexion accentuated her hazel eyes. She wore her brown hair in a ponytail on the days she didn't have it done at the beauty parlor. Her hands and toes were painted red. C-Note watched her as she glided into the kitchen.

"You hungry?" she asked. "I'm baking blueberry muffins."

The smell of the muffins hung thick in the air, making his belly grumble.

"Don't mind if I do," he said, sounding like a cowboy.

"Would you like coffee, milk, or juice?" she asked with the sound of dishes rattling.

"Milk," he said offhandedly.

Moments later, she appeared with a plate in one hand, glass in the other. She handed him the plate and set the milk on a table next to the sofa he sat on. Then she disappeared back into the kitchen and came right back out with another plate bearing another muffin and a mug filled with hot coffee. Lowering herself into an easy chair, she sat just a few feet away from C-Note with her legs crossed. The split in her robe revealed a tan thigh, and C-Note couldn't help but stare at it.

Honey Bee smiled seductively. "How long you think the house down the street will last?" she asked, trying to take C-Note's mind off her thigh. Although he looked, she knew he wouldn't touch. She had tried several times in the past. He always chose to keep it all business and no pleasure, because he had already had a woman. In her mind, though, she knew it was just a matter of time.

C-Note swallowed his first bite of muffin. "Ain't no telling how long it'll last," he said finally. "This neighborhood does have neighborhood watch, right?"

Honey Bee nodded her head up and down. He picked up the milk and took a light swallow. "Then I don't think it will last too long."

Honey Bee set her plate down and picked up her mug, sipped quietly, and set it back on the tray she had next to her chair. She seemed to be thinking. Then she said, "I just hope those young boys can hold water if the shit hits the fan." She stared at C-Note questioningly.

"Young boys?" C-Note said stiffly. "Them niggas is a few years younger than I am. I told them the consequences beforehand, and they made their own choice. Plus, I don't plan on keepin' the spot until it gets raided. I'm goin' to switch it once it gets too hot."

Honey Bee smiled slyly. "I guess you know what you're doin'," she said rigidly. "They started with an ounce a day. Now they're up to three."

C-Note didn't comment. He just continued to eat his muffin. He knew his boys would hold their water if it came down to it. Would Honey Bee? He finished his muffin and milk. Honey Bee took his dishes back to the kitchen. If everything went according to plan, then he should be alright. All Honey Bee did was watch the spot down the street.

When Rock Bottom and Black (the two boys working the spot) were either through or low on work, Honey Bee would meet up with the two at a meeting spot, collect the money, and restock them with more dope for the spot. It was a simple task and everybody was making money.

She was back from the kitchen, sitting again in her chair. "So how's life at home?" she asked, showing that shapely thigh again.

C-Note smiled. He knew she wasn't the type to give up so easy. She was a good-natured nuisance. "All right," he replied. "Why do you ask?"

She threw him a lewd smile. "Just checkin' to see if you're ready for a mature woman." She was trying to weaken his resolve. She uncrossed her legs, giving C-Note a brief glimpse between her thick thighs. She wore no panties, and C-Note could feel the bulge between his legs growing. She had a magnificent body for a woman her age—plump, bronze breasts and silky, jet-black hair at her groin.

C-Note found his throat dry and hard to swallow. He licked his lips to moisten them. "Woman, you won't stop at anything, will you?"

She laughed in a husky voice, legs parting again. "Not until I get that meat in between your legs." She had her eyes fixed on his hard-on. He watched intently as she put one foot on the easy chair, cocking her leg open. One of her hands fell between her golden thick thighs, and she began to rub herself vigorously, her fingers moving in and out of her soft spot. C-Note felt himself about to bust as he watched Honey Bee play between her legs. He knew she was trying to seduce him, and she was doing a damn good job at it.

C-Note got up and covered the short distance to where she was. As he stood in front of her, his mind was whirling. Honey Bee had his pants down to his ankles and his dick in her mouth before he realized he was giving in to her wants. She was moaning, sucking, and kissing. C-Note's mind flashed, and he quickly backed up, out of her reach.

What am I doin'? How has she got me this far? Am I REALLY this weak for pussy? These questions raced through his mind in an instant. He hastily pulled up his pants while Honey Bee fought to try to keep them down.

"Oh, please! Oh, please! Oh, *pleease!* Just let me suck it!" she begged repeatedly, one hand groping for his dick, the other tugging at his pants.

C-Note was almost tempted to slap her upside the head to bring her to her senses since it seemed she went into an uncontrollable frenzy. He became very angry. "Crazy bitch!" he yelled, pushing her away violently. "You done flipped ya fuckin' wig?"

She stared up at C-Note with unseeing eyes, as if in a different world. Then she spread her legs and began to play with herself, and at the same time, beg for C-Note to hit on her. He couldn't believe his eyes or ears and began to hurry back to the door he first came through. Hastily, he twisted the locks, opened the door, and the last thing he saw was Honey Bee convulsing and shaking violently in ecstasy as she brought herself to her own orgasm. C-Note stepped out the door, shutting it, and hurried to his car ready to leave. He couldn't trust himself any longer had he stayed and watched Honey Bee perform her own freak show.

C-Note sped home with hope that his son, Christian, was still fast sleep. If he were, he told himself, then he could release his horniness on Sheila for a while to soothe the erection he still had from the visions of the freak scene he had just witnessed with Honey Bee.

He made it home in record time, only to find Christian wide awake. Cursing to himself, he had to settle for a cold shower. He thought of going back to Honey Bee's, but he taught himself to never mix business with pleasure. So C-Note showered and dressed. Since Sheila was downstairs making breakfast for Christian, he picked up his private phone and punched some digits.

"Hello," said a voice after the first ring.

"C-Note speakin.'"

The voice at the other end spoke. "I'm ready for breakfast, that is, if you're ready to eat."

C-Note smiled. "I'm starving. I'll be there in about an hour." He hung up the phone and immediately called Two-Down and Little Poke.

"The food is cookin,' " he said when the phone was answered. "I just need the final ingredients as soon as possible."

Little Poke had answered. "You lucky you caught me," he said half-unenthused. "I was just leavin' for the rest of the day. I'll be by there wit' the final ingredients in about ten to fifteen minutes."

They both hung up with no more words spoken. C-Note hoped his dope talk wasn't too transparent. He rarely talked on the phone and doubted that the Feds were listening. Then he went to the closet, grabbed a gym bag half-filled with money, sat on the bed, and began counting out the rubber-banded stacks of money. This time, instead of buying one kilo, he was buying four. So he counted out fifty one thousand-dollar stacks, which only took several minutes to count as he waited anxiously for Poke to bring the remaining four thousand.

Between Two-Down and Poke, they had seventy-five hundred for the work they had sold the day before. The extra thirty-five hundred C-Note reflected would go to his early retirement fund. At the rate he was going, it wouldn't be long before he could quit the game and live a normal life without always having to look over his shoulder, he thought, as he stuffed the money back into the bag. After zipping up the bag, he went downstairs, ate one of the breakfast sandwiches Sheila had made, and waited patiently for Poke to arrive with the rest of the money.

chapter

2

C-Note woke up the next morning highly pissed. It was a cold, cloudy morning and that only made things worse. All the workers at his dope spots had answered their pages and called back. All except one. *Scrappy*. Everybody else had come by when C-Note gave them the word and picked up the product that kept their spots rollin' day and night. All but Scrappy. C-Note paged him continuously, but he never called back.

Therefore, C-Note had to put his family in jeopardy by keeping the dope at his home. That was one of his main "Don't do" rules in the game of hustling. Even Honey Bee's horny ass had showed up when he had asked her to come retrieve the poison from his house. By the time all the workers had finished with whatever they had to do, they had found the time to come pick up the product. It was a little past ten p.m. when the last worker dropped by. And so, C-Note found himself stuck with Scrappy's shit overnight. He padded to the bathroom for his morning piss. The tiles on the floor were cold, and this, too, angered him more, increasing his frustrations. He cursed.

He was in such a hurry to get to the bathroom that he didn't bother lifting the toilet seat and ended up pissing all over it. His day was already starting off bad, and he wondered how much worse it would get. After cleaning up his mess, he was on his way back to get in bed when his private phone shrilled. Already he could feel a slight headache starting to pound his temples.

C-Note walked the short distance to his private phone and picked up on the beginning of the third ring. His phone had never rung so much, nor this early, since he had it.

"What?" a voice snapped rudely into the mouthpiece, greeting his ears.

C-Note recognized Scrappy's voice instantly. "What?" he repeated smartly. "Nigga, *you* the one who called me!" C-Note was driven into a fury by Scrappy's attitude. "I called you last night, asshole! Where the fuck were you?" C-Note asked smartly.

Scrappy seemed a bit shaken. "Oh, my phone was in my pants on vibrate. An' I didn't know it went off."

Fury bubbled inside C-Note as he tried to control his rage. "You're the only one out of the whole crew that didn't show up las' night. Nor did you even bother to call an' say you were too busy to make it." C-Note paused, trying to regain his composure. "Where are you at this very minute?"

Scrappy snorted into the phone. "Does all that really matter right now?" he asked C-Note sarcastically.

C-Note had to stop himself from slamming down the phone in Scrappy's face. "Yeah, it matters, Mr.-Fuck-Everything-Up! The shit is still sittin' in my goddamn house, an' I want it out of here ASAP!" Although C-Note couldn't see this, he was willing to bet Scrappy was on the other end of the phone smiling while he raged. Scrappy even sounded chipper when he spoke.

"Don't get your balls in an uproar! I'm at one of my broads' houses. I can get dressed an' be there within an hour."

There was a lot of bitterness in C-Note's voice. "You jus' hurry up an' do that!" He slammed the phone down with a bang.

Sheila rolled over in the bed. "Talkin' to Scrappy, huh?" she asked to confirm what she already knew.

C-Note slid on a pair of sweat pants and sat on the edge of the bed. "Wouldn't you know it?" he said, turning to Sheila. "I think this nigga is really tryin' to find out what makes me tick." He got up and went to his dresser, opened one of the drawers, and pulled out a gun, then chambered a round. "And he's gonna find out jus' what that is."

Sheila got out of the bed in one swift motion and wrapped her arms around C-Note's waist. "Please don't do nothin' to that idiot that'll make our family suffer in the long run." She looked at him with pleading eyes. "He really ain't worth it. An' if you hurt him and go to jail …" Her voice trailed off as tears began to flow down her cheeks.

As he watched her crying, he knew what she said was true. Not only would he suffer, they all would. Sheila, Christian, and himself. C-Note's solemn face cringed. Slowly, he put the gun back in the drawer. Sheila was relieved but pained.

"If he upsets you so much, you should really not put yourself in a situation by dealin' with him. He's not the friend you think him to be."

He made an openhanded gesture but said nothing in response. He knew she was right. She usually was. All his life he'd known Scrappy to be a born troublemaker. He was one of the meanest, dirtiest, and most vicious of his class. But like C-Note, he showed an interest in making money and C-Note thought he could help his once-best friend to achieve the luxuries of the ghetto.

Ever since C-Note could remember, back when they both joined the dope game as partners, Scrappy had always fucked over the money. The big man on the block would front the two of them a hundred dollars' worth of crack apiece. Off the hundred, they were required to pay back seventy dollars, the rest being theirs. Almost all the time, C-Note paid for what was given to him. But Scrappy never did pay the majority of the time, and he brought problems upon himself. While C-Note was on the corner hustling, Scrappy was off in one of the many vacant houses using his crack for blow jobs and sex. And as C-Note thought about it, Scrappy still hadn't changed after all these years. He tried to look on the bright side—but there wasn't one. C-Note had only just realized the magnitude of the problem.

He smoothed his goatee with his thumb and forefinger. The anxiety and tension in Sheila's voice increased as she said, "Sooner or later, he's gonna backstab you. He's just waitin' for the right time."

It was painfully disturbing to hear this. Sheila was clear and precise. He sat there wondering why he had let himself in for so much grief. He knew the game was up in pretending he still had a best friend. He knew it was absurd to think so. Brooding, he said, "Yeah, I'm startin' to recognize and realize the reality of the situation. It has dawned on me that he either takes me for stupid or foolish, maybe both, and sooner or later one of us is goin' to wind up hurt." C-Note sighed despairingly.

He made his way to Sheila's side, filling bad-tempered and perturbed. He felt torn, and for once, he was at a loss for words. Sheila shuddered with fear. She knew this was the beginning of his troubles and hoped everything would work out. Finally, she rose and smiled sadly. "Since I'm up, I'll fix you breakfast. And maybe that'll help you feel somewhat better."

C-Note said nothing. He just continued to brood. The memories of his once-upon-a-time best friend melted his heart.

⌬━◄►

SCRAPPY SAT IN the car passenger seat of one of his many girlfriends. His stony face stared unseeing out the window as the woman maneuvered through the L.A. streets. Scrappy was in deep contemplation, and the female he was with knew better than to say something when he was in one of his vile moods. She was uncomfortable, knowing at any time he could fly into a violent rage—like he did sometimes. Then he would curse her, strike her, and even spit on her. It seemed so unfair he blamed her, but she told herself over and over that it was really other reasons causing this behavior. She still wondered why she was even with someone who treated her so badly. The mere idea made her heart pound.

Scrappy's harsh voice made her jump as she quickly came out her thoughts. "When your stupid ass get to Rosecrans, make a left," he said firmly.

She said nothing but obeyed his orders. The next time, she told herself—and then quickly checked herself at once. "There *won't* be a next time," she silently promised herself. Even if she did fill incomplete and unfulfilled without him, she wouldn't put up with this type of treatment anymore. She would be no longer scared, and that brought a glow of pleasure to her face. She smiled openly, because she knew in her mind that this would be her last time in the presence of the psychopath who rode in her passenger seat.

Scrappy's mind raced a million miles a second, juggling thoughts. He fought the impulse to reach over and slap the bitch who was driving, because on her face he could see the smug smirk that had formed at the corner of her lips. But he curbed his urge and brought his mind back to the problem at hand. Since as far back as he could remember, he and Fat Boy, or C-Note, as he now liked to be called, had been the best of friends. But now that he, C-Note, had met that corrupt bitch, Sheila, and started making big money, things had definitely changed. Scrappy cast his eyes leftward towards the driver, who remained tight-lipped.

He smiled evilly as his mind raced wildly. C-Note always tried to play head honcho, Scrappy reflected, using the power of money to exert his authority and superior manner. It was always something or other, Scrappy thought. Like when C-Note told him he was disassociating himself from the 'hood they had grown up in. *How could he?* Scrappy wondered coldly. It was uncalled for.

The driver's scared, but soft voice brought him out of his thoughts. "We're on Rosecrans; which way now?" Scrappy gave her the directions and then went back to his mulling. He knew his best friend had his limits. And from the earlier conversation on the phone, Scrappy knew he had stretched the rubber band too far.

The doorbell rang. C-Note got up from the kitchen table and went to answer the door. Scrappy stood poised, with a straight face. C-Note opened the screen door, and Scrappy walked in, saying nothing as he passed C-Note. He took a seat on the leather sofa, and C-Note did the same across from him. They both sat facing each other across the glass coffee table. Sheila came out of the kitchen on her way back upstairs to their room. She gave Scrappy a generic "Hello" and never broke stride.

Scrappy slightly flinched, then mumbled in the same generic voice, "Hi, how ya doin?"

C-Note's eyes were hard and alert, his brow furrowing in deep thought. Scrappy smiled guilty, noting C-Note's discomfiture. His tone was arrogant. "I know you got somethin' to say, so say it!" he said with undisguised venom.

C-Note began to browse through his thoughts, thinking of the wisest course of action. His voice was a mixture of sadness and scorn. "First of all," C-Note began, "if we're gonna face the facts, let's face them all. Obviously, somewhere, the two of us have a problem. Your sudden irrational behavior just ain't for nothin'. So if there is somethin' you got to say me, well, then, I suggest you get it off your chest, because I won't have my cash faucet bein' turned off for some bullshit."

Scrappy's eyes darted nervously. He looked troubled and took a moment to comment. His manner was straightforward. "The money changed you," he said flatly. "You deal wit' niggas from the other side. You stopped representin' the 'hood. You think you can tell people what to do and when to do it. And you talk any ole way to people." Scrappy paused briefly, his lips moving twice as fast as his brain. "And the bit—" he caught himself, "I mean, the broad upstairs has fouled up yo' head. Fat Boy, it's you who's changed." Scrappy knew C-Note hated being called by his old nickname, but did so just to piss him off anyway.

C-Note let the thoughts of what Scrappy said wash over him. He found himself choosing his words with care. He knew what Scrappy said was a twisted version of the truth. He wondered what would happen if he could see himself as others saw him. His voice was flat, all businesslike, and professional.

"Scrap, you've known me almost as long as I've known myself. And vice versa. And not once have I come at you wrong when you've done nothin' wrong." There was a tiny pause while he changed tactics. "Just like you, I've spent all my life toiling in the ghetto streets. If there was money to be made, I included you. Now, it seems since I'm more family-oriented and not bangin' the 'hood no more, you consider me a pushover. You, of all people, know the treacheries of my personal life. I can't live without tryin' to be true to what I do."

There was an awkward silence, and then C-Note continued. "I thought by puttin' you in the game as deep as I was that our friendship would become stronger, where we could both make a living and somethin' of our lives. But somewhere down the line, you lost love for everything, Scrap. Not only foes, but friends, too. I never pulled any cheap tricks on you. You knew next to nothing about real money and now you're baskin' in enough of it to pay your bills, trick with your women, and stack some to the cut."

C-Note's eyes blazed while Scrappy listened to his spiel with a dignified air. "Plenty of sleepless nights of plannin' and longin' had gone into my strategy of gettin' rich, and as my best friend, I brought you along for the ride. Deep down, I can't lie, because you've fucked so many people in the past, but I cherished a glimmer of hope that you'd by now have learned how to play the game. The stakes are high, and no matter what the cost—I mean, whatever the situation is—I won't stand to be made a fool of."

Scrappy replied in a voice of controlled anger and obvious distaste. A gleam of excitement, mixed with anger, came into his eyes. "First off, I'm the one who's sellin' the dope night and day. I'm the one riskin' my ass. If the spot gets raided, who's goin' to jail?" Before C-Note could answer, Scrappy plunged on. "*Me*—that's who! If one of those crazy-ass smokers get sprung and want some shit on credit and I don't give it to 'em, who you think got to deal with the brunt of their rage? *Me*— that's who! If I got to dump the shit into the acid or down the toilet, who has to pay you for it? *Me*—that's—"

C-Note cut in and cut him off. "Come off that bullshit, Scrap. Everything is fifty-fifty. If a loss is to be taken involving the Po-Po's, you know I accept the loss without chargin' you. And if there is a loss involving yourself, I even go outta my way to split that up wit' you."

Scrappy's face set in hard lines of determination. "And what about the police and goin' to jail?" he asked tersely. "I'll be locked up and doin' time while you're still out here doin' 'yo' thang,' as you call it." Rebellion flashed in his eyes, and it was now Scrappy's turn to stare hard at C-Note.

C-Note wondered if Scrappy had orchestrated this in the past, always nursing these thoughts. Or had they just been what was on his mind and that was the sudden reason for his hostility? C-Note couldn't decipher his thoughts. His mind rapidly tossed over Scrappy's possibilities. Then his own thoughts began to strike him like blows. I hadn't been the one needing and asking for help. *I wasn't the one making him want to sell dope*, C-Note told himself. Scrappy was in it just as deep as he was. Because if Scrappy were to get busted, what were the odds of him not talking?—especially with the hidden resentment he was now showing.

C-Note became angry, his voice flat as if he didn't care. "Nigga, it ain't like I'm holdin' a pistol to yo' head makin' you sell dope. You doin' it for the same reason I am. To make money! Now if you feel you're getting the short end of the stick, nigga, you can bounce!"

Scrappy shifted uneasily on the sofa as C-Note rolled on. "'Cause what you won't do, somebody else will."

Scrappy stared at C-Note disbelievingly. When he spoke, his voice was like glass. It had a cutting edge. "Nigga, don't you ever forget you and I originated from the same dirt. The ghetto! And despite all my misgivings, I can do with or without you. I'm totally aware of my misdeeds and myself, unlike you. I think what you need is some considerable soul-searchin'. You need to find out what you are and who you are, 'cause most definitely, you done went soft."

C-Note wanted to let out a stream of obscenities, but just as he was ready to fly into one of his fits of rage, the doorbell rang. He got up from the sofa and hurried over to the door, opening it. It was the woman who had brought Scrappy to C-Note's house.

"Could you tell Scrappy it's been longer than the ten minutes he said it was going to take, and I have to be on my way to work." She shifted from foot to foot nervously. Scrappy was up and at the door in a flash as C-Note opened the screen door for her to come in.

"Wait yo' stupid ass in the car!" he yelled at her, his face a mask of anger. "I don't give a fuck where you got to be! You jus' wait out there until I get through, crazy-ass broad!"

C-Note couldn't believe his ears. Had he misjudged his friend? Was he *really crazy*? C-Note knew, by rules of the game, that you didn't get into other people's affairs. But as he stood there looking at the girl in his doorway ready to burst into tears, he couldn't help but feel sorry for her. She seemed so fragile that she was ready to break.

C-Note's mind thought quickly. "Scrappy, why don't you let her roll on to work since we ain't nearly finished with our conversation? Why hold her up? I'll run you back to the pad." Scrappy shot him a look that would kill, if looks could do so. But before Scrappy could refuse, C-Note rolled on. "We still have plenty to talk about. And surely you wouldn't want her to lose her job."

As bad as Scrappy wanted to say fuck her and her job, he didn't say it. He knew if he did, she'd know how he truly felt about her. Plus, C-Note had cleverly maneuvered him out of position, allowing him no choice but to let her go.

"Go on," he said finally. "But make sure you call me tonight when yo' ass get off work."

C-Note watched as her face registered a hint of surprise. "Okay," she said hastily and was off the porch and headed for her car instantly.

Scrappy moved back to the sofa while C-Note shut the door. He was tired of going back and forth with Scrappy, trying to get him to see eye to eye. He began compose in his mind what he was going to say to Scrappy. C-Note finally decided on what course of action to take, and he knew his best friend was going to be argumentative. No more small talk and talks of how long they'd been friends. No more ridiculous talks of how he was trying to help Scrappy and all the other bullshit that floated around in his mind. He knew he had to assert aggression. His way or no way. No more weak points.

C-Note licked his dry lips, while Scrappy was not attempting to disguise his contempt. He just sat with a smirk on his face, not showing any concern whatsoever.

"Despite all the setbacks I've had while tryin' to bring up your cash flow, I'm unable to keep bein' taken so lightly. You must have thought I've taken leave from my senses." C-Note paused for sometime, as if weighing up what he should say.

"I've tried my best to be fair, but all you got in your head is my changes and my problems, when really you should be working on your goddamn self."

Scrappy looked as if he wished to make some protest, but C-Note waved an agitated hand, indicating he was not finished. "I don't begin to know what kind of world you are livin' in! But it is one not of the real world. Fantasy, I might say, because you really believe that people are to do all your bidding for you, jump when you say jump, or move when you say move. You're fucked-up in the head is what I'm gettin' at. And you should seek some professional help before someone who isn't as nice as me winds up offin' you."

C-Note was greeted with a look of either surprise or anger. Scrappy was not in the habit of being told what to do. He tried to appear unruffled. Like himself, C-Note realized he was dealing with someone from the underworld. Scrappy's unreserved assurance made him feel more confident.

"Why does one always think the worst in these situations?" Scrappy asked, shaking his head from side to side.

C-Note looked puzzled. "Nigga, what are you talkin' about?"

Scrappy's sinister laugh sent chill bumps down C-Note's back. "Who the fuck do you think you are, some kind of street psychologist?" he asked, still laughing. "Right now, I'm at the top of my game," Scrappy went on, "so if you feel there's a snag in what we got goin' on," Scrappy paused for a brief second, "I mean what 'you' got goin' on, then jus' say what that problem is."

C-Note saw this was going no place, but he felt he had to persist. "Then why is it, Scrappy, we keep havin' these silly-ass bitch arguments over bullshit?" C-Note asked, becoming heated. "'Cause the animosity you got towards me ain't hidden anymore. Let's stop the lollygaggin' and this beatin' around the bush shit. Is all this over somethin' I done to you, or is it over somethin' I got an' you want?"

Scrappy feigned surprised. "Nigga, whatever you got, I can most certainly get," Scrappy said hotly.

C-Note stared him eye to eye. "Is all this over my broad?" C-Note asked coldly.

Scrappy couldn't contain his anger any longer and lashed out with bottled-up resentment. "Yo' bitch? Yo' *bitch*? Nigga, yo' broad is damaged goods. She ain't about shit! She's got yo' nose so open, I can see that pea-sized brain of yours. If I wanted her, I could've had her. But that was one time there I showed you love."

Scrappy was insulting and rude, and C-Note took it with a smile as he stirred himself up to try to keep control.

"I don't have the least notion of why you would really believe that half-ass daydream of yours."

C-Note knew Scrappy had a talent for needlessly annoying people, just as he was doing now.

"Scrappy, those are unhealthy delusions you have stored away in that empty head of yours," C-Note said mockingly. "I think you should really check on gettin' some help for your mind."

Scrappy laughed cryptically as a radiant look of triumph flashed on his face. C-Note, too, had to smile at the simplicity of the situation. Did Scrappy really believe he could have had Sheila if he had wanted to? The unexpected question that formed in C-Note's mind made him laugh.

"So, this is the reason for the personal dislike?" C-Note asked, still laughing.

Scrappy drew his lips into a sneering smile. "There ain't no personal dislike," Scrappy said, his tone underlining the stupidity of the remark. "I just object to becomin' a doormat to others. In other words, bein' walked all over an' stepped on."

C-Note knew these were more crazy feelings Scrappy had been harboring. Unlike himself, Scrappy didn't believe C-Note was helping him at all.

"You know life is a risk. Every mornin' you wake up, you're takin' a risk. You jus' can't live without takin' risks," C-Note said matter-of-factly. "And all I was doin' was tryin' to cut down on your risks of takin' a loss. But seein' you feel used, here's the deal. You can bring your own money to the table and buy your own work. And since I started the spot, I'm goin' to put a worker in there to sell my shit. And you, you can do your own thang."

C-Note paused to let his words sink into Scrappy's hard head. Scrappy's smile turned wolfish, but C-Note wasn't through. "And let's get this straight from the giddy-up. You have your customers ask for you. And my worker'll have his clients ask for him. And whoever they ask for gets the sale."

They both locked stares before C-Note rolled on. "An' absolutely no short-stoppin' the smokers."

Scrappy smiled that smile again. "Perfect proposition," Scrappy stated, sounding somewhat enthused.

"Oh, yeah ..." C-Note added as an afterthought, "since things will be run this way from now on, you're required to pay half of the nine hundred fifty-dollar rent. Plus half on all the bills every month."

Scrappy gave him a calculated look. Outside, he remained cool, but on the inside, he was steaming. He was trying to camouflage his feelings, but C-Note knew him too well.

"No problem," Scrappy said through clenched teeth. "The money I'll be makin' after the first month will be enough to pay my half of the rent for five years. I ain't trippin.'"

C-Note felt an air of calm and contentment. He knew from previous times before that it was just a matter of time before Scrappy fucked something up and things would start to go wrong. He also felt a mixture of pride and sorrow and was bewildered by this new set of emotions.

Scrappy, C-Note knew, wasn't deeply committed or loyal to the game of hustling. That's why he, Scrappy, was still falling through the air without a single thing to latch onto. No stability, physically or emotionally. It was just a matter of time, C-Note mused to himself, before Scrappy fell again and he wouldn't be there to catch him as he did over the past many years.

C-Note stood up, ready to go. "You're now the captain of your own ship. Let's just hope when times get hard, you can steer your ship from the danger of the rough waters tryin' to sink it."

Scrappy only pretended to relax, folding his arms across his broad chest. "The waters ain't so rough when you got a navigational system," he said smartly. "'Cause you can jus' go right around those rough waters with smoothness." He broke into wild laughter at his quick rejoinder.

The two men left C-Note's house not best friends anymore, but only business partners in the trial-and-error game of hustling.

As C-Note drove Scrappy back to the spot, the conversation was at a standstill. Recollections of the past engulfed him as Scrappy rode tight-lipped, staring out the window, entrenched in his own thoughts. The days of the calendar had been wiped away by time, but those were the good old days, and time could not wipe those memories from his mind. C-Note's mind drifted as he tried to reconstruct the events of his past ...

They were in the sixth-grade, the same elementary school, the same class. They lived on the same street, just different sides of the street, and just a few houses down and across from each other. C-Note would stop by Scrappy's house in the morning so they could walk together to school. Scrappy's parents worked, so they'd be gone when C-Note got there. This particular morning, Scrappy had asked C-Note to come in, which was not allowed while his parents weren't home. C-Note knew instantly that Scrappy was up to something.

Scrappy first took C-Note into his parents' room, where he showed off and played with his father's .3030 rifle he kept under the bed. After loading it and unloading it several times, he then took C-Note in their garage that they had converted into a storage and sitting room. It had a bar and furniture, a place for a washer and dryer, and a place where feed was kept for the various animals his father raised. Scrappy's smile was devious as he went behind the bar and came out with a bottle of vodka. His eyes gleamed with excitement.

"You wanna taste?" he asked eagerly, then turned the bottle to his lips. C-Note didn't like the taste. He had tasted his grandfather's bottle before.

"That's all right," C-Note said, trying to be nonchalant.

Scrappy swigged again, then went behind the bar, put the vodka up, and came back out with two small cans of beer. He tossed C-Note one, then opened one for himself. "I know you ain't gone punk-out on a beer. We drink beer all the time."

Scrappy downed half the beer in one swallow. C-Note set the can of beer on the bar. "It's too early to be drinkin'," C-Note said. "You know how one beer do me, Scrap." Scrappy's face squinched up in a mask of fury. Without saying a word, he stormed out of the sitting-storage room and went into the house.

C-Note thought he was going to get his books for school and they'd be on their way. Instead, Scrappy came back out with his father's rifle in hand. C-Note knew he was drunk. In the past, it had taken Scrappy much less to get drunk. C-Note was unable to hide his surprise.

Scrappy loaded the gun slowly while he stood there watching. After he loaded it, Scrappy scowled, "So you ain't gone drink wit' me?" He aimed the gun right at C-Note's chest.

Shaking, C-Note picked up the can of beer and opened it. "Drink it nonstop," Scrappy said, with the rifle still fixed on him. C-Note did as he was told as panic bubbled inside him. He had no other choice. He stood spooked and helpless, rooted to the spot.

Scrappy laughed coldly at the stark fear that was on C-Note's face. C-Note knew his friend had a sadistic sense of humor and might have shot him if he had refused to drink the beer. After that, Scrappy unloaded the gun and went to put it back in his parents' room.

C-Note didn't stick around. As soon as Scrappy was out of sight, he ran off to school, wondering if he should tell their sixth-grade teacher. C-Note knew if he told that Scrappy would be in deep trouble, not only with the school, but his parents as well. So he said nothing about the incident.

At recess, Scrappy told all their friends about what happened and they teased him the rest of the day about it. After school, C-Note was walking home by himself. He stopped at the ice-cream truck that parked at the corner of his block to spend the dollar he had earned cleaning out the flowerbeds. Scrappy and several of their friends walked up, laughing and heckling him as he was about to make his purchase. Scrappy spotted the dollar in his hand.

"Buy me somethin' off the ice-cream truck," Scrappy stated instead of asking. C-Note whirled around at him.

"Are you nuts?" C-Note asked, not wanting to believe his own ears.

Scrappy snorted sarcastically. "That's why yo' punk ass was scared shitless this mornin.'"

C-Note tried his best to ignore the laughter comin' from behind him. But Scrappy couldn't leave well enough alone and thumped C-Note behind the ear. C-Note couldn't contain his rage any longer. He turned on Scrappy, unleashing all his pent-up rage and anger and embarrassment. The first blow to his nose sent Scrappy flying. C-Note was on him before Scrappy could hit the ground, pounding his fist into his face relentlessly.

Scrappy didn't have a chance, and it took several other parents who had been walking their children home to stop the beating C-Note was giving Scrappy. The friends who had been laughing with Scrappy now looked at C-Note through different eyes. All through elementary school, Scrappy had been terrorizing and bullying almost everyone at school. Now, everyone cheered openly as they watched the defeated Scrappy, nose and mouth bleeding, cowardly run home. That day C-Note never forgot, and now while taking Scrappy home, he knew Scrappy hadn't forgotten either. The pain he experienced that day had been a longtime remembrance, and a terrible one, and Scrappy wouldn't let it end as quietly now as he had done many years ago.

Scrappy stared through the window, deep in his own thoughts. It was tough to keep despair from his mind when things were going a bit awry. His negative thoughts, memories, and feelings resurfaced. He had an itch that needed to be scratched, and he wouldn't stop until he was at the top of his game; that is, until his good fortune came calling. Scrappy knew the scales had to be balanced, and he couldn't think of any other solace to offer himself but to be in C-Note's shoes, or to be over him. He planned to use C-Note for more profitable pursuits, but he had opened his mouth too soon and prematurely showed his hand.

He told himself he should've guessed C-Note's reaction to what was going down. But instead, he had let his actions fly, and he had faith in the outcome of the matter at hand. However, he didn't want to become too chancy, so he sat reflecting on how he'd always come out victorious over all the years of befriending the truly stupid C-Note.

They were in the tenth-grade and went to different high schools. He knew someone at his school who was selling a hot Honda CR 125 dirt bike. Only problem was, he didn't have the money himself to buy it. With his smooth manipulation and his exaggerated friendliness, he conned C-Note into purchasing the stolen motorcycle. He even charmed C-Note into hiding the dirt bike at his house so C-Note's grandparents wouldn't be suspicious of where he'd gotten the money to buy the bike.

After about a few weeks of keeping the dirt bike at his house, Scrappy began to daily ride it on the streets. Eventually, he was stopped by the sheriff for riding on the streets without a license and the law took the dirt bike into the police impound. He never paid C-Note back.

And then there was the time he had wanted some FILA shoes. He took most of his dope money to buy the shoes. He and C-Note had been in the alley serving dope when the dope man pulled up, demanding his money and he didn't have it. The dope man grabbed a fistful of his shirt, and with his other hand, slapped him hard upside his head. C-Note had always been a loyal friend. Running to the secret spot where they kept their .25 automatic, C-Note drew it on the dope man, who laughed at the thought of being shot.

"Little nigga, if you know what's right, you'll bring me dat' gun," said the dope man as he let go of Scrappy's shirt. He watched carefully as C-Note chambered a bullet.

"Blast on his ass!" Scrappy yelled through swelling lips to his best friend. The dope man's face registered surprise and then fear when he saw C-Note was about to pull the trigger.

The dope man quickly spoke. "All I want is my money," he began in a shaky voice. "I didn't come here for y'all to be pullin' a gun on a nigga." The dope man's eyes were pleading.

"Scrappy been owin' me for well over a month now, an' he still ain't thought about payin' me my money. Look it!" The dope man pointed to Scrappy's feet. "The nigga can buy new shoes, but he can't even pay me for my product I gave'em."

C-Note started to lower the gun, knowing the dope man made a good point.

"Shoot the muthafucka!" Scrappy yelled again, stepping up next to C-Note.

"Look at my fuckin' face." The dope man put both hands in the air, like the police used to have a suspect do back in the days before they started shooting.

Scrappy tried reaching for the gun, but C-Note moved it away. Scrappy could see the ever-increasing dismay written on the dope man's face. He also saw that C-Note was starting to feel sorry for the dope man. If he had the gun right at that moment, he would'a shot both their asses. As usual, Scrappy noticed his best friend wanted to take charge of things.

"Check this out," C-Note began. "What if I jus' reach in my pocket an' pay you? Would you consider forgettin' what happened out here today?"

The dope man smiled agreeably. Scrappy exploded instantly, putting together all the vile words and phrases he knew.

"Let's jus' kill'em now and we ain't got to worry about him comin' back," Scrappy barked.

C-Note shook his head sadly. "For a few measly bucks?" C-Note asked. The dope man was watching the confrontation between the two, wide-eyed.

"The son of a bitch was gonna kill me!" Scrappy stated heatedly.

C-Note reached in his pocket and brought out his bankroll. "How much he owe you?"

The dope man licked his lips greedily. "One fifty."

C-Note counted out the wad of money in his hand. "It's a hundred and thirty-three dollars. Is that cool?"

The dope man shook his head up and down and reached for the money. C-Note gave it to him.

"I hope you don't try an' get combative," he said as he watched the dope man fold the money and stuff it in his pocket, "'cause next time, you might not be so fortunate."

The dope man had to summon up his nerve. "You ain't got to worry. There won't be a next time." And he rushed off without another word.

Scrappy had made false promises of paying C-Note back. So it was that day he told himself that C-Note was so idiotic and that he could be manipulated easily. And then all he had to do was play on his best friend's sympathy and obtain total control over his streets and his money. Then he would be smarter and more cunning than C-Note would ever be.

C-Note stopped the car in front of the dope spot. He spoke in a quiet but fierce voice. "The rules are set Scrap. If you're late on anything, you gots to go."

Scrappy's face was a mask of stubbornness. He opened the door and got out. Before closing the door, he spoke with malice in his voice. "You should know by now, Fat Boy, that I don't abide by anybody's rules but my own." Before C-Note could say something, he slammed the door and started up the walkway to the house.

C-Note shook his head sadly, put the car in gear, and headed back home. What he foresaw wasn't good, and he just hoped he wouldn't be on the losing end of the stick, because he was ready to die for what he had spent so many years to accomplish. He also wondered if Scrappy would be willing to die trying to take over his position, to gain what he had accomplished. C-Note smiled coldly, because he knew that one of their days was numbered and wondered if he should retire from the game earlier than he expected.

chapter

3

The next few months whisked by. C-Note got his cousin, Cat-Daddy, to run his spot with Scrappy. Cat-Daddy was in college and the few months he had off from school he joined the dope game. Cat-Daddy's plan was to save enough money to get him through the last two years of college.

Things with Scrappy and the game were slowly deteriorating. Scrappy's mouth was also a problem with Cat-Daddy. Cat-Daddy complained to C-Note all the time. C-Note tried to assure him that it wouldn't be much longer, because he, himself, was retiring from the game in the next couple of months. Cat-Daddy was making good money, so he told himself not to let Scrappy's rage and resentment towards his cousin get to him. He pretended to be unperturbed. This was an opportunity he couldn't let slip through his fingers, no matter how much shit Scrappy talked.

Scrappy was quick to sense other people's moods. Since day one, he knew C-Note's cousin, Cat-Daddy, would be in the way of his plans. Plus, he didn't like Cat-Daddy anyway, because he was making the money that should have been going into his own pockets. Every day Cat was there tortured him. It seemed unfair Cat-Daddy was gettin' more money than he was. But in truth, Scrappy knew it would make no difference, because in time, he knew C-Note's treasures and everything he loved so dearly would be his. And C-Note would be up shit creek without a paddle. A spasm of joy raked his body just thinking about it. He laughed to himself eerily with delight at his inner thoughts.

C-Note was feeling especially subtle today. His dope connection had finally trusted him enough to give him the dope without using any of his own money upfront. The money he'd make would only add to the money he was already saving to retire out of the dope game. Twelve kilos, two for each one of his dope houses. Instead of flooding the dope houses with too much dope, he only distributed one kilo to each of the houses. The others kilos he stashed at a safe house. It was his good judgment not to have that much work in one place. His street smarts taught him better, and he told his workers the same. He smiled guiltily, because now, they all were wholly committed to helping him push the poison on the streets. After this last big sting, he told himself, he would change his life, his environment, and his friends, and start up a new path to a new state, as well as to new friends and a new life.

C-Note stood in the kitchen, blabbing to Cat-Daddy as he went through the procedures of showing him how to make powder into crack rock. Cat-Daddy wanted to bypass the chitchat, but C-Note ignored the crazy looks Cat-Daddy was giving him.

"With these last twelve chickens," C-Note was saying as he put hot water into the beaker, "I'm through wit' the game of hustlin' when I'm done movin' the rest of this shit. I'm buyin' me a house and a Benz, putting up a hundred gees for the kid, and investin' the rest."

Cat-Daddy shook his head sadly. "You know Scrappy is in his room with one of his chickenheads?"

C-Note continued to play with the beaker. "I don't give a shit!" he stated. "After I'm through wit' the last of dis shit, he can have this spot an' everything in it."

"You jus' don't know where to draw the line, do you?" Cat-Daddy asked solemnly.

C-Note could hear the disapproval in his voice. He walked from the stove to the sink, turning on the cold water. "Listen, Scrappy's doin' his own thang. What do he care what I got goin' on?"

Cat-Daddy shrugged his shoulders. "All I'm sayin'," he paused to look over his shoulder, "is that it's too soon to celebrate or count your eggs before they hatch. Anything can go wrong. That's a lot of shit."

C-Note felt untouchable. "You never cease to amaze me. You can be so unimaginative."

Cat-Daddy drummed his fingers on the countertop next to the sink. He felt himself getting cross but didn't say anything. C-Note took the rock out the beaker and wrapped it in a towel, drying it. He looked over at Cat-Daddy.

"Now, that wasn't hard, was it?" he said, giving Cat-Daddy a silly grin. "It don't take no rocket scientist to cook this bullshit," he added as he poured more drugs into the beaker. He walked to the table and sat down while Cat-Daddy began the process all over again using the beaker and knife.

Trouble finally erupted. Scrappy came stumbling into the kitchen in just his boxer shorts. He stared at the dope on the counter, his eyes never leaving the drugs, and said, "I thought I heard my name bein' mentioned."

Cat-Daddy shot C-Note a sideward glance, but continued to cook. Scrappy walked to the refrigerator, grabbed a bottle of Corona, opened it, and swigged. He wiped his mouth with the back of his other hand. "That sure is a lot of dope there," he said pointing with the hand that held the Corona. "I hope you're takin' most of it wit' you when leave, 'cause that's too much shit to be keepin' around here. Especially as hot as it is around here." Scrappy's appraising eyes lingered on the piles of white powder.

C-Note could feel his frustration mounting. He switched his attention back to Cat-Daddy and went right on talking as if Scrappy hadn't spoken. "It ain't like I'm countin' eggs," he said sarcastically. "I'm countin' money! An' until all this shit is gone and sold, only then will I be satisfied."

Cat-Daddy pulled the beaker out of the boiling water, walked to the sink, and stuck the glass under the cool current coming out of the faucet. Scrappy stood there looking troubled but didn't say anything. However, his eyes glimmered like a hot flame. C-Note rolled on intently with his recital to Cat-Daddy.

"I felt, I wanted, I hoped, and I dreamed of fairytale fantasies. I harped on the fact that I wasn't satisfied with life's expectations, that somehow, I had fallen far from my estimation. I felt I needed so much and had so little, therefore, I felt I was losin' the battle of livin' a real life. And as you know, I'm not a man who takes defeat philosophically. More importantly, I refuse to glamorize my way of life, but it's the only way I've ever made money. It's all I know."

Scrappy snorted, then laughed bitterly. C-Note bit his lip to keep from saying something smart to Scrappy. Cat-Daddy was scooping more powder into the beaker, but was still listening with open ears.

"How ironic," Cat-Daddy said. "I know how you feel, sort of. I'm in the same predicament. Here I am, tryin' to get money so I can make it through school and have a better life, too. So I guess we're in the same boat, huh?"

Scrappy wildly laughed out loud, then swigged from his beer again before he spoke. "What do two ghetto hopeless-ass niggas know about another life, a better life? All you damn fools know is the streets, and that's all you gonna ever know."

C-Note sat cool and let things play out.

"Now I woulda' believed you," Scrappy plunged on sarcastically, "if you two said you could tell me how to survive in jail or on the streets. But that 'better life' shit—" he broke off, roaring with laughter. He was laughing so hard at what he considered was his own joke, beer leaked from his nose and mouth as he held on to the doorjamb to keep himself from falling over from laughter.

C-Note sighed, shaking his head solemnly in protest. Cat-Daddy was back at the stove, smiling slightly as his eyes went from C-Note to Scrappy. C-Note's eyes were blazing with wrath.

"Don't be like this senseless idiot who's at a loss with stupid-ass thinking such as his," C-Note snapped curtly, pointing a thumb at Scrappy. "His own emotions are confused, and to make matter worse, he don't know his ass from a hole in the ground." C-Note paused to let his forceful words sink in.

But Scrappy laughed on, not caring what C-Note said. C-Note gazed at him blankly in frustration. "You have so many lessons to learn in life. I just hope you live long enough to learn 'em all."

Scrappy's laughter quickly stilled. He narrowed his eyes and stared at C-Note keenly. C-Note caught his reaction and quickly rolled on while he felt he had Scrappy up against the ropes.

"See, Cat-Daddy, a nigga like this," he nodded at Scrappy with his head this time, "is an unstable character. He looks out at the world, and he thinks he's not part of it, nor could he ever be. He's always puttin' himself in chancy situations. Always findin' himself caught up in a struggle he can't identify with, or don't want to identify with. Not only can't he be loyal to others, but he's not capable of even bein' loyal to himself."

Scrappy's face creased with anger. "Fuck you!" he barked as C-Note smiled at his increasing displeasure. C-Note definitely knew which buttons to push. Cat-Daddy watched quietly, enjoying the scene. He thought he was the only person to argue with Scrappy on a constant basis. Scrappy's sharp gaze focused on C-Note disapprovingly.

"As rumor has it," Scrappy started, his chest rising with each breath he inhaled, "you play a role long enough you become that character you play. Ain't that right, sucka?"

C-Note gulped at his censure and then smiled bravely. "Truly, Scrap, you don't really think of me as a sucka? 'Cause if you do, I think we got a problem that needs addressin'. Suckas get licked, an' that's somethin' I don't plan on havin' done by you or any other nigga on these streets." C-Note stared hard into Scrappy's now-expressionless face. C-Note yearned inside for him to rise and take the bait. And sensing it, Scrappy's instincts told him better. He laughed quite loudly to cover the fact that he wasn't certain whether or not he was ready to take C-Note on. So instead, he turned up his beer again.

Looking to Cat-Daddy for assistance, Scrappy said half-jokingly, "He started the hecklin', and now he wanna fight." Scrappy sighed and shook his head sadly. He gulped his beer again, turned, and walked away, mumbling something under his breath. C-Note couldn't hear what he said. Cat-Daddy was smiling like the cat that ate the canary.

"That's the first time I ever seen him walk away losin' an argument," Cat said amazed. "He never seems to cease runnin' his mouth." C-Note shrugged his shoulders as Cat continued to talk. "I guess he knows that two people who think they know everything and disagree on everything can't both always be right."

Cat-Daddy smiled at his ingenious comment. "I guess you are right," C-Note said matter-of-factly, "'cause if he wouldn't have walked out, we woulda' been arguin' like two broads screwin' the same dick."

Cat-Daddy laughed and countered. "Yeah! Or vice versa, two dicks fightin' over one cunt." Now they both laughed. C-Note couldn't stand to be made a fool of. Thinking out loud, he said, "Scrappy really believes me to be soft. After all the years we done dirt together, he of all people should be the first to know I shouldn't be taken lightly."

C-Note paused while Cat-Daddy ran cold water over the beaker. "He's on the brink of ruin. He likes gamblin' wit' his life when the stakes are high. He won't get it into his hard head that jus''cause you got money, people are goin' to respect you. You got to give respect to get respect. An' that's somethin' he jus' don't give."

C-Note paused again, deeply thinking. "Remember, Cat, it's always better to have a good name than to have lots of money. Your name is all you got when you are born. And it's all you'll have when you die. The money will only be remembered by those who get some. But your name will be remembered forever for the person you were."

Cat-Daddy smiled slyly. "And where did my cousin—the philosopher—steal that line from?"

SCRAPPY WALKED INTO the room he occupied, slammed the door, and sat heavily on the edge of the bed. The female who had been sleeping sat up with a startle at the sound of the door. She was about to say something about the noise until she caught the look on his face and thought better of it. She'd seen that look plenty of times in the past and knew instantly that Scrappy was mad about something—something she didn't care to know about in fear he would take his anger out on her, just as he'd done before. She eased back down on the pillow, pulling the covers up to her chin and rolled completely over to her side of the bed, her back to him. No, she knew better than to speak, because to speak was to arouse his anger. She closed her eyes and quickly tried to force herself back to sleep.

He sat at the edge of the bed fuming, anger clouding his face and eyes. He had a mind to go back into the kitchen and blow the brains out of both them sorry niggas. But he was conscious that he'd have to kill the bitch in his bed as well, and that was just too many bodies to dispose of. He was in a rotten frame of mind.

Fat Boy, or C-Note, as he liked to be called, came off with that mumbo-jumbo bullshit and had tried to put him on the spot again. And Scrappy had enjoyed it not at all. Frustration and anger welled in him, almost to the point where he was stark-raving mad. He wished, he told himself, that the bitch in his bed had said something stupid so he could've relieved all his pent-up frustration on her head. But the bitch wasn't nearly as stupid as he thought she was, he mused, laughing to himself. She'd done what was best; she rolled over and took her nappy-head ass back to sleep.

He was frozen by rage. Fat Boy had again tried to make a fool out of him in front of an audience. The knots in his gut tightened while droplets of sweat formed on his forehead. He felt jittery, tired of exaggerating his friendship for his use-to-be best friend. Those days were over. Now it was about survival of the fittest, and he felt he was the fittest. He became almost neurotic at the thoughts that surfed his brain, his anger slowly dissolving as his mind juggled the pleasures of the future he had planned. He climbed into bed and lay wide awake, his heartbeat soaring. He could not remember being so enthusiastic at such a cleverly fiendish idea before. He closed his eyes, feeling pleased and proud with a contented smile on his face, sleep coming instantly as he closed his eyes.

It was still early when C-Note left Cat-Daddy at the spot. The sky periodically blazed with lightning, threatening rain. The wind raised a steady whoooo as C-Note walked up the driveway to the back of a heavily barred house. The house needed major work, he noted, as he stood on the back porch, checking out its dilapidated condition. Too late, he told himself, because after these couple of weeks, or maybe even a few days, it would be the owner's problem once again.

He rang the doorbell, but nobody answered. Instead of ringing it again, this time, he pounded on the barred door with his fist. In unison, the three pit bulls tied to the gate, tree, and a doghouse began to bark. C-Note turned his head to watch the dogs, making sure none of them broke free. Where the mailbox had been on the barred door, it was now converted into a six-inch slot, which was barely big enough for the biggest hand to fit through. A metal piece was attached on the inside, allowing the occupant inside access to opening and closing the slot at will. The inside of the door was painted black and the inside of the house was lit so dimly that it was impossible to see in. The slide slid open finally.

"Who dat?" asked a voice C-Note was quite familiar with.

"Cash-Notes," he answered, and waited while the locks were being unbolted. He finally heard the two 2 x 4s being removed from behind the door, then the door opened.

"Da' way you beatin' and da' dogs barkin', we thought you was da' police."

C-Note stepped in, trying to focus his eyes in the darkness. The only thing that appeared clearly visible was the mouth of the person he was talking to. The gold and diamonds sparkled even without light.

"What brangs you on dis side of town so early?" he asked C-Note, handing him a foldout chair. C-Note unfolded the chair and sat down.

"Jus' checkin' on my spots. Nothin' else to do, really."

Goldmouth smiled. "Shittt! If you ain't got nothin' else to do, you can brang yo' rich ass down in here an' help me an' Footwork pop off some of dis shit."

C-Note smiled, "You know I ain't gettin' down like this no more—rock houses played out."

The gold smile flashed again. "Dat's what you thank! Beer?"

C-Note shook his head and goldmouth got up and opened the refrigerator. The light from inside cast a ghostly illumination as he grabbed a bottle of MGD and sat back down. He opened his beer. C-Note watched his big frame silhouetted in the dark. His name was Kevin, but he liked to be called by his nickname, Do-A-Deal. He was close to six feet tall, and every bit of two-hundred thirty pounds and so black that he was blue. His best friend and partner in crime's name was Footwork.

Footwork was the total opposite of Do-A-Deal physically, but mentally, they thought and acted alike in most ways. Both were from the country part of Dallas, Texas, and both were loyal to the game that they chose to be their occupation.

C-Note smiled as he reflected on how he'd met the two. "Bawy, what you smilin' fo'? I can see yo' ass over d'ere grinnin' in da dark."

The gold smile flashed again. "You oughta' know by now, Pitch Black is my cousin," Do-A-Deal said jokingly, turning up the bottle.

"Yeah, I know," C-Note said, and then added, "I was jus' trippin' off how we met. Crazy, ain't it?"

Do-A-Deal thought for a brief few seconds. "Crazy ain't even da half of it," he said thoughtfully. Neither one said anything; both were lost in time, thinking back to that day.

Do-A-Deal and Footwork had driven out here from Texas. They had pooled all their money together to buy a kilo, and wound up buying two pounds of baking soda and cake mix. They had no idea that the female Footwork was involved with and who had set up the transaction was in on the bogus deal. When they arrived back at their hotel with what they thought was cocaine, she was long gone and nowhere to be found. They both sensed something wasn't right. Do-A-Deal immediately walked over to where Footwork had hidden the rest of their money that was for the trip back home. Nothing. Then reality struck.

Do-A-Deal crossed the room to the table where Footwork had set the kilo and began to rip the tape off the package. Once open, he stuck his finger in the powdery substance and moaned aloud. "Fuckin' cake batter!" he half-yelled, half-cried.

Footwork was crushed and devastated. "Don't worry," he told Do-A-Deal sadly, "I'll sell all my jewelry to get us home. Then I'll sell my two rides and my motorcycle and that should take care of yo' half of what was lost."

The two took what little money they had in their pockets and went to eat breakfast at the M&M restaurant that was down the street from their hotel. C-Note had already sat down with Sheila and his son when the two came in and were seated at a table next to his. The young black waiter flirted openly with Sheila as he brought their food.

"Anything else?" the waiter asked, the question posed to Sheila more than he.

C-Note tried to curb his tongue, but found he couldn't. "Yeah, there's somethin' else," C-Note said smugly. "You can have my broad if you can bus' her midair. Seein' how you all in her face and givin' her so much attention, you should be able to talk her right from up under me, playboy."

The waiter frowned slightly, but didn't move. The two who had been seated next to C-Note were in an uproar, laughing to almost tears.

"Bring ya' sorry ass over here an' do yo' job," said the big one with the gold in his mouth.

"Yeah," the smaller of the two quickly added, "'cause you sho' don't know what to do wit' a woman that fine. 'Cause he just gave you the opportunity to get at her an' you jus' standin' d'ere lookin' stupid."

They both cracked up laughing as C-Note turned around and glared at them. The smaller of the two shrugged his shoulders. "Jus' tellin' the truth," he said matter-of-factly as the waiter hurriedly moved over to their table.

C-Note went back to eating his food, while Sheila toyed with hers, somewhat embarrassed. When they finally finished,

Sheila went to the car, and C-Note paid for the breakfast. Just as he was about to walk out the door, the bigger man of the two who had been sitting next to him called out, "Hey! Hold on! Can I holla' at you for a minute?"

C-Note wondered what he could want as he watched the big hulk of a man and his smaller friend lumber over to him. "Let's step outside," the big man said and held the door open for C-Note. Once outside, the big hulk produce three gold chain necklaces, the same ones C-Note had seen his friend wearing.

"I got dee's solid gold chains I'm sellin'," he said, practically shoving the necklaces in C-Note's hand. "Now befoe you say anything, I want you to check out the quality and the weight."

C-Note examined the necklaces closely.

"Me and my partna' ain't from here. We from out of state. And we need the scrilla to get back home."

C-Note was about to say something but was cut off. "Dem' two herringbones are an inch thick. And dat rope is solid gold all da way through." He paused briefly to see if C-Note was buying his spiel. "All I want is three-fifty for all dem."

It was a deal C-Note could not resist. He figured he'd give Sheila one of the herringbones and the rope and the other herringbone to this grandmother. "It's all good," C-Note began, "but there's one problem."

The two friends exchanged a quick, mystified look. "And what's dat?" the big guy asked somewhat nervously, afraid his sales pitch was about to be turned down. C-Note smiled thoughtfully, "I ain't got three-fifty on me. But if you wanna follow me to my girl's spot, I'll take the necklaces off your hands."

The hulk thought about it for only a split second, then said, "Let me get a box for my food and pay for it, and I'll be right out."

C-Note had taken them through backstreets all the way to Sheila's neighborhood, sure they wouldn't be able to find their way back to her spot if they tried. C-Note had told Sheila to go in and count out the money they were requesting, then to go back upstairs and sit with the nine millimeter in hand just in case the two had planned on some shady shit. After making sure Sheila was upstairs, C-Note let the two in.

While they had been waiting outside on the porch for Sheila to count up the money, C-Note found out the names of both the men. Do-A-Deal was the bigger of the two, and the one who had approached him about buying the necklaces. Footwork, the smaller one, was the one who had clowned the waiter at the restaurant. At first, they seemed hesitant, afraid to come in, but then went on in. Both were surprised and impressed.

"Nice crib," Do-A-Deal complimented.

"Yeah, nice setup!" Footwork chimed in.

C-Note picked up the cash lying on the table and put it in Do-A-Deal's big paw. In return, he handed C-Note the necklaces. C-Note immediately went to the kitchen, reached onto the top of a cabinet, and brought out his digital scale. The two out-of-towners exchanged knowing glances.

"Jus' checkin' the weight on these chains," C-Note confessed openly. "I don't wanna be payin' too much for something I can get cheaper from somewhere else. You know what I mean?" C-Note looked both men squarely in their eyes.

Seeing the scale made Do-A-Deal and Footwork relax a little more. And that's when the two opened up and told him everything from the business they were doing in Texas to the time they got finagled out of their cash. The sincerity in their voices told him that they weren't lying. Also, the fact that they were selling their gold cemented their story. They had been thrown a curveball, and C-Note felt sorry for them. It was too late for sympathetic remarks he figured, but a tidal wave of emotion engulfed him.

"Here," C-Note said, handing two of the necklaces back to Do-A-Deal. "If you're true to the game, you'll take my number down, and when you get your ends together, you can shoot my three-fifty back. And I'll do the same with your other necklace."

Neither could believe he was so trusting. "Shit! I wish we'd of known you from da git-go," Footwork said impulsively. "We wouldn't be up shit creek wit'out a paddle right now."

C-Note smiled his sad smile. "You live to learn," he advised firmly, and then handed them both a piece of paper with his number on it. "When y'all ready to separate the real from the fake, give me a call."

And that was how they all met.

It had been thirteen months ago since that incident, C-Note reflected. "Seems like years," Do-A-Deal added, as if reading his mind.

"I know," C-Note answered. "One side of me wanted to not trust you. The other side, my good side, made me."

Do-A-Deal sipped his beer and smiled.

"When y'all called me two months later and said y'all had jus' moved out here, I had written y'all off for dead," C-Note said sincerely.

Do-A-Deal's expression pained. "I knew you thought we was chickenshit," he said lamentably, "but how we was gonna pay you back was all we talked about on our drive home. That, and how we were gonna git' some real money too. But you were our main concern. You looked out for us in a time of need, an' for that, we wanted to make good."

C-Note felt embarrassed by his sentimental feeling, and Do-A-Deal recognized his feelings as well. "You've been like a brother to me and Footwork, and I can't begin to tell you how much love we got for you." Do-A-Deal paused, his own feelings becoming involved. "You helped us get our cash right. Took us places. Showed us the do's and don'ts of L.A. And treated us wit' the utmost respect. I can from myself tell you how much I appreciate you as well as respect you for the knowledge and game you gave us. Without it, ain't no tellin' where we'd be."

They both sat in awkward silence for a while. Finally, C-Note spoke. "I told you a while ago I wasn't gonna be in this game forever. 'Cause this sellin' dope shit don't last forever. I'm glad y'all got y'all paper right, 'cause after this last sack a' dope, I'm truly givin' up the game."

Do-A-Deal flashed his best smile. "It's all good," he delightfully enthused. "You know me and 'Works been savin' our money, and we was ready to quit too. Moms got her house, and we got our record shop and some. So it couldn't be a more perfect time to jump outta da game." Do-A-Deal got up, went to the refrigerator and grabbed another beer.

C-Note felt his life simplifying. He pondered this briefly, as if it mattered. From day one, life had handed him a shitty deal, and he knew it wasn't over until it was over. He made himself sound as casual as he could.

"I'm really glad you got what you wanted outta dis game," he said and meant it. He stood up, ready to leave. "I know you're barley startin' on that kilo I gave you the other day, but I don't feel too safe where they are. So can I bring you the other one I said I had for you?"

Do-A-Deal pushed back the chair he was sitting in and stood up as well, wickedly smiling from ear to ear. "Ya' damn right you can bring it! The more the merrier, and the merrier the more money." They both broke out into laughter and then embraced, and C-Note departed, feeling extraordinarily better than he had in a long time.

chapter

4

Since he was already deep in L.A., C-Note decided to stop by a couple of other spots he had a stake in. Va-Voom and Leeway grew up and lived in the forties, off Central Ave. Both were good friends of one another, but both chose to have a spot of their own. Their spots were right around the corner from each other, and if they had wanted to, all either one had to do was jump into his neighbor's backyard, walk to the back fence, hop over it, and be in his friend's backyard.

Both were good-natured nuisances to each other. They competed in everything. If one busted with a new car, a few days later, you could expect to see the other with a newer car. To them, everything was competition. Clothes, jewelry, cars, women, as well as just seeing who could live life best. And they both had plenty of everything. On weekends a couple of times a month, the two would get together and take their women at that time out for a little fun. Something to relieve the stress and strain of the dope game, they said.

Leeway once told C-Note how Va-Voom and he had gone out one Saturday. He mentioned how he felt the woman he was with didn't compare to the woman Va-Voom was with, so he dumped her and found new a star. The next time they had all went out, Leeway said, he felt surely he was winning the ongoing battle. But in the following weeks to come, his friend, Va-Voom had done the same thing, finding an even better-looking woman than the one he had had. And as a result of the ongoing situation, Leeway told him, neither of the two ever took the same woman out more than twice.

C-Note had laughed and wondered if the story he was told were true. However, he noted they both made formidable opponents for one another.

C-Note parked the car at the curb in front of Va-Voom's house. The house had been built in the early '50s, but was immaculately remodeled. A 1995 Chevy Impala sat in the driveway and a '63 Chevy Impala sat on the front lawn, lowered to the ground.

Va-Voom sat on a ragged, sagging recliner chair on his front porch. His voice matched that of the character in which his name came from off the Felix the Cat cartoon. Va-Voom looked suspicious for a second as C-Note got out of the car. His suspicion changed in a flash, though, when he saw who it was.

"Nigga, what you doin' on this side of town?" Va-Voom's voice boomed as he walked midway up the walkway to greet C-Note with a sturdy hand clasp and a short hug.

"I was checkin' out my folks not too far from here, so I came to see what's crackin wit' you," C-Note said as they both walked back to the porch.

Va-Voom sat in his old recliner, while C-Note stood up an orange milk crate and sat on it. Once he was comfortable again, Va-Voom reached down and picked up a glass plate, which contained every bit of two ounces of crack cocaine, a single-edge razor blade, and dozens of 1 x 1 inch baggies. Right next to the recliner, on the wooded floor of the porch, was an AK-47 assault rifle. Two extra clips lay in between the gun and the recliner. Va-Voom started stuffing the baggies with cutup cocaine rocks.

"What's all the heat for?" C-Note asked quizzically.

Va-Voom didn't even look up; he just continued to stuff the baggies. "Young punk in da 'hood been seeing too much." Va-Voom paused as if he weren't going to say anything else. C-Note was about to change the subject when he continued on, still stuffing the baggies with rocks.

"A few of the older homies got out of jail, and they hatin'. They expect a muthafucka to take care of their grown, sorry asses."

C-Note shook his head solemnly. *Same thing, just different 'hoods,* he thought to himself. He'd been through it so many times himself. Remembering those days, he was suddenly overcome with mixed emotions. "How you plan to handle it?" he asked Va-Voom frankly while staring at the gun.

Va-Voom finally looked up from packaging his rocks and smiled coldly. "Wit' dat dere," he said, pointing at the AK with a nod of the head.

C-Note smiled crookedly. "That'll back them off once that kay starts to spittin.'" C-Note had firsthand experience of the streets and knew what Va-Voom said was the truth. To be under fire of an AK was a frightening experience, especially if you lived to tell about it.

"I guess you got the right arsenal," C-Note said as an afterthought.

Va-Voom again looked up from his packaging process, smiled wolfishly, and said, "That ain't shit compared to the weapons I got in the house."

Sitting there, panic started to bubble inside C-Note's head. What if someone came gunning and Va-Voom was unable to make it to the AK? He quickly fought down the panicky feelings and changed the subject to soothe his mind.

"What's up wit' Leeway?" C-Note asked.

Now Va-Voom was cutting smaller rocks from a larger one. He didn't bother to look up. "Same shit," Va-Voom said scathingly. "They tried to shoot up his house, but it wound up bein' a shootout. Leeway woulda' got they ass too, if he'd been shootin' wit' Betsy over there." He nodded to the AK-47 again and then quickly rolled on.

"But all he had at the time was a lousy-ass Tec-22, which barely put a hole in their car."

C-Note could hardly believe what he was hearing. "Why didn't y'all call an' tell me the spot got shot up?"

Cutting up his dope still, Va-Voom said smartly, "'Cause' it ain't like we don't know how to handle shit like this. Dis ain't nothin' new to Leeway an' me. We grew up our whole lives goin' thru shootouts, an' one more ain't gonna change shit anyway. Plus, they came thru shootin' wit' a .38 or a .32 revolver. It sounded like they were poppin' firecrackers, dawg."

C-Note stared blankly at Va-Voom. "It's my fight as well, so that makes me involved. I ain't scared of gunplay."

Va-Voom's head jerked up, a serious look on his face. "Of that I'm quite certain," he replied smartly. "Me and Leeway got this under headlock. We know jus' who to eliminate and all our problems will be solved." The wolfish grin was back.

C-Note hunched his shoulders. "If you say y'all need me, you know where I'm at."

"Sure do," Va-Voom said sarcastically, continuing to cut his rocks. C-Note ran down his game plan, just as he had done with Do-A-Deal. And just as Do-A-Deal, Va-Voom was all for having more work. "A bird in hand beats one in the stash marinathin,'" he said, laughing at what he considered a joke.

C-Note stood up, ready to leave, and shook his head pitifully.

"What?" Va-Voom asked, concerned.

C-Note laughed mirthlessly. "That was the sorriest shit I heard all week, Voom. The gunplay must be strippin' you of your usual good humor."

Va-Voom didn't say anything. A small piece of rationality bit at him. Maybe C-Note was right. Was he losing his mind to these mean streets? Has his humor deteriorated? His face was bewildered by his own questions. Quickly his mood changed. Va-Voom knew he had firsthand knowledge and the best experience of the street. He was self-assured and quickly shook the moment of doubt.

"C-Note," he said standing up after he set the plate down, "these fools are the hardhead type. And you know the sayin' goes. A hardhead makes a soft ass. An' when I get through wit' 'em, you can bet they'll be soft as doctors' cotton." He roared again at his so-called humor as C-Note hurried his pace and made a hasty getaway.

He pulled around the corner and parked in Leeway's driveway behind his car. As he got out of the car, C-Note saw someone peek through the venetian blinds. Then he heard the locks to the door being unlocked as he walked across the dirt lawn. As he walked up the steps to the porch, the door swung open. Leeway stood in the jamb, grinning from ear to ear.

"Look it what the wind blew in," he jeered as C-Note stepped past him through the door.

"I jus' left from ya' boy Voom's joint and figured I'd drop by here too."

The house was dark, and the only light was from a dim lamp on a wooden table. C-Note let out a low whistle as his eyes caught sight of the weapons on Leeway's floor.

"I take it Voom has told you the situation," Leeway said, sitting on a fairly new tan leather sofa.

"Yeah," C-Note replied, still looking at the arsenal. There were more than a dozen guns laid on the floor in front of the sofa he was sitting on. "Looks like you're gonna take on Afghanistan or Iraq wit' all dat shit." He bent over and picked up the biggest gun of them all.

"Is this the same gun Scarface had in his movie?" C-Note asked, checking it out admiringly.

Leeway loved to boast idly. His lips curled in the corners to form a cruel smile. "Damn, right!" he stated proudly. "M-16 wit' a grenade launcher. Fully automatic, too, and ready to tear some shit up! So be careful wit' that thang 'cause it's loaded, too."

C-Note observed the gun more closely. "These damn things are brand-new."

A gleam of excitement flashed in Leeway's eyes. "I know! I jus' bought all this shit from my folks." Leeway gestured to the guns on the floor.

C-Note laid the M-16 back in its place and hefted up a Glock-34 with an infrared beam on it. He liked the feel of the gun in his hand. "Man, Lee-baby, sell me this one," C-Note said aiming the red beam at the venetian blinds.

Leeway shook his head side to side, smiling. "No-can-do, big baby. That's my favorite one, too." Leeway bent down and picked up a gray, stainless steel automatic. "Here's a .45-caliber Ruger wit' silencer and infrared. I can sell you this." Leeway handed the gun to C-Note and picked up another. "Or this .380 Beretta."

The .45 seemed three times heavier than the Glock he had first picked up. He played with the big gun for a few seconds. It reminded him of a Colt .45 he once had but that was taken by the police. Now he took the black .380 from Leeway's hand, playing with it the same way he had with the .45.

"Nigga, you actin' like you some kind of gun expert. And you probably don't know jack shit about no guns." They both broke out laughing at Leeway's remarks, because what he said was 100 percent pure truth.

C-Note set the gun back down and asked, "Can I get both of 'em?" hoping that Leeway wouldn't try an' stick his whole hand in his pocket and charge him up the ass for both guns.

Leeway seemed to contemplate the question for a moment. Then said, "Yeah, we'll jus' take it off the ..." Leeway paused again in deep thought. After a few seconds of thinking, he continued, "Six hundred! I think that's a cool price for two new guns." He looked at C-Note questioningly and asked, "Is it alright if I take the six hundred off the bill I owe you?"

C-Note felt he couldn't argue with that. "Good deal," he said quickly, shaking Leeway's hand to seal the deal before he could change his mind. He felt he had to be nosy, and asked, "Where you get the hookup on all these straps?"

Leeway grinned wryly. He knew he could trust C-Note, just as C-Note had trusted him many a time. "My uncle," Leeway said smiling. "He's a crooked sheriff's deputy, and he's got the inside plug."

C-Note believed everything Leeway said. He'd known Leeway to be a bragger, not a liar. C-Note then shifted the scene to the reason for having the guns. "Voom says y'all know the source of the problem."

Leeway's lips twisted into a sneer. "Damn right we do! And when I go over to Voom's later on, I'm gonna make a small bet of a few gees jus' for fun to see who'll be the first of us two to get this muthafucka."

C-Note didn't reply. He was at a loss for words and didn't know how to respond. "Once we get'em," Leeway went on, "everybody else gonna back up. The only reason they trippin' now is 'cause they scared of this fool 'cause he just got out da' pen and he got a little size on him."

Leeway picked the Glock up, cocked one eye, and aimed the gun on his make-believe target on one of the walls. "But this right here," he said, nodding his head to the gun in his extended hand, "is gonna show him size ain't shit!"

C-Note told himself whoever this dude was, he was in for a world of shit, fucking with these two loonies with guns. As if reading his mind, Leeway said, "Uh-huh, ole boy is in for a shit-storm fucking wit' me and the Voom. The damn fool don't even recognize real gangstas even when they right in his face."

C-Note didn't say anything for some time, as if weighing up what he was going to say. "I just hope you are as lucky as you are confident," he said to Leeway, now standing up, ready to make his exit. "Because no matter how many guns you got, it all boils down to who gets the first draw." He picked up the .380 and the .45, tucking them in his waistband. Leeway appeared to have a perpetual beam on his face.

"Ya' know, you're right a lot of the times. But this time ain't one of them times. This cat ain't jus' up against one gunner, but two. So, therefore, it shortens his odds drastically."

They walked to the door, and C-Note gave him the rundown on the real reason he had come by there. Like the rest of the people he supplied with drugs, Leeway wanted his share of the dope.

"Yeah, I sure can use the money off the extra byrd. Those guns will put a nice dent in my pockets on my profits from the first kilo, which, by the way, I still got three-quarters of. But bills, car note, and baby mammas is gonna drain the remaining profits from that.

"So on the second one, I can stack some extra cheddar and get ready to move myself. This bullshit around here is too full'a drama; it's always keepin' a muthafucka in some kind of cahoots."

They both stepped out on to the porch, and Leeway tensed. He then quickly turned around and went back into the house, picked up the Glock, and came back out, smiling slyly. "Almost caught me slippin," he said, looking up and down the street for any signs of possible danger.

His reactions caused C-Note to check out the street as well. He felt sort of ill prepared at being in the line of danger. "I know exactly how you feel," C-Note said, stepping off the porch and heading for his car. "The 'hood'll definitely take you under."

He got in his car and started to back out the driveway. Leeway held up a fist before disappearing back through his front door as C-Note sped off, driving carefully. Inwardly, he was overcome with a sudden sadness. Money was again the cause of so many problems. Not only with him, he reflected, but with everyone. All were afflicted by a disease that only money could cure, and casualties would be the only physical evidence in the struggle for the almighty dollar.

The days of the calendar were wiped away by time. To begin with, everything seemed to be going dreamily. No one at the time could resist all the dope C-Note was pushing on them, mainly because everyone wanted the same thing. Money! And just as C-Note was thinking about "The Big Sting," so were all those who had never in their lives touched two kilos. He knew how they were thinking, because he, too, was thinking the same way, but on a larger scale. This was his ultimate come-up for all his years on the streets hustling rocks just to get where he was today. Plus he knew he was helping everyone who was helping him to sell the dope to fulfill a dream, a goal, and to achieve whatever it was they were selling dope for. It was never far from the back of his thoughts how the final prize so often lands in your lap just when you least expect it.

His far-fetched ideas were coming true, the obsession that somehow, someway, he would beat the game made him sense victory. He was feeling oddly calm and yet thrilled by apprehension. C-Note felt wearily satisfied, because after this last "Big Sting," no longer would he be part of the dope game. That insatiable hunger for money would finally be fulfilled. No more dope. No more games. No more bullshit. He could finally start on the path to a new life, a new environment, and new friends. He could change the direction of his life, attain some positive attributes so he could one day reflect back on his life and proclaim he wasn't one of the statistics that said he would wind up dead, locked up, or broke. He knew where to draw the line. For years, he'd lived dangerously in the roughest parts of the streets, always taking the roughest paths through life, and now, the dangerous, lengthy process was almost over.

If invested correctly, he had more than enough money to last him a lifetime. C-Note knew—he never forgot that tears were a way of life to the black man. He just hoped with all his heart that he would not falter in the battle of life. His desire was to live his best in the most excellent way possible for his family and for himself. He earnestly desired to finally become solid, dependable, and have a strong sense of duty.

Now he was anticipating his fair chance to undo his

past, to perform his family duties, to develop some character, integrity, and honesty before it was too late. There was no way possible that this world would ever balance itself out, and he knew that. But he wouldn't worry about that now. He had to fill the holes in his soul first. All he wanted was to be free from fears, insecurities, guilt, shame, and resentments. And only then would the dream of getting out make his spirits soar.

chapter

5

Thunder cannoned and the wind whipped the trees mercilessly as the rain tapped on the window. Sheila and C-Note had been to a party the night before and arrived home rather late. The dreary weather helped their blissful sleeping. Unfortunately, C-Note's private phone came to life, interrupting the peacefulness of the morning.

"Awww!" Sheila moaned, rolling over and putting her pillow over her head. C-Note sat up, debating with himself whether he should silence the phone once and for all by yanking it out of the socket.

"Answer that damn phone!" Sheila's muffled voice screamed from under the pillow as the phone shrilled again. C-Note quickly answered it before it could pierce the quietness another time.

"Hello" he said sourly into the mouthpiece.

"What's up?" was the reply on the other end.

C-Note felt himself getting agitated. "Fuck the formalities! Who is this?"

The voice on the other end coughed nervously before answering with a shaky voice, "Cat-Daddy."

C-Note was about to ask why was he calling so early when Cat-Daddy rushed on. "I'm here at the spot an' Scrappy wants me to help him work on gettin' a car." He paused slightly, and when C-Note said nothing, he went on. "He wanted your car, too. You know the one for three thousand three hundred and seventy-five dollars. He's been buggin' me all last night an' all this mornin'. I tried callin' last night, but no one answered. I told him I couldn't make a decision like that until I consulted you, by it bein' your car 'n' all."

C-Note wondered if Scrappy was doing this on purpose? Scrappy knew he hated to be awakened at such an early hour and perhaps thought he could get him to make an unwise choice this way. But he was awake now, and only angered more. "What the hell's wrong wit' the car dealer he's been dealin' wit'?" C-Note asked harshly. He heard Cat-Daddy ask Scrappy the same question.

Then, moments later, "He said his car dealer is out of town and won't be back for several days."

C-Note smiled to himself, because Cat-Daddy had remembered to talk in code over the phone. In so many words, Cat-Daddy was telling him that Scrappy wanted to buy nine ounces, a quarter of a kilo for $3,375. The same price he had been paying. And that Scrappy's connection for the product was out of town. But that wasn't his problem, C-Note thought bitterly. It would also mean more money for Cat-Daddy to make, since Scrappy would be out of dope. Cat-Daddy's voice brought him out of his thoughts.

"Whatcha' want me to do?"

C-Note thought briefly for a few seconds. "Tell him I can't sell the car whole like that anymore. I got to break it down so I can make my money. It'll be five-hundred apiece for the parts he wants. And he can buy all the parts he wants at that price." He heard Cat-Daddy chuckle lightly, then there was mumbling in the background. Next, he heard Scrappy's voice spewing obscenities.

Seconds later, Scrappy was on the phone himself. "That's fucked-up the way you tryin' to charge a nigga up," Scrappy said testily. "Downright chickenshit! Straight chickenshit!"

C-Note spoke in a quiet but fierce voice. "Call it what you want, nigga! You ain't part of the team no more. So, I ain't got no deals for you. Your price is the same as the next man's price, and that's about best as I can do."

Silence now took over as C-Note listened to the rain splatter against the window, feeling pleasure at Scrappy's rage. He knew his best friend was stark-raving mad and hoped he didn't try no funny business with Cat-Daddy. Finally, after a few moments of total silence, he spoke. "It's all good," Scrappy said sourly. "Every dog has his day, and yours is soon to come."

Before C-Note could reply, Cat-Daddy came back on the line. "So sell the car to'em part by part?"

C-Note didn't care if Scrappy was mad. That was part of the game. "Damn right! Ain't no love," C-Note said. They talked briefly for a few more moments, and then hung up. Still tired, he climbed back into the bed, listening to the gloomy weather. He wondered to himself if the solemn weather could be a sign of a bad day that had already begun.

On the other side of town just as C-Note was hanging up the phone, a hard knock on the barred door brought Two-Down back to the attention of business. "These damn smokers jus' don't quit," he said meekly, putting the PlayStation on pause and standing up. He stretched like a cat before walking to the door and peeking through the peephole. The weather and the barred door made it hard to see. Little Poke sat on the couch with the second controller of the PlayStation in his hand, smoking a Black & Mild cigar.

"I know," he said to Two-Down's remark. "They're puffin' like chimneys or a broke stove. In rain, sleet, or snow, that crack keeps them comin' no matter what."

The door pounded again, and Two-Down cracked the wood door barely enough for his head to fit through. Instantly he recognized one of the neighborhood smokers. "It's Mike," he said over his shoulder to Poke, as he began to unbolt the door locks.

"Shit, Poke, we ain't never made this much cash in one morning ever," he enthused with a wide grin on his face, "let alone on a rainy day." He pushed the barred door open and stepped aside to let Mike in. Usually, he or Little Poke would serve them right through the bars. But since it was raining, they figured they wouldn't leave their clients standing out in the rain. That would be bad for business.

As Mike stepped through the door, Two-Down knew off the bat something was wrong by the look on Mike's sucked-up face. Before Two-Down could react to anything, it was too late. Two masked gunmen had been standing out of sight next to the door and were right on Mike's heels as he came through the door with their guns raised. Little Poke was also late to react, as he jumped up from where he had been sitting and tried to dash to the back room where their guns were kept.

The first gunman was on him quick and grabbed him by his shirt and slammed the butt of his gun into Poke's face and head. Blood squirted out of his head onto the walls before he crumbled to the floor.

"Sit the fuck on the couch, both of you!" The second gunman ordered, waving the pistol in his hand at Two-

Down and Mike the smoker. Two-Down did as he was told, noticing as he sat down the silencers on their guns. The first gunman reached into a black nylon jacket he was wearing and produced several pair of handcuffs.

"Help ya' man off the floor," the second gunman said. "Both of you!" Two-Down and Mike the smoker lifted Poke off the floor and sat him on the couch.

Mike the smoker began to plead with Two-Down. "I ain't have nothin' to do with this shit." Mike was near tears. "I was comin' to get me two doves when they forced me to come to y'all do'e." He reached into his pocket and brought out the two twenty-dollar bills to prove he was telling the truth.

"Shut the fuck up!" said the first gunman, then whacked him on the head with his gun. His partner had his gun aimed directly at Two-Down. The first gunman took the forty dollars that fell to the floor from the smoker's hand and put a pair of the handcuffs on Mike's wrists. Quickly he did the same to Two-Down, and then to Little Poke. The second gunman still had his gun trained on Two-Down.

"Search'em and make sure they ain't heated," he said to the first gunman, who began immediately to do what he was told.

"I know y'all ain't in here without gats. Where you two keep your gats at?"

Two-Down had a faint smirk on his face. "You mean, where are the straps at?" he said, correcting the first gunman and being sarcastic as well.

The gunman's hand was a blur as it struck Two-Down in the jaw. "Keep up that jive bullshit an' you might not see tomorrow."

Blood trickled out the corner of Two-Down's mouth as his hurt turned to frustration. "And you bett'a hope I don't see tomorrow! 'Cause if I do, yo' ass gonna be mine."

The gunman who hit Two-Down laughed coldly.

"That's why yo' ass is wearin' that mask; you scared to show yo' face."

The second gunman produced a roll of electrical tape. "Tape their mouths and their feet," he said, tossing the first gunman the tape. Little Poke let out a moan of pain. Slowly he sat up on the couch, taking in the whole scene. An injured look came over his face as the gunman put tape around his ankles and a strip across his mouth.

Mike the smoker began to plead again. "Please," he said almost crying, "I ain't got nothing to do wit' this! Why am I bein' tied up? I ain't seen nothin', I don't know nothin', an' I ain't gonna say nothin'. Can I just please go?"

The first gunman grinned savagely. "Jus' shut the fuck up!" he said as he pointed his gun at the three of them on the couch.

Once everybody's legs were tied and mouths taped, the second gunman pulled off his ski mask and tucked the gun in his waistband for easy access. The first gunman followed suit, taking off his mask as well. Two-Down looked at Little Poke and hunched his shoulder. Little Poke shook his bloody head from side to side.

The first gunman disappeared into the back room, while the other sat across from the three on the couch. Poke watched him with murder in his heart as Two-Down seethed with anger from the hit to the jaw from the first gunman. Tears streamed down Mike the smoker's face as he thought about how rapidly his life was falling apart. First the dope, and now this. All was quiet for a moment, and all that could be heard was the rain and wind outside, and the first gunman occasionally moving around in one of the back rooms.

The second gunman relaxed, crossing his feet and folding his arms across his chest. His voice was menacing and almost quiet. "Let me begin simply," he said calmly, seeming even more relaxed as he went on. "There are several ways this robbery can turn out. Or should I call it 'Jack Move,' as you boys here in Cali like to refer to it as." He paused, smiling devilishly.

"First of all, this can be simple, or we can make it difficult."

Two-Down could feel a wetness at the seat of his pants. He glanced over at Mike the smoker and noticed he had pissed his pants.

"All we want is the dope and money, and I expect the two of you to tell me where it is."

Poke wiped the blood from his face onto his shirt.

"And if you choose not to tell me," the gunman said smoothly, leaning forward slightly, "then we'll have to resort to torture. And Larry jus' loves hurtin' people."

The first gunman was coming through the door from one of the back rooms with several guns in his hands when he heard his name mentioned. "You call me, Johnny?" he asked. Two-Down shot Poke a look as if to say, did you catch their names? Poke quickly winked back, letting Two-Down know that he had.

Johnny spoke. "Naw, Larry, I didn't call you. I was jus' tellin' de's two boys how you like ta hurt people."

Larry smiled humorlessly as he set the weapons on the floor at Johnny's feet. "I couldn't find the dope or the money. What's dat smell?" Larry asked, turning to the three men on the couch.

Two-Down looked at the man in between him and Poke who was crying in muffed sobs. "Goddamn!" Johnny shouted, standing up and moving next to Larry. "This muthafucka done shitted on his self!"

Larry moved a short distance and stood in front of the frightened dope fiend. He began to viciously slap the smoker repeatedly, causing both Two-Down and Poke to wince at every blow. "Nasty sum' bitch! Who you thank wanna smell yo' shit?" Larry continued his beating. "All you had to do," smack, smack, "was tell somebody you had to shit." Whack! Whack! Whack!

"That's plenty," Johnny said mildly, having seen enough. Two-Down and Poke sat there boiling, clenching their teeth, unable to speak. But their eyes told it all. Johnny saw their anger and smiled. "Now who's gonna be the first one to tell me where the cash and dope is?"

Larry half removed the tape from Two-Down's mouth. "Since you only got hit in the jaw, and you're not as beat up as these two," he pointed to Mike the smoker, whose face was now swelling, and then to Poke, whose head was leaking like a broken faucet, "why don'cha make it light on yourself and tell me what I wanna hear."

Two-Down put together all the vile words and phrases he knew, right before Larry was able to place a big fist on his nose to shut him up. Blood splattered over the smoker and Poke. Mike the smoker was so scared, he began to pass gas uncontrollably.

Johnny sat back down on the couch again, enjoying the scene unfold before his cold, dark eyes. Larry covered Two-Down's mouth once again and moved down in front of Poke. "Now, I know you really don't wanna lose too much more blood, do ya'?" Larry asked Poke dementedly as his eyes sparkled with glee at the sight of blood. He peeled the tape half back from Poke's mouth.

"Go fuck ya'self!" Poke spat through swollen lips.

Larry replaced the tape back across his lips, then he slammed his big fist in between Poke's eyes, breaking his nose just as he did with Two-Down. Blood flew everywhere as Mike the smoker continued to pass gas and sob behind the tape that covered his mouth.

Larry bent down, grabbed the smoker by his arm, and lifted him off the couch. He frantically shook his head and made all kinds of grunt noises as Larry half dragged and half carried him to the back room. Johnny sat back smiling, watching. In a moment, Larry reappeared solo.

"That damn dope fiend in there is in an emotional frenzy. He done gone jus' bout crazy!" Larry said, taking a seat next to Johnny. The two were overconfident, Two-Down thought. If only he had his ...

"Larry, here, is known for his wild, spontaneous behavior. He can get—"

Someone banged on the door. Little Poke jumped up instantly and made a dash for the door, forgetting that his legs were tied. He fell. And almost instantly, Larry was on top of him, kicking him viciously several times in the rib cage.

The door banged again. Larry looked to Johnny, questioning what to do. The banging on the barred door grew louder. Johnny gestured for Larry to keep it quiet. Silently, he got up and went to the door. Peeking through the hole, he could barely see a female smoker on the porch. Her clothes were ragged, and her hair disheveled. Her face looked exhausted from continuous days of being on a crack spree. Johnny cracked the door.

"Ain't nothin' happenin'," he said to the lady on the porch.

"Awww, shit!" she stormed. "Now I got to walk a half mile in this damn rain to get what I want. Fuck! Shit! Dammit to hell!"

Johnny laughed coolly. "Well, sis', we out right now. But come back in few hours an' we should be back on the ball." She stood there, trying to see through the crack as if she didn't believe what she was hearing.

Johnny shut the door and watched her through the peephole. She stood there longer than necessary. Johnny hoped it was because of the rain. Finally she stepped off the porch and disappeared down the street. He turned back to Larry, who had a foot planted on Poke's throat.

"She's gone," he said, heading back to the couch and sitting in the same spot, "but I don't trust it. She may have heard you two wrestlin' around in here." He paused, thinking to himself.

"Let's get this over wit' and be gone. Since they're not gonna take the easy way out, we gonna have to give it to'em the hard way."

Larry pulled Poke off the floor with simple ease. "Since you tried to play like a track star, you gonna be first to witness that we ain't playin'," Larry said, dragging him into the back room.

The smoker sat at the head of the bed, his eyes bloodshot from crying. Larry yelled for Johnny to bring Two-Down in there as well, so he, too, could witness what was about to happen. They were all in the same room now, and Johnny covered the door with his silenced weapon in hand. Mike the smoker's eyes got as big as saucers when Larry walked over to him and grabbed his arm. Before the smoker knew what was happening, Larry shot him in between the legs, blowing off his dick. Mike the smoker crumbled to the ground in pain, withering, shaking, and sobbing. Blood soaked the carpet underneath him.

Larry laughed smugly at the sight before his eyes squirming on the floor. "He looks like a damn fish floppin' around outta water," he said jokingly. Johnny's cold eyes didn't flinch, and now they began to show a tremor of excitement. He drew his lips into a sadistic smile.

"Now Larry and me is tryin' to make dis light as possible. One of you two is next, and Larry ain't gonna be as nice to you as he was to this crackhead." Two-Down's eyes threatened to explode, while Poke leaned against a wall, overwhelmed by the bleeding smoker on the floor. A twinge of guilt hammered at his conscience as he thought about the pain the smoker must be feeling. But even as he thought about revenge, Poke knew it was an unhealthy delusion to believe they would get out of this alive. Larry again removed the tape from Two-Down's mouth.

"OK, I'll ask one last time. Where is the dope and the money at?"

Two-Down felt a maniac force building inside himself. "Go fuck yourself! I ain't tellin' you shit!"

Larry's lips curled into a sneer. Before he could put the tape back across Two-Down's mouth, a wad of spit hit him on the upper lip and nose. The spit hung from his nose, stretching like a rubber band before falling to the floor. Larry's left hand came up so quick Two-Down didn't know he was knocked out cold before he hit the floor. He lay there unconscious.

"Since he wanna be a badass, he's the first one for the treatment." Larry dug around in his pocket. "Make his friend get on his knees," Larry said to Johnny, pointing at Poke, "and put the gun to his head. And if he moves off his knees, kill'em!"

A swat from Johnny's gun helped Poke get to his knees more swiftly. Out of his pocket, Larry pulled a box cutter. Poke shook his head that was still foggy from the blow. Larry pinned Two-Down's unconscious body to the floor by straddling him. Slowly, he began to carve long, deep slits into Two-Down's arm. The razor blade sank deep in his skin. From his hand up to his forearm, Larry sank the razor blade as deep as it would go into Two-Down's flesh, cutting veins, nerves, and muscle. Blood gushed from the wound onto the floor like a busted water pipe.

Larry turned to look at Poke with childish excitement in his eyes, with Two-Down's blood covering his hands and clothes. The tears ran freely down Poke's face. He dared not to move with the gun pressed in the soft part of the back of his neck.

"I'm gonna cut this nigga up like a pig if you don't tell me where the shit is!"

Poke was too shocked by all the blood to respond instantly, so Larry turned back around and sliced a gaping hole in Two-Down's face from his temple to his jaw. Two-Down lay still, unconscious, as if he were dead.

"You ready to talk?" Larry cracked, enjoying the moment and the sight of blood.

Poke had seen enough. He knew that if he didn't give in, not only would they kill Two-Down, but him as well. Maybe—just maybe—they would let them live if he told them where the dope and money were. Poke nodded his head up and down. Johnny removed the tape.

"Smart man, my man," Johnny said almost gleefully. "All this could've been avoided if you two wouldna' have been so stubborn. All we wanted were the goods." Johnny sat on the edge of the bed, while Larry stood up over both the bleeding bodies. His clothes were drenched with blood. Poke's face was an expression of utter panic as his gaze darted here and there.

"Where you got the shit hid?" Larry asked, moving towards Poke.

It took Poke several seconds to find his voice. "In the—the closet," he stammered.

Larry's eyebrows wrinkled menacingly. "Bullshit! I done looked in there already."

Johnny's smooth voice spoke up. "Why don't you get up and show Larry where it's at, my man, so we can be outta here, and you can help your friends."

Poke struggled off his knees to his feet and Larry dragged him to the closet while Johnny held open the door. "Look in the sleeve of the black Raider jacket that's close to the wall."

Poke watched while Larry went through the jacket. He pulled from the sleeve a plastic Footlocker bag full of money. Before Larry could ask where the dope was at, Poke said ruefully, "All the dope is in the freezer, in a Ms. Smith pie box."

Larry handed Johnny the bag of money and went to the kitchen. Within a minute, he was back. "Is this everything?" he asked, opening the box and turning it upside down so the contents fell out on the bed. He began to count the individually wrapped dope packets.

Before Larry could finish counting, Poke said, "Twenty-four ounces and a little bit over twenty-two thousand in cash in the bag."

Larry and Johnny exchanged a triumphant look. Then Larry rapidly started tossing the dope in the bag Johnny held open. Afterwards, Johnny tucked the bag inside his jacket. "You," Johnny said pointing his gun at Poke, "come with me."

With the bloody box cutter, Larry bent down and cut the tape on his feet. Poke hesitated at first, uncertain. Then he followed.

"Sit down," Johnny said. He picked up the weapons Larry had found when they first came in, placed one of the guns in his waistband, and put the other in the bag with the money and dope. Johnny crossed the room and peeked out the window. All clear. Poke was wondering why the hell Larry was still in the other room when Johnny came back and sat on the couch across from him.

"Business is business," Johnny said in that smooth voice of his, "an' this is business."

Larry came out of the room. "It's a done deal in there," he said, sneaking Johnny a wink, which Poke caught. Poke seemed to take a moment to process the situation.

"Surely you didn't believe life could defeat death?"

Poke looked at the piece of shit smiling at him. He thought he ought to say something in his own defense, but couldn't bring himself to say anything, because he knew when they had taken off their ski masks and showed their faces, that he and the others wouldn't leave the house alive. Poke moistened his lips as he watched the two carefully.

"Philosophizing," Johnny was saying, "I guess that's what you can call it. But Larry and me, we call it survivin'. Eatin'. Makin' ends meet the best possible way." He paused, looking Poke squarely in the eye. "And now we're enemies because of the pain I inflicted."

He raised the silenced gun in his hand, aiming it at Poke's head. "So as enemies, I'm left with no choice other than to eliminate you." The first bullet went right through the left eye, exiting the back of the head and splattering blood over the walls and couch. The second bullet ripped the upper right cheekbone completely off his face, blood and puss and gore making his face hideous and gruesome, with a demonic grin still on his lips. The final bullet tore his throat open, leaving his vocal cords and major vessels exposed to the naked eye.

Smiling, Larry looked at Johnny. "Those two in the back room don't look near as bad as this one does."

Larry was pointing to the body on the couch, "Maybe I should go back an' rearrange their faces as well," he said now laughing loudly. Johnny waved it off and stood, ready to go.

"Naw," he said heading for the door, "there'll be plenty more bodies soon. You can have the honors from now on when it comes to the killin' part. My stomach can't take too much more."

Larry's face gleamed demonically. "One down and five to go," he said laughing and joking as they left the house.

⊙══⊀⊱

SHE MURMURED CURSES to herself for being addicted to a drug that made her do anything and go to any lengths to obtain it. The rain drenched her as she splashed through puddle after puddle in her twenty-minute, half-mile journey. But as she walked, she also thought of the quality and quantity of dope she'd be getting for her money's worth. C-Note's spots had the bomb always, and if your money was right, you could even get enough to make double your money. But doubling her money wasn't on her mind. Smoking crack was. She cursed again, this time aloud, causing another smoker who was walking by to stare.

Poke and Two-Down had just told her that they would be working 24/7 for the next week, and then when she went back to spend the hundred she had made off a white trick, they were out. Yeah, she told herself, she'd raise hell if she walked all this distance and Cat-Daddy didn't have any crack either. Then she lied to herself. "Maybe I'll jus' stop smokin' rocks altogether." She laughed out loud as she turned the last corner, because she knew even if she went to hell, or wherever it is you went when you're dead, that if they had crack, she'd be putting on the hits forever and ever.

chapter
6

Sheila had just finished dressing their son as C-Note rushed her to hurry up. She had been up since early morning, when C-Note's private phone had awakened them. Neither one fell back asleep, so they made love in the stormy weather to pass the morning away. Now they were on their way to the movies. A "family day," C-Note liked to call it. Sheila had just put their son's jacket on and was slipping her arms into her own leather coat when his private phone came to life. They were on the way out of the bedroom door. Sheila looked at him knowingly.

"Can you not answer it this time? We're on our way out, remember? Every time that phone rings, it's always business."

C-Note gave an apologetic smile. "I promise, whatever it is, it'll have to wait," he said, crossing the room to the phone. He picked it up on the beginning of the third ring. "Hello?"

The same voice from earlier that morning said those same words, "What up?"

C-Note glanced at Sheila, who, in turn, stared back. "What up, Cat-Daddy? I was jus' walkin' out the door wit' Sheila and Christian." C-Note thought instantly that Cat-

Daddy was calling for Scrappy again by the way he hesitated. Sheila's face cringed in anger.

"Somethin' is up," Cat-Daddy said worriedly. "Kim came by here a few hours ago mad 'cause she had to walk all the way here to buy the part for her car. She said she went to Two-Down and Poke's place, and somebody she didn't know answered the door and said that the car wasn't runnin'. She also said that thirty minutes prior to that, both Two-Down and Poke had been there and that the car was guaranteed to be running whenever she was ready to drive."

Cat-Daddy was silent briefly. Sheila eyed C-Note impatiently. He went on. "You and I both know that neither one of them lets nobody drive their car. Plus, I've been callin' every thirty minutes to see if they made it back. But nobody's answering."

C-Note was quiet, deep in thought. He could hear Cat-Daddy talking to someone in the background. "Who is that?" he asked Cat-Daddy.

"Scrappy wanted to use the phone. I told'em he's got to wait."

"He didn't hear what you were tellin' me, did he?"

"Naw. He jus' walked in the kitchen wantin' to use the phone."

C-Note breathed a silent sigh of relief. "Good! That's good." Again he was in deep thought. He had forgotten about Sheila standing there. He looked up, and she appeared troubled.

She spoke her mind. "I hope this damn call don't ruin our day. It' been weeks since we've all been out together."

C-Note's mind was in a turmoil. He felt a peculiar stirring in his stomach. "Listen, Cat-Daddy," he said, eying Sheila with an unflinching gaze, "we'll stop by there on our way to the movies an' check out everything. I'll see if everything is all fine."

Cat-Daddy sounded relieved. "Do that, and call me when you get the word on them." He paused. "Knowin' them, they probably got a couple of young hoochies over."

In the back of his mind, C-Note knew that wasn't the case, but he told Cat-Daddy that he was probably right, because that's what he wanted to hear. They hung up, C-Note promising to call when he got word. He turned, and Sheila was eying him coldly. It took him a few seconds to regain his composure.

"Hey," he said pleasantly, "if you would have hurried up, we would've been long gone. But you chose to take your sweet time."

She didn't speak, and he made himself sound as casual as he could. "We are just gonna stop by Two-Down an Poke's joint along the way. That's it—I promise."

She eyed him keenly. "Yeah, well, come on then," she said heatedly. "I'm sick and tired of your shitty-ass promises. There's not too much reality to 'em." She started down the stairs, not waiting for a smart rejoinder from him.

As if it were an omen, Sheila said nothing the whole way. C-Note turned on the street and instantly knew by all the law enforcement and paramedics surrounding the spot that something tragic happened. He parked a few houses down and sat there staring with fear and pain in his eyes. He knew the yellow tape that the police used that said "DO NOT CROSS" meant a murder had occurred. Sheila shifted uneasily in her seat, but didn't say anything. She looked guarded, and she could see C-Note's self-control about to crack. Fear swelled in his eyes.

"I should'a known somethin' crazy happened," he said, jarring the silence. She gave him one of her sweet smiles, saying in a voice that was too sympathetic, "You don't know if anything crazy has happened. The police could just be raiding the place, and they might've got away."

He didn't buy her sympathetic remarks. He sat feeling helpless and stunned. "If nothin' crazy ain't happened, then why would they need a coroner's van with the Los Angeles County seal on the door?"

Sheila was unconvinced. "Then why don't you go see what happened? Or what is happening."

Taking her advice, he got out of the car and walked up to a crowd of neighbors who were being nosy. C-Note noticed the old lady who lived across the street from the spot with several other older neighbors, so he walked over to the old lady, wondering if she might remember him from the times he had spoken to her on his many visits to the spot while she had been working in her garden. He remembered Two-Down and Poke telling him her name. So he approached her, using it.

"Hi, Mrs. Ables," he said in a voice that was smooth and polite. She eyed him suspiciously at first, then as he came closer, recognition dawned.

"Oh, hi, son," she said, then shook her small head gravely. "They done found them two young boys you always come to see in there dead as cattle in a slaughterhouse." She shook her head again and shuddered as if she were cold. "They's ain't the only one found. It was an older man, too."

The other neighbors looked on as she told the story. "That man over there in the back of that police car," Mrs. Able said, pointing to a black-and-white with a man in the backseat, "says he came over for one reason or another to talk to one of them boys." She paused, then added conspiratorially, "Probably came to buy some of that stuff dem boys was sellin'." A few of the neighbors' heads nodded up and down in agreement to what she had said. It was her story and she was telling it.

"Dat man says he walked up to the door and knocked and the door came open." She paused again, and C-Note almost said, "Just tell the damn story, would you?"

"He said soon as he walked in the house, it was a dead body on the livin'-room sofa." She shook her head sadly.

"Nigger in da police car was probably gonna steal everything that wasn't nailed down if he hadn't seen those there dead bodies," said an older man standing with the bunch.

C-Note wondered curiously how these old folks had found out so much. "You sure Two—" he caught himself.

"Are you positive those two young boys are dead?" said another older lady.

He restrained himself from saying something foul to the old people with their wisecracks, because this, to them, was entertainment. Real-life and better than any TV show. Now they had something to talk about for weeks to come. He thanked Mrs. Able and slowly headed back to his car. He knew if there was any dope or money in the house, it was lost to the police. But the dope and money were the least of his problems. How was he goin' to explain what happened to the parents of the dead men? That was his big issue, because he, himself, didn't know what happened. But in the back of his mind, he knew that the drugs he had put in their hands had something to do with it. And he promised himself he wouldn't rest until he found out who had committed such a bold act.

━━━◦━

SHEILA COULD SEE that he was still highly upset over the killing of his "two boys," as he called them. He moped around the house feeling guilty and sad. "You've paid for the funeral. What more can you do?" she asked as she cleaned the dinner dishes off the table, putting them in the water in the sink. His tone did not invite discussion.

"Find the son of a bitch who done it!" he snapped.

She concealed her emotions, hoping he wouldn't go out and do something stupid. She knew it was a sore point to touch on, but she had to make him see how stupid he was thinking. Turning to look at him, she said just as snappishly, "An' how in the hell are you gonna do that?" They locked stares, Sheila not giving in one bit. "If the damn homicide detective can't find the bastard or bastards who did this, what makes you so smart that you can?"

C-Note was amazed—and appalled—by her frankness. He looked mildly offended by her words. He stood. "There's a snag somewhere, a loose piece of thread. And once I start pullin', it'll all come unwound. That you can believe."

Stubborn. She said nothing else because she knew he was the hardheaded type. She cherished a secret, faint hope that he'd start thinking sensibly. And if he didn't, everything that they dreamed about would be ruined, destroyed. And the sad part was, she could see it happening, but she couldn't stop it from happening. He'd have to see it on his own.

━━━◦━

Low-Bone sat on the love seat at his and C-Note's dope house, brooding. It had only been days since Two-Down and Poke had been brutally murdered, and he couldn't believe the two we're actually dead. His stomach twisted in knots of frustration, because he wondered constantly over the past few days who could've done such a thing. It was on his mind like a nagging toothache. It was a bold step to take for whoever it was. The image of death stuck with him; it had the effect of pure terror. If he was going to die, he wanted to die quickly. Not painfully like the news had said Poke and Two-Down must have experienced.

Low-Bone checked his watch. It was 1:28 am. He was unsure of whether to stay a little longer or leave because the clientele picked up around three in the morning. And that's usually when he caught the big sales. But he was tired, plus he had already met his quota for the day, which was twenty-five hundred dollars. Ever since C-Note had given him the two kilos, he'd been able to make the size of his rocks bigger, therefore causing his business to pick up dramatically when the word got out. Although business was good, he decided to call it quits for the night, go home, and sleep until three in the afternoon. Maybe I should just stay the night, he wondered. But quickly he rejected the thought. He never made it a habit to sleep in a dope house, and he wasn't about to start now.

He gathered up all the money he had made in the past week and put it in several velvet Crown Royal bags with the yellow string used for tightening the bags. Six bags he counted, all with three thousand or better in each one, each bag containing that day's profits. He knew the stash in his Thunderbird could hold up to eight Crown Royal bags filled with money, so the six was no problem.

By nature, he was a cautious man. But he refused to carry a gun on him at all times because of the new gun laws, and on top of that, he already had two felony strikes. One more and ... So he kept his gun in the stash spot in his car and in the house. If cops came in the house, they couldn't prove that the guns were his. Everything was in a smoker's name, and he was just visiting, for all the authorities knew. And the stash in his car, they'd never find it. That's what he had paid all that money for. He made sure everything was safe and secure, lit a cigarette, and was ready to head home.

All was quiet in the wee hours of the morning as he strolled quickly across the short distance to his car to stick his key into the lock on the door when he noticed it was already unlocked. *Must've left it open earlier,* he thought to himself, then got in. He stuck the key in the ignition, because to trigger the stash, he had to have the radio on and the power as well. With his head looking down, Low-Bone didn't even see the man who was on the backseat floor pop up, clad in all black. The silencer muzzle touched the back of his neck.

"Raise your hands slowly from under dat seat," said the unfamiliar voice. "I'm sure you don't wanna die. An' I sure I don't wanna kill ya. So make it easy on the both of us, will ya'?"

Low-Bone did as he was told. He was too frightened to turn around. At first, he thought it was a police officer, setting him up in some kind of sting operation. But then he stole a look in the rearview mirror and found it to be a jacker, dressed from head to toe in all black. Even his eyes were barely visible in the night.

"Don't make no sudden moves," said the man in his backseat, "an everythin' should be alright. What was that you have in the brown grocery sack?"

Low-Bone's heart thumped so loudly, he wondered if the cat in the backseat could hear it. "It was ... uh ... money," he said shakily, unable to contain the fear he felt. He wondered if he had jinxed himself by constantly thinking about Two-Down and Poke.

"Slowly set the bag on the passenger seat," the man said, his gun still touching Low-Bone's neck. "Where's the dope? In the bag, too?"

Low-Bone managed to look both baffled and surprised at the same time. "Dope? Wh—what dope are you talkin' about?"

The man in the backseat hit him on the head with the silenced barrel of the gun, but not too hard. "Listen," the man in all black said smoothly, "you can make this hard on yourself, or you can make it easy, as I told you before." He paused to let his words sink in. Seeing he had Low-Bone's full attention, he continued. "Look closely in the bushes, right under your picture window." Low-Bone did as instructed and saw a man camouflaged and hiding there, in all black as well.

"That's my partner," said the man in the backseat. "He's waitin' for my signal." Low-Bone stared out the window.

"A signal for what?" he asked, now glancing back in the rearview mirror. The lips in the black ski mask curled into a sneer. "Are you gonna cooperate, or are you gonna play crazy as you're doin' now by askin', 'what dope?'"

Low-Bone was not attempting to hide his fear. There was something eerie about the man in his backseat. He was plagued by waves of fear. Low-Bone tried to change tactic. "The dope is in the house. You can take the money, and I'll give you the keys to the house. Just let me go while y'all're in the house."

The man in the backseat laughed mirthlessly. "We can't do that," he said dismissively. "You might do somethin' like wake a neighbor or call the police."

Now it was Low-Bone's turn to laugh humorlessly. "I can't do no shit like dat," he said in his most convincing voice. "What am I goin' say? 'Hey! I've been robbed for twenty gee an' some dope. Could ya' hurry on over?'"

The man in backseat shook his head unreasonably. "Can't do it," he said.

The conversation came to a standstill, with Low-Bone trying to think of some way to get out of the sticky situation. Then it occurred to him. Could this be linked with the Two-Down's and Poke's thing? And could these two be the same people who kill them? Now his heart really began to pound his chest. He was almost sure the man in the back could hear it. Low-Bone tried again to shift the scene.

"Okay. Say I tell you where the dope is, and you let me stay out here while your partna' goes in and get it. Then y'all can be on your way, and then who am I goin' to tell? Nobody."

The man in the backseat had heard enough. He knew the man in the front seat was talking out of fear and ignorance. Did he take him for a fool? "This gun has a silencer on it, so listen, and listen to me close."

Low-Bone was all ears. He didn't want to upset the man holding the gun behind him.

"Now if I wanted to kill you, I could have already and no one would'a heard a thing. I then could've gone into the house and searched it and when done, left." He paused, hoping Low-Bone was seeing the picture the way he was painting it. "But that ain't the deal here. We jus' want the dope and money an' won't hurt no one in the process. You feel me?"

Low-Bone's head rose up and down, slowly. He didn't believe the man in the backseat, but what choice did he have? He stared blindly into the night.

"Now, when we get outta the car," he told Low-Bone, making his voice smooth and convincing, "I don't want you to make no sudden moves, no screamin' or yellin' or no tryin' to play hero. Because if you try any of what I jus' said, I'll kill you wit' no hesitation."

Low-Bone looked at him through the rearview mirror. He tried to seem unruffled, but his imagination began to drift, thinking weird and crazy thoughts.

"Let's go!" said the man in back of him, breaking into his frightened thoughts. Low-Bone opened the door and stepped out. He briefly considered breaking and running away, but those thoughts were immediately dispelled when the second gunman who had been in the bushes was at his side the instant he had got out, his gun jammed in Low-Bone's ribs.

"Shit!" he muttered to himself as he walked to the door with both men close on his heels. They reached the door and Low-Bone just stood there. "Open the damn door!" said the other man who had been hiding in the bushes.

"He said don't make no sudden moves," Low-Bone said smartly, reaching into the left pocket with the keys, "if I didn't wanna be shot."

The gunman waved his hand in a manner that indicated he didn't want to hear what Low-Bone was saying. Low-Bone opened both doors, then stepped to the side, letting the gunman who had been in his car go in first. Then Low-Bone went in behind him, and the other gunman last. "Turn some lights on, Johnny," said the gunman who had come in last.

The one called Johnny stopped what he was doing and looked hard at the other gunman. "What the fuck do you think I'm doin'?" Johnny stated coldly, hating being told what to do. "You jus' get out the cuffs an' tape an' take care of securing ole boy."

The other gunman did what he was told while Johnny went searching through the house. From a back room, Johnny yelled, "Larry, make sho' there ain't no guns hid under that couch you got'em on."

Low-Bone knew that something was not right. They were now using names, and the one called Larry who had put the handcuffs on his wrists and the tape on his mouth was now taking off his ski mask. Panic bubbled in him. He was in a hopeless situation. Johnny appeared, mask off.

"Okay, now. Where's the dope?" Johnny asked, falling into the plush love seat. Low-Bone cursed himself again for having the misfortune to be caught like he had. There was no point in self-pity now, he told himself, because in truth, he knew it would make no difference. His face looked blank for a moment; then it cleared.

Larry removed the tape from Low-Bone's mouth, who said with fury in his voice, "Why should I tell you, an' you're probably still gonna kill me anyway?" Larry's gun hand came down like an anvil on the back of Low-Bone's neck. The pain raked his body. A faint sheen of sweat appeared on top of his forehead, and he was breathing hard.

Very smoothly Johnny's voice said, "You can be argumentative all you want, but I can assure that we got ways to make you talk."

Low-Bone laughed loudly and eerily. He was no longer enraged, because he knew the two planned to kill him anyway. He suddenly felt oddly calm, his face distorted into a grimace of hatred. His voice was like iron. "Both of y'all can go fuck yourselves in the ass, because I ain't tellin' you shit!" Low-

Bone laughed again cold and heartlessly. "An' when you two are done here on earth, I'll be waitin' for y'all both in hell, right along with the devil."

Larry looked spooked now.

"Whoever sent y'all forgot to tell y'all one thing," Low-Bone smiled cruelly, "that *I'm* the devil's advocate."

Now Larry was *beyond* scared; he was petrified. His only fear was talk about going to hell and burning forever. His mother said the Bible talked about it constantly, so he knew it was true. Larry's breath came in gasps now, and his stomach cramped with tension.

"Let's jus' leave, Johnny," Larry said with a sick look on his face. "We ain't done nothin' to 'em, so we ain't got to worry about seein' him in hell."

Johnny stared at Larry aghast. He then threw Low-Bone a look of scorn, who, in return, laughed wickedly. Low-Bone noted the panic in Larry's voice and plunged on. "You can trust me on this one, Larry," Low-Bone said smiling wolfishly, "if you lay a hand on me to harm me in any type way, *I'll* be your judge, jury, and executioner when you arrive in hell." He paused to glance at Johnny, who shook his head sadly at his friend.

Larry shuddered with fear.

"I'll have a personal request to have you pulled down. Surely God don't want no cold-blooded murderers up in heaven."

Larry became extremely uncomfortable under the penetrating stare of Low-Bone and the wild talk of hell. His visions tortured him. "I'm outta here!" Larry said, heading for the door in which he had come through. Johnny couldn't believe his friend's stupidity. His eyes clouded with frustrated rage as he stood up to his friend.

"Are you fuckin' crazy?" he snapped sharply, looking Larry square in the eye. "We're here now, so we're gonna get what we came here for."

There was a murmur of surprise. "Let's jus' get the fuck outta here!" Larry groaned.

Low-Bone sat on the sofa, smiling devilishly. He sensed victory. For once, Johnny was at a loss for words. He felt torn. The mere idea of his friend being so scared about the talk of hell made him wonder, *What if we got caught and the police threatened Larry with hell?* Johnny already knew the answer to that question. They'd never see daylight again. Johnny was now teed off at both Larry and Low-Bone. With spitefulness in his eyes, he gave Low-Bone a dirty look.

"Look," he said, turning back to Larry, his voice going back to normal, "I'll do all the dirty work wit' this cat here," he nodded his head at Low-Bone. "You jus' collect the dope once he tells us where it's at."

Low-Bone laughed harshly. "I ain't tellin' you shit!" Johnny turned back to him, giving him an ugly grin. "That's what you think."

Larry still looked troubled and terrified. Johnny, thinking it best to give Larry something to do, said, "Go fill up the bathtub."

Larry quickly exited the room. Johnny turned to Low-Bone. "Now you're gonna pay for those cutthroat maneuvers." Johnny was sneering. "And make it all *hot* water," he yelled to Larry who was in the bathroom.

Low-Bone was licked, and he knew it. Through the years, he'd lived dangerously by gang banging, dope slanging, and any other activity that wasn't legal. His dark eyes were questioning, face expressionless. Inside, he was stinging with humiliation and anger. With no hint of hope, it was as if he were sinking slow in a deep abyss. He knew now, life was a slender thread to hang on to, and it was slipping through his fingers.

Johnny grinned crookedly at his victim. He felt he held the ultimate power. He could feel it surging through his body, heating his blood. *He was* in the position to make one laugh, cry, or be angry. And *that* power took more than just charm; it took brains as well. And he had both.

The atmosphere was thick with emotion, each man lost in his own thoughts. Larry's voice coming from the bathroom brought both men back to the moment.

"Get up!" Johnny said rashly, grabbing him by his arm. Low-Bone had a faraway look in his eyes as Johnny pushed him towards the bathroom. "You got one more chance to tell me where the dope is at," Johnny said, forcing Low-Bone into the bathroom. With the three of them in there, the bathroom was instantly crowded. Larry saw and knew the plot hatching in his partner's evil mind.

"I'll wait in the hallway," Larry said, pushing past the two.

Low-Bone appeared calm, grinning evilly. "Like I said, I ain't tellin' you where shit is."

Johnny hunched his shoulders as if to say, I told ya so. He placed another strip of tape across Low-Bone's lips. "I guess you'll have to find out the hard way," Johnny said, then shoved him into the scalding water. Low-bone tried to wrestle free, but Johnny's brute strength was just too much for him. Low-Bone lay sprawled on his back, his head barely above the scalding water, and Johnny held on firmly to his cuffed hands with one wet foot on Low-Bone's throat, ready to send his head underneath the water with the slightest force of his body weight. Low-Bone suddenly became breathless with the cold hand of fear gripping his heart. His face was suffused with grief and horror. Johnny glowed with pleasure at the face looking up at him, eyes wide and bulging.

"Drownin' is one of the worst possible ways to die," he said, his voice calm and low. "Now, I'll bet you're gonna tell me where you got the goods stashed, huh?"

Low-Bone's eyes flashed anger and rebellion. Johnny's voice almost rose to a shout. "Stupid asshole," he said with sudden viciousness, than pushed Low-Bone's head under water with his foot still on his throat, pulling on the handcuffs while he did this. He held him under for thirty seconds, and then eased up the pressure on his foot, letting Low-Bone's head barely surface above water. Johnny laughed coldly at the sight of him struggling to fill his lungs with air.

"Horrible, ain't it?" he asked as smoothly as a snake when his lungs and eyes cleared. It took Low-Bone a few seconds to digest that. He hadn't planned it would be this bad. He tried to tell himself it was a tactic of intimidation and that they wouldn't kill him because they wouldn't get what they wanted. He'd have to hold his breath, no matter what.

"All you have to do," Johnny began, "is to shake your head up and down, and I'll pull you outta the water." He paused to grin again crookedly. "That is, once we have the dope." A tingle went down Low-Bone's spine. It seemed he could see through the head down to the heart of this man with his foot on his neck. And he knew he was lying.

"Suit yourself," Johnny said, pushing his head back beneath the water. Only this time, he held him under until Low-Bone started to squirm for dear life. Water splashed everywhere, and Johnny lost his balance on the wet tiled floor. He fell into the bathtub on top of Low-Bone, still holding fast to his cuffed hands. "Larry!" he yelled angrily, "bring yo' ass in here an' help me with this muthafucka. He done got me soakin' wet fumblin' wit' his ass."

Larry stepped into the bathroom and had to suppress a laugh. Johnny was in the bathtub on top of Low-Bone, their legs entwined, and Johnny was holding tightly to his cuffed hands, wrestling with him. Larry rushed to help his friend.

"Damn, Johnny, you let him yank you in the water like dis?" he jeered, pulling Johnny out of the bathtub. Johnny went cold with anger. His friend had insulted him, berated him.

"No, dumb ass, he didn't yank me into the fuckin' tub. I slipped and fell in."

Larry cracked a wiseass smile. He had a mind that comprehended. Low-Bone looked at the two wretchedly through unseeing eyes. He understood that the Fates did as they willed. But he couldn't take no more of the punishment. His mouth was taped, so that made things even worse. Plus, he now knew terror and if he was going to die, he didn't want to do it by drowning. Too late, though, Johnny was mad.

"Hold his legs, Larry," he said, putting his foot back on Low-Bone's throat. His eyes blazed with wrath. "I'll teach his ass to wanna hold out on where the shit is." Again he pushed Low-Bone's head under the water, using the toilet for extra support and leverage.

Seconds ticked by like minutes. Low-Bone was no match against the two holding him submerged under water. Just as life was leaving him, he felt a burst of air fill his lungs. Johnny stood over him, pulling the tape from his mouth.

"It ain't time to die yet," he said smiling gleefully. "We gonna keep bringin' you back every time until you tell us." It took Low-Bone several minutes to cough all the water out of his lungs before he spoke.

"Move the pillows on the couch. On the back to the right, there's a zipper. The dope is in there."

Johnny smiled with bubbling excitement. Larry let go of his legs.

"Never fails," Johnny said, then told Larry to go check to make sure they hadn't been lied to.

Low-Bone gazed blankly at Johnny in shock. The fright of being so close to death made him want to live now more than ever. Tears ran freely down his cheeks and blended with the water already on his face. He felt a pang of regret over how he had spent his life. And now, he knew that although he had told them where the dope was, he wouldn't be given any more chances at undoing his past, his ruined life. He had corrupted many, and now it was his time to pay for that corruption. His thirst for life was going unquenched, and he began to cry almost silently.

Johnny saw him crying and laughed, satisfied. "Mr. Tough Guy finally broke down like the bitch he really is," Johnny said mockingly. Low-Bone was too deep within himself to hear what Johnny had said.

Larry reappeared in the bathroom doorjamb with a small, black sports bag. "I got it," he said, holding the bag open for Johnny to see its contents.

Low-Bone still cried softly and had not seen Larry come back into the bathroom. "What the hell is he cryin' for?" Larry asked, as if he were concerned.

Johnny laughed harshly and grabbed Low-Bone's cuffed hands while sticking his foot on his throat again. Low-Bone looked up at Johnny glassy-eyed, knowing that his time had finally come.

"Grab his legs!" Johnny told Larry as he pushed Low-Bone's head under water. "You know why he is cryin'?"

Johnny laughed ominously. "'Cause he got a date wit' the Grim Reaper, an' Mr. Grim gonna take that ass on the first date." Johnny looked into the tortured eyes of Low-Bone and grinned sadistically.

Black despair washed over Low-Bone's face and his endless tomorrows finally arrived. He had suffered a lifetime of dismal failure, and his conscience could no longer bear the burden. All of his nightmarish life was ending, and he was beginning to feel somewhat relieved. A faint smiled curled the edges of Low-Bone's mouth as he looked up into the steely, merciless eyes of Johnny as he ceased to struggle. For reasons he could not fathom, Low-Bone wondered why all of a sudden he felt so happy. His head began to swim with dizziness, and then the darkness crept in. Just as he closed his eyes for good, he knew why he was so happy. Because he knew it wouldn't be long before he saw the man with the foot on his neck in hell with him.

chapter

7

C-Note awoke with a startle. The thunder clapped in the sky, sounding like gunshot. He glanced around the room cautiously. Sheila was nowhere to be found, but Christian lay next to him, sound asleep, undisturbed by the rain pelting the windows and the loud noise of crashing thunder. He stretched feebly and then got out of the bed to go take a piss. Downstairs, he could hear the vacuum running in the living room and wondered how long Sheila had been awake.

After flushing the toilet, he went back and parked himself on the bed. For some reason he could not fathom, a heavy weight seem to be pressing on him. Then it came to him. He hadn't talk to Cat-Daddy in almost a week. Cat had told him he would be going to Vegas for few days with his new girlfriend and would give him a call when he got back. That was six days ago, so C-Note wanted to know what the hell was going on. He knew it wasn't normal for Cat to be missing money.

He reached for his private phone and dialed Cat's cell phone. His answering machine picked up on the first ring. So he left a message, telling Cat to call as soon as he got the message. C-Note then dialed the dope spot Cat and Scrappy shared. The phone rang several times, and right when C-Note decided to hang-up, Scrappy picked up the phone.

"What?" he growled into the mouthpiece, sounding half-sleep.

C-Note smiled for the first time that morning. "Let me speak to Cat."

Scrappy instantly recognized his voice. "The nigga ain't here," he said dismissively, "and ain't been here fo' some days."

C-Note's voice was devoid of all emotions. "Alright then, tell him to call me when you see him."

Scrappy laughed impulsively. "I ain't tellin' him shit. I ain't one of your muthafuckin' Do-Boys."

An expression of alertness came over C-Note's face. He was amused by his old friend's anger. "Look, stupid ass," he started to say, but then the phone was slammed down in his face. He shook his head sadly. Scrappy sounded as though lunacy had taken hold of him. C-Note thought he was a proven example of what crazy was. He quickly put Scrappy to the back of his mind and called Cat's house phone.

"Shit!" he said annoyed as his answering machine picked up again. He left another message, hung up, and dialed Low-Bone's number. Low-Bone's sister answered the phone.

"Hello."

"Hey, Tee! Is Low at the joint?"

She knew his voice and said, using his old nickname, "I haven't seen him this morning, F.B. He didn't come home last night."

C-Note didn't mind her calling him F.B, because he'd known her since she was a toddler, and because she didn't know he had changed his nickname.

"Thanks," he said thoughtfully, "tell'em I called."

"Will do," she said and hung up.

Just as he hung the phone, Sheila came strolling in the room with the vacuum in her hand. "What's wrong with you?" she asked, puzzled, with a concerned look on her face. She could see that his anguish was apparent.

"Nothin' that concerns you," he snappily replied while lying back down in bed. Sheila stared at him unflinchingly but said nothing because of so much that had happened of late. Instead, she turned and stomped out of the room. He lay there wondering what the fuck was going on. First, Cat didn't answer, and now, Low-Bone, too. He tried to calm down, to talk himself out of his feelings. Finally, he got up and walked to his bedroom window to look out. The sun hid behind the dark churning clouds. The wind and rain blew hard, the wind increasing until it sounded haunting. His gut feeling told him that this day was not going to be a good day at all.

<hr />

JOHNNY HEARD SOMEONE at the door fumbling with the locks. He reached under his pillow and grabbed his gun, aiming it at the door. He cocked his gun right as the door swung open.

"Nigga, you almost got shot sneakin' in here like dat," he said, smiling, then lowering his gun.

"Aw, nigga, you wouldn't shoot ya' family," his cousin said jokingly as he closed the door, "especially after I done hooked you wit' all this easy money."

Johnny smiled again. "Damn right, I wouldn't. But the way you creepin' up in here, I thought you might've been someone else."

His cousin looked around the dirty living room. "Where's Larry at?" he asked questioningly.

Johnny pointed over his shoulder with his thumb. "Dat nigga's in the room asleep. We had a long night last night."

Johnny's cousin sat on a recliner chair across from him, eyes sparkling. "So, how did everything work out?" he asked Johnny eagerly.

Johnny got up, still smiling, reached behind the couch he was sleeping on, and grabbed a duffle bag. He tossed the bag to his cousin. "Here, see for ya' self."

His cousin caught the bag and opened it. "Whewwweee," he said, as he pulled out stacks of money and Ziploc bags full of dope. "This is a grip of shit," he said with his eyes bulging. "How much is it?"

Johnny hunched his shoulders. "Me and Larry ain't counted it yet. Shit! We ain't had time."

Larry came out of the room in his boxer short and socks, scratching his balls. "What's up, peoples?" he said, sitting next to Johnny.

"This money," his cousin replied, holding up several stacks of dough.

Johnny got up and turned the TV on. "These rooms have paper-thin walls," he said, sitting back down.

"I see where ya' comin' from," his cousin said knowingly. He poured out the rest of the contents from the duffle bag. "We gonna be rich by the time we get through jackin' these niggas."

Larry smiled slyly and said joyously, "Gettin' this easy money sho' is fun."

Johnny's smile was erased from his face almost instantly. "Nigga, you almost shit ya' pants last night when dat nigga started talkin' about that devil bullshit."

Larry's face went sad, and Johnny rolled on. "You should've seen the look on this nigga's face when that fool started talkin' about goin' to hell." Johnny paused to catch his breath, he was laughing hard now. "He was ready to run outta the fuckin' house an' leave all the dope an money behind."

Their cousin began laughing too. Larry didn't like being made fun of. "Fuck both y'all pussies!" he said hotly.

"Fuck you, too!" Johnny managed to say in between laughs.

Larry was about to say something when their cousin waved him off. "Enough of the jokes," he said seriously. "I got one more lick for y'all. That is, if y'all are up to it."

Larry shook his head solemnly. "I think we should call it quits while we're ahead."

Johnny made his expression stern and his voice cold. "Muthafucka, are you crazy? Dis here is free money, and we gonna get all we can get before we go back to Louisiana."

Larry looked hurt. "You can take yo' country ass back wit' yo' share of the money, but I'm stayin'."

Johnny and his cousin both looked at Larry.

"You can go back if you want to," his cousin offered, "but that's up to you. Because either way you go, me an' Johnny gonna get this money."

Larry tried not to think bitterly about his weaknesses. He suffered a moment's doubt before saying, with a broad grin, "Count me in, 'cause I do need some more strip club money."

⌖

C-Note got dressed and quickly left the house. He didn't wanna hear the shit Sheila had to say. That would've only just pissed him off even more. The rain-slickened streets caused drivers to drive slower than usual, so he cursed out loud to himself. On a trip that normally took him twenty minutes, it now turned into an hour.

Finally, he pulled the Q-45 in Cat's driveway and called into the house from his cell phone. "Shit!" he cursed darkly as the answering machine picked up again on the first ring. C-Note backed the car out of the driveway and then decided to drop by his and Low-Bone's spot. In the back of his mind, he just knew something wasn't right.

The ride took a little over ten minutes, and C-Note was glad he didn't have to deal with the freeway again. He noticed Low-Bone's car in the driveway as he pulled to the curb and parked. "Nigga must be laid up wit' some broad," he thought out loud as he walked to the door. He banged on the door three times, his code, to let Low-Bone know he was coming in just in case he did have a woman over. Then he stuck his key in the door and turned the lock.

⚬

"I'm TIRED OF eatin' fuckin' M&M's every damn day," Footwork argued as he put on his tee shirt. "We eat that shit at least five days a week."

Do-A-Deal looked up at him from tying his shoe. "And we certainly ain't eatin' at the Servin' Spoon either," Do-A-Deal counted stiffly. "We ate breakfast there every mornin' last week, an' I ain't eatin' lunch there, too."

Footwork shrugged his shoulders. "Okay, then, so what we gonna eat?"

Do-A-Deal slid on a lightweight jacket. "Beats the fuck outta me," he said walking to the back door. Footwork grabbed his windbreaker from off the back of one of the kitchen table chairs and followed Do-A-Deal out the door. The three dogs tied up began to bark relentlessly at the sight of their owners.

"Shut the fuck up!" Footwork hollered over his shoulder. "I'll feed you mutts when I get back." They walked down the short driveway to the car.

"Let's get some Mexican food," Do-A-Deal said hopefully, hoping Footwork wouldn't disagree.

"That's perfect," Footwork said, opening the car door. "Let's hit up Ramona's. The food there is cool."

Do-A-Deal started the car and backed out of the driveway. Their minds were so occupied with eating that they didn't even pay any attention to the two men sitting in the car right across the street from their house.

***

C-Note opened the door and knew instantly that something was wrong. Pillows from the couch were thrown everywhere. Chairs were overturned, and the living room was flooded with water. He also noticed the door to the refrigerator was open. He walked cautiously to the kitchen first, trying not to touch anything.

Food from the icebox was everywhere. C-Note left the kitchen and went to the hall. Water was coming from the bathroom as he made his way towards the door. His chest pounded so hard he thought his heart might come through his skin. When he got to the doorway and looked in, he froze. Low-Bone's swollen face looked at him from under the water. His body had doubled its size and blood and mucus was coming out of his smiling mouth, nose, and ears. C-Note couldn't believe what he was seeing. His eyes teared. Seeing his friend like this punched a hole in his heart. He wanted to kill whoever was behind the murder of his longtime friend.

He just didn't know what to do. His mind was racing as fast as a Nascar in its final laps. He backed out of the doorway and went back to the door he had come through earlier, where he wiped the doorknob clean with his shirt, peeked outside, then closed the door behind him just as he had found it. Still in a state of shock, he got in his car and just drove, not knowing where to go or what to do. After driving for two hours, he decided to pull over to a phone booth and made an anonymous call to the sheriff's station.

⌐═←

JOHNNY AND LARRY watched the car as it backed out of the driveway and drove right past them. "They didn't even look our way," Larry chimed with an ugly smile spreading across his face. "Grab them bags of steaks in the backseat," Johnny urged Larry, "or them damn dawgs gonna bark they fuckin' asses off."

Larry did what he was told. "What did you put in dem steaks?" he asked dumbly.

Johnny shook his head in disgust. "What the fuck does it matter?" he asked rashly, "as long as it kills those mutts they got back there."

Larry was shocked by the venom in Johnny's voice. Anger clouded his face momentarily. He knew Johnny had a talent for needlessly annoying people and figured him to be nervous. "You know we can take what we got an' call it quits while we're still ahead," Larry said sheepishly.

A slow, grim smile lit Johnny's face. "You scared, ain't you, huh?" he asked Larry, smiling wildly.

There was a snort of disgust from Larry. "Nigga, I thought you were scared long as it's taken you to get outta the car."

He opened the car door and got out, taking the bags of steaks with him. Johnny opened his door and followed him across the street and down the driveway. Larry reached over the wrought iron fence and unlatched the gate. "I hope these muthafuckas are tied up like our peeps said," Larry said shakily, peeking his head through the gate.

The dogs started barking wildly at the sight of both men as they stepped through the gate. "Hurry an' throw'em the fuckin' steaks," Johnny advised edgily, "so they can stop all that fuckin' barkin.'"

Larry reached into the bag and pulled out the steaks. He flung a steak to each of the three dogs. "Goddamn," Larry stated with amazement, "look like these mutts ain't ate in weeks the way they tearin' into them steaks."

"You ain't never lied," Johnny replied jokingly. "Give'um the rest of them."

Larry dug back in the bag and tossed the dogs the remaining steaks. Within seconds, the tainted steaks took affect. "Oh, shit!" Larry cracked. "Look at the dog tied to the tree," he said pointing a finger at that dog. "Is that his guts he's heaving up?" Larry asked, shocked.

Johnny's face twisted in total disgust. "How the hell would I know?" he replied feebly.

As they watched, all three dogs begin to convulse and regurgitate blood. Low moans of pain could barely be heard through the swollen necks of the dogs as their stomachs came through their mouths and out onto the ground where they lay. "Where in tha' hell did you get those damn steaks from?" Larry asked, still stunned by the sight of the now-dead dogs.

"One of our people got the cyanide tablets from a smoker of his who works in a pharmacy. He assured us that would do the trick nice and quick."

Larry just shook his head slowly from side to side.

"But I added some cocaine and heroin, too, jus' ta be on the safe side," Johnny said with a fiendish smile.

Larry had seen enough. He turned and made his way to the back door, turning the handle to see if it were locked. "Would'ya look at this?" he said in amazement as the door swung open. "These bold muthafuckas must really think they can't be touched."

Johnny's fiendish grin broadened as he stepped past Larry into the house. "We'll jus' see about that, won't we?"

⚬═◄►

SHEILA HAD JUST finished washing the last plate when all of a sudden the window began to vibrate. Dishes rattled together in the dish drainer as the vibrating grew stronger and stronger. At first, she thought it was the big earthquake that everybody in California talked about until she realized it was somebody's sound system. She set the plate in the sink and walked to the living room, pushing the white curtain aside. Then she peeked out the picture window and saw a black XLT Cadillac truck on black and chrome wheels pulling up in front of her house. The sun reflected off the chrome, causing her eyes to squint in order to get a better look. Several moments later, Sheila recognized Cat-Daddy sitting behind the steering wheel of the truck. She walked to the stairs and boomed out, "Cat's outside, babe, in a nice-ass truck."

C-Note had heard the racket as well and had looked out the window, too, from up in his room. "I'll be down in a sec," he yelled back while slipping on a pair of sweat pants. "And could you ask him not play his music so loud the next time he's by here? You know how the neighbors like to bitch an' complain about everything." He held himself from flying into a rage. What he wanted to say was, "Fuck the neighbors! And fuck what she was bumpin' her gums about!" He decided the argument with Cat would be enough, so he kept his mouth closed.

C-Note glided down the stairs, taking them two at a time. Before Cat-Daddy could ring the doorbell, he snatched the door open. "Where the fuck you been where you can't return a muthafucka's phone call?"

Cat stood stock-still, caught off-guard. Before he could say anything, C-Note raged on. "I've been callin' an' leavin' messages, and you couldn't see what the hell I was blowin' your phone up for?"

Cat walked past C-Note into the house, his face contoured with fury. He felt dismal and bewildered. "What the fuck is all the yellin' for? You knew I was goin' to Vegas, so what's the big deal?"

"What's the big deal? *What's the big deal!*" C-Note couldn't suppress his anger any longer. "Nigga, if you would'a called back, you would'a known somebody been hittin' the dope spots. An' whoever it is has been killin' all the niggas workin'um!"

Cat fidgeted, then shook his head in perplexity. He sat on the long sofa, and C-Note sat across from him with a look of disdain etched on his face as rage overcame him, changing his facial features and his voice.

"What the hell does that have to do with me? You lookin' at me all funny an' shit like I had somethin' to do wit' it!" Now it was Cat's turn to be furious.

"Nigga, like I said, me an' Snake was in Vegas."

C-Note's face was suddenly colder with menace. He glowered at Cat as if he cared nothing about hiding his feelings. The volatile quiet stillness collected around them. Cat could feel the anger moving through him as if it were a hot liquid. C-Note's eyes passed over him slowly, lingeringly.

"You never said nothing about Snake goin' to Vegas wit' you before."

Something happened in Cat's face. His voice held a mixture of sarcasm and malice. "I don't remember when you became my muthafuckin' daddy. I ain't gotta report what the fuck I'm doin' every hour on the hour to you. I'm definitely not a bitch, and I sure ain't got no pussy like one." His face appeared monstrous.

C-Note stared at Cat as if he were about to go mad. There was something cold and disenchanted, and even malicious in his gaze. "Nigga, you do a great Houdini disappearin' act wit' our scandalous cousin, don't call nobody back, and then come pullin' up at my joint in a fifty thousand-dollar truck. What the fuck would you think?"

Cat's face crumpled in confusion at first, and then went into a dark chill of disbelief. "I jus know you ain't thinkin' what I hope you ain't thinkin'," Cat said scathingly, his face becoming disfigured and strange looking, "'cause if I wanted to rob you, nigga, it would'a happened a long time ago."

C-Note's eyes narrowed slightly and a cold apprehension came over him. He went on remorselessly. "And what's that supposed to mean?" he asked Cat, mystified by his last remarks.

"Jus' what the fuck I said! I didn't bite my tongue." He shot Cat a look of poisonous fury, but then had to rein in his temper for the moment. He hadn't wanted to get into a verbal sparring match with Cat, but it was already too late.

When he spoke, C-Note's voice was like bile. "Cousin or no cousin, if I find out you and Snake got anything to do wit' this, you better have your funeral arrangements all mapped out. It won't be no talkin' next time—that I can guarantee!"

Cat stood up with a look of irritation glued to his face. A fierce anger rose in his chest as he stood frozen like a snowman. He spoke in a voice low, filled with a mixture of coolness and contempt. Slowly he shook his head from side to side as his eyes fell on his cousin's face.

"Making threats and false accusations ain't gonna get you nowhere. If it was *anybody*, I mean anybody else, you'd be a dead muthafucka sittin' there." Cat paused for what seemed to be an interminable duration. He was in a pure rage, staring at C-Note intently, his face full of feelings, his chest heaving up and down under his shirt. His eyes took on a look of cold intelligence.

"You're gonna need me before I need you. I'm outta here, 'cause you're two words from me downin' yo' ass right here and now."

Cat turned and stomped to the door with a frown and a look of grave intensity on his face. He whirled around just as he reached the door. "Fuck you!" he said without emotion and stormed out of the house back to his truck.

A look of sadness, like a shadow, fleeted across C-Note's face. He fell into a deep bout of depression. He tried to calm down, to talk himself out of his feelings, but he knew the heart of men. He didn't need to know science or algebra or literature or geometry. But what he did know was something you couldn't find in the books, and that was how to survive in the ruthless-ass streets. Like all true, real hustlers, C-Note knew when it came to money, your own mama would feed you to the wolves for the almighty dollar.

chapter

8

Do-A-Deal pulled the car into the driveway in a hurry to get in the house to eat his food. He reached for the bag of food on the seat next to him and hopped out of the car while Footwork stretched to the back to retrieve his food from the backseat.

"Lock the car up, Work," he said, slamming his door before Footwork could complain.

Footwork got out of the car and hit power lock switch and the shut his door. "Yo' fat ass must be hungry," Footwork cracked playfully, "'cause I ain't seen you move that fast in years."

Footwork brought up the rear as Do-A-Deal went through the gate and opened up the back door. "You always worryin' about lockin' up that piece-a-shit car of yours; you need to start lockin' up the damn house."

Do-A-Deal sat at the table, ignoring Footwork's snide remarks. He knew Footwork complained about itty-bitty things on a daily basis. Footwork set his food on the table and went to the refrigerator, opening it. "What you want to drink, lard ass?" he asked, grabbing himself a beer.

"Diet Pepsi," Do-A-Deal replied gruffly, chewing on a mouthful of food.

Footwork's face crumpled like the face of a child about to cry. "You order two burritos, two enchiladas with rice and beans and a taco. What the hell is a Diet Pepsi gonna do?"

Do-A-Deal shot him a stupid look. "Jus' hand me the goddamn soda, would you? And keep that smart aleck shit to yourself."

Footwork set the drinks on the table and began opening up his food when he realized he hadn't heard the dogs barking when they came through the gate. He stood up and walked over to the kitchen window. "*What the fuck—*" was all that came out of his mouth.

Johnny pushed open the broom closet door holding an ominous-looking nine millimeter aimed right at Footwork's face. Instantly, Do-A-Deal jumped up ready to fly into action, but Larry had sprung from his hiding place in the living room just seconds before. He grabbed Do-A-Deal by the back of his jacket and brought his gun down on Do-A-Deal's head with all his might. Blood splattered over Footwork and the walls before Do-A-Deal could hit the floor. His blood dripped down Larry's face as he stood there with a savage grin spread from ear to ear.

"What's goin' on here? Who the hell are you? An' what the fuck y'all doin' in my crib?" Footwork tried to act calmly while his thoughts and his brain stumbled over themselves. A low moan escaped from Do-A-Deal's mouth as he rolled over in his own puddle of blood and tried to push himself onto his knees.

"Stay the fuck on the floor!" Larry barked, putting his size 12 foot squarely in the middle of Do-A-Deal's back, pushing him roughly back onto the floor.

Remorselessly, Larry kicked him in the open gash on his head. Do-A-Deal stiffened in a spasm of shock and pain.

"Have a seat," Johnny said to Footwork, waving the gun toward the chair Do-A-Deal had just been sitting in. "An' I'll be the one askin' questions, not you."

Footwork slowly stepped over his best friend and parked himself in the chair. He could hear guttural sounds coming from Do-A-Deal's chest—tiny, low, gurgling, choking breaths.

"Man, whatever it is, we ain't done it," Footwork pleaded, his eyes darting back and forth, sweeping the kitchen for a way out.

"Put the cuffs on dat nigga, Larry. Looks like he might have a little jackrabbit in his ass."

Larry reached in his back pocket and brought out a pair of handcuffs, quickly sliding them on Footwork's wrists.

"Man, what is this about? We ain't—"

That was as far as Footwork got. Larry's gigantic hand had slapped him so hard in the mouth, his head twisted viciously to the side.

"Now we gonna do the talkin', not you," Larry snarled, playing the bad-guy role.

Johnny, playing the good guy, interjected soothingly, "Come on, Larry, give'em a break and a chance to cooperate. I'm pretty sure he don't wanna get hit no more, or his partner, either."

Larry shot Johnny a dumb look. He had no idea what Johnny was up to. "Johnny, he ain't gonna—"

"Shut the fuck up, would you?" Johnny said indignantly, cutting him off midsentence. "Let me do the talkin'. You want somethin' to do? Get his pal there an' find somewhere to tie'em up."

Larry reached down and grabbed the half-conscious man by the back of his neck like a rag doll. They disappeared through the door leading to the living room. Johnny turned his attention back on the handcuffed Footwork.

"I hope you don't make this more than what it is. I think you know why an' what we're here for. We want the bait you got that brought us two sharks here."

Footwork shook his head sadly with an expression of utter panic across his face. Never in this world would he have believed that this could be happening to him. He tried to stir himself up with confidence to keep control of his sanity. "You got the wrong folks, black," Footwork said miserably. "Me an' my boy ain't got nothin'; we ain't even from out here."

Johnny laughed mirthlessly, slowly shaking his head from side to side. Suddenly, his face became stern and his voice cold. "Don't give me that bullshit! I know what the fuck's up, and I know you get your work from C-Note."

Footwork's face registered a slight sign of shock. All he could do was remain speechless. Johnny's voice brought him back to reality with a hard bump.

"Not only for your friend's sake but yours as well, I suggest you tell me where the money and dope are. I really don't wanna put Larry to work no more than I have to."

A faint look of irritation crossed Footwork's face. "Look, dude, I don't know nothin' about no money and dope. An' furthermore, I ain't heard of no muthafucka name C-Note! I'm tellin' you, black, you got the wrong spot."

"Have it your way," Johnny said rashly before bringing his gun down on Footwork's forehead. Footwork slid off the chair and crumpled to the floor, but not before Johnny could kick him in the stomach. Footwork balled up in a fetal position, moaning in agony. The commotion in the kitchen brought Larry running with his gun ready.

"What the shit's goin' on?" he asked.

Johnny slammed his foot again into the man's stomach. "Stupid sonnavabitch thinks I'm some kind'a dumbass," he hissed to Larry. "I'm gone make his life flash before his eyes if he keeps tryin' to make a fool outta me. Set his ass back in that chair."

Larry scooped Footwork up and sat him back on the chair roughly. Johnny was silent for sometime, as if weighing up what he should say. Larry waited and watched awkwardly for Johnny's next move, his patience growing rapidly shorter.

"I can make him talk," Larry said as he wrapped his two giant hands around Footwork's neck, squeezing tightly.

As Footwork started to squirm in his chair, Johnny waved a hand, indicating Larry should stop. His eyes showed no hint of anger. A maniacal curl spread across his lips. "Now, where were we?" he said, sitting down in the chair opposite Footwork. "Am I gonna have to have Larry choke the answers outta you? I wanna hear you. Or are you gonna make this light on yourself?" Johnny could see the fear coursing through Footwork's veins.

Footwork was beginning to see it was becoming a no-win situation. He was furious he let himself get caught up in such a sucker's position. He knew if he kept up the charade, it could be a move he'd live to regret. He eyeballed Johnny vindictively, his eyes looking like black jewels.

"I ain't tellin' you shit until I can see Do-A-Deal an' make sure this gorilla ain't done nothing stupid."

Larry punched Footwork in the side of the head with a heavy fist. "Yo' mama's the fuckin' gorilla," he said tetchily.

Footwork's jaw was set tight. "I ain't tellin' you shit if this muthafucka puts his damn hands on me one more time! I don't give a fuck what you do to me—kill me, beat me, shoot me—I won't say a fuckin' word."

Johnny laughed, but his eyes were steely. A dark glow of cunningness flashed on his face. "Never say 'never,'" he said laughing raucously, his laughter echoing menacingly. "Me an' ole Larry, here, can make you do things you'd never thought you'd do with simple ease. Matter of fact, would you like a small sample?"

Panic took hold of Footwork. His eyes narrowed with suspicion and dread, while his mind jumbled with frightening images of his longtime friend Do-A-Deal. He now scented his own defeat. "Jus' let me see Do-A-Deal, an' I'll give you everything we got."

Johnny could hardly conceal his pleasure. "Take'em to see his partna' so we can be gettin' the fuck outta here."

Larry stood Footwork up by the neck, mad because Johnny had given in to his ultimatum. He violently shoved Footwork through the kitchen door. "Ya' boy is in the basement," he said with icy conviction, following close behind as Footwork led the way. Johnny followed as well, hoping in the back of his mind that Larry wouldn't do anything stupid before they got what they came for. On the floor of the basement, Do-A-Deal lay hog-tied in a pool of his own blood.

"What the fuck you done to him?" Footwork asked with utmost seriousness as he spun around to face Larry.

Johnny was too slow to stop Larry, who grabbed Footwork by the front of his handcuffs and kicked him square in the balls. Footwork hit the basement floor with a thud. Larry quickly rolled Footwork on his stomach while stretching his handcuffed hands out in front of him. Then he tied a piece of rope he had leftover from tying Do-A-Deal up to the handcuffs. Pulling out another pair of cuffs, he attached them around Footwork's thin ankles. Running the rope between the cuffs on his ankles, Larry pulled with all his strength, bringing Footwork's hands to his ankles. Footwork's collarbone snapped and popped out of his skin while Larry hurried to tie a knot.

"How you like that?" he asked emphatically with an evil smirk on his face.

Pain ripped through Footwork's shoulder, causing him to spew obscenities through clenched teeth. "You ignorant fuck! You ain't nothing but a piece a shit who needs to be flushed out of life once and for all."

Johnny roared to life with laughter, unable to control himself from laughing. Growing angrier by the wild laughter of his friend, Larry walked over to two tanks sitting in the far corner. After twisting the valve on each tank, he began to unwrap the lengthy green and red hose. He walked back over to where Do-A-Deal lay. Johnny watched intensely, still unable to stop laughing.

"We'll see who gets the last laugh, muthafucka," Larry said doggedly as his eyes searched the room for the striker. "I had metal shop class from the eighth-grade until I dropped out," he added just as he saw the striker lying in a Craftsman toolbox next to the oxygen and acetylene tanks. He grabbed the striker and turned a few knobs on the torch handle.

Johnny's laughter came to an abrupt stop when he heard the hissing sound coming out of the torch head. "What the fuck you doin'? Turn that shit off!"

Now, it was Larry's turn to laugh. He put the striker to the torch head and lit a flame. The gas and oxygen combined made an intense blue and yellow flame. Larry turned the knob again to adjust it, causing the flame to turn all blue. Johnny's eyes bulged in horror, as did Footwork's. He had known his cousin was an expert in torture, but he had never thought Larry to be so shockingly heinous.

With his eyes lit with fire, Larry put the 6,200-degree flame to Do-A-Deal's thigh. The unconscious man abruptly woke with a scream of certain death and then passed out again from sheer pain. The acrid, disgusting smell of burning flesh and thick gray smoke quickly filled the room. Johnny had to cover his mouth with the back of his hand to keep from vomiting. Tears ran freely down Footwork's face as he watched the thick blood run out of Do-A-Deal's leg. He couldn't help but feel that he was trapped in some terrible nightmare, his imagination stretched beyond it worst limits.

"It's in the shoe box, the Nike shoe box, third one from the floor," he cried despairingly. "The money is under the big screen TV in the living room. The carpet comes out, and the floor lifts up."

Larry gave Johnny a look of "I told ya' so," as Johnny hurried past him, wanting to escape the horrid stench of burnt flesh which filled the room. Panic bubbled inside of Footwork as he pushed the bile back down his throat. He fought down the panicky feeling with a small piece of rational sense biting at him.

"Come on, man, I told you where the money and dope is, jus' take it an' leave," Footwork pleaded, sounding unsure of himself, his voice faltering. A look of hopelessness was ingrained on his face.

Larry smile evilly from ear to ear. His voice went flat as if he didn't care. "I see you don't find shit so funny no more. I'm waitin'. Crack another joke, funnyman."

Larry roared with laughter, while all Footwork could do was cry brokenheartedly. A cold apprehension came over him somewhere in the back of his distracted mind. A voice told him he wouldn't go on living another day after this one. Footwork wondered how a person could be so cold, so unfeeling. He felt entitled to an explanation.

"Why?" he asked sorrowfully, shaking his head. "Why does a person do this? For money?" He felt sick with disgust.

Larry frowned, somewhat awestruck by his question. He nodded his big head grimly, smiling deviously. "How dare you accuse me of doin' such harsh acts for money. Unlike you, my motives are straight to the point. You're no better than me. In fact, you're worse than I am. You kill people deliberately, slowly, torturing them for years. Me, I get right to the point." A faint smile of pride danced across Larry's face.

Footwork desperately searched for something to say. His resentment burned hot, and it showed. "Don't try an' compare your sick-ass thinking to sellin' dope. They're not even close." He watched the insanity gleam wickedly in Larry's eyes.

Johnny came rushing into the room just then with a green pillowcase slung over his shoulder. "Let's roll! I got the money an' the goods. We been here too fuckin' long as is anyway."

Johnny turned to leave, but Larry stopped him. "We can't leave these niggas here. They saw our face." Johnny set the pillowcase down. He wiped droplets of sweat from his forehead. He hoped Larry wasn't thinking his usual psychotic thoughts. He could almost see a sadistic plan brewing in Larry's mind.

"What you gonna do wit'em?" Johnny asked wryly, grinning impishly.

"Wait by the back door," Larry answered, smiling slyly. "I'll be done here in less than a minute."

Johnny picked up the pillowcase. "Jus' hurry the fuck up, whatever you do." He disappeared through the door. Larry went for a roll of duct tape he had seen in the toolbox. Footwork knew it was his last chance at life and began to scream hysterically at the top of his lungs. Angry, Larry kicked Footwork in the mouth, knocking out several teeth. He reached down and quickly wrapped up his bloody mouth with the duct tape. Then, he hurried to the two basement windows and sealed them as best he could with the tape.

Smiling, Larry grabbed the torch hose and torch head and wrapped tape around the lever which released the gas and oxygen. In one corner of the room were two extra acetylene tanks. Just opposite, were two oxygen tanks as well. He could smell the acetylene from the torch head as it quickly filled the room. He opened the valves as far as he could on all four tanks and quickly headed for the door. Footwork's bloodied face tried to plead with him.

"If you're lucky," Larry said sarcastically, "you'll pass out from the gas by the time it hits this flame." He reached down and opened the little door that covered the pilot on the water heater, then turned the pilot all the way up to full blast.

"Jus' like the fiends you sell dope to, I'm givin' you the same treatment, a for sure and prolonged death. See ya', wouldn't wanna be ya.'" He snickered maliciously as he closed the door.

Across from the basement door was a linen closet. Opening it, he found an old bath towel and stuffed it under the crack of the basement door, then took off to find Johnny, who was standing in the kitchen doorway, regarding him suspiciously.

"What did ya' do?" he asked Larry with a leering grin.

There was a smug smile on Larry's face as he turned on all the pilots to the stove and oven.

"Don't worry about it! Let's jus' get the fuck outta here," he said, darting past Johnny and out the door. Johnny slammed the door shut and rushed to catch up with Larry, who was already out of the gate and moving rapidly down the driveway toward their car across the street.

"Slow the fuck down!" Johnny hissed angrily thorough clenched teeth. "You don't wanna cause an attraction to us." He looked around nervously, hoping that no one was paying any attention to them.

Larry didn't break stride. "Fuck causin' an attraction! You better put a move on it, or else you won't be livin' long enough to be worried about who saw us an' what they saw!" He turned his head in time to see Johnny pick up the pace behind him. Without delay, they got into the car and drove off.

"What the hell was that all about?" Johnny protested, ill-tempered and teed-off. "You gonna get us busted wit' your bullshit shenanigans."

A wicked, slow smile lit Larry's face. He could see Johnny's expression was set for a scornful protest, so he remained silent, hoping Johnny would, too. Larry pulled to the end of the street and stopped at a stop sign. He looked both ways and then made a right turn.

Just as Johnny opened his mouth to continue to argue, an earthshaking explosion violently shook the car and the houses around them. Stunned, Johnny looked over his shoulder, his jaw hanging in shock as he watched the dark mushroom cloud of smoke rising into the air where the house once stood. Slowly, he turned back to Larry, who wore a comic expression of amusement and savage glee plastered across his face.

Johnny now realized how easily his perception changed. In his mind, Larry was truly a madman who had an unquenchable thirst for death.

chapter

9

Sheila was unwilling to admit she was in a no-win situation. She had overheard the brief argument between her man and Cat. She'd been on the phone with his other cousin, Snake's, wife, Diane. Diane had been telling her how Snake and Cat-Daddy had won big in Las Vegas and how both had bought matching Cadillac SUVs in cash. The only difference between the two SUVs she said was Snake's Cadillac was white and Cat's was black. She bragged to Sheila about the bumpin' sound system and the big flashy rims.

But Sheila had said nothing, instead, just absorbing it all in as Diane's jaws flapped continuously. After hanging up the phone with Diane, she wanted to go upstairs and tell C-Note what she had just heard firsthand from Diane. She could hear him upstairs stomping around and slamming things down, and she knew sooner or later she'd have to make an intense decision. To her, something was seriously wrong. She replayed C-Note and Cat arguing in her head and wondered why Cat had not mentioned to her man about Snake buying an SUV when C-Note brought it up to him. Sheila wondered if Cat and Snake were hiding something.

The door slammed, and she realized C-Note had left. After mulling over whether to tell him about his cousin, Snake, or to just let him find out on his own, she decided to ask the opinion of someone she looked up to and admired. Her older sister, Janice. Up until two years ago, before Janice had got married, they had been inseparable. Because of Janice's husband's occupation and her man's occupation, the two agreed to keep them away from each whenever possible. Janice had married a narcotics detective.

Sheila had known of her sister's disapproval of the man she had chosen. But like the loving big sister she was, Janice never said anything to her about it, nor had she said anything bad about C-Note. But like any concerned sibling, Janice was always worried about the kind of people that were involved in drug selling. The "cutthroats," she and her husband liked to call them.

Sheila almost laughed when Janice and her husband, John, came up with code words and little secret things to do in case she was ever in any danger. The two of them even convinced C-Note to learn the code words to help ensure that Sheila and Christian would be as safe as possible. He bitched at first, Sheila remembered, but then agreed to, just to shut the three of them up. Ever since after then, C-Note and John had become slightly cordial with one another. At family gatherings, the two would talk about sports and current events, while always avoiding the topic of each other's occupation.

Picking up the phone, Sheila felt a moment of unease. However, she quickly put her feelings aside and called Janice. When Janice finally answered, Sheila opened up, telling her everything from the argument C-Note had with Cat, to Diane running her mouth about Snake. Janice listened closely to it all. Like Sheila, she, too, thought it strange both cousins go missing for a week and then show up all of a sudden the big winners from their Vegas trip. Janice found herself without any answers, but submerged into a sea of questions. After talking for an hour on the phone, they both hung up, still not sure what to do, and Sheila was in an even more distracted mood. She pursed her lips skeptically before finally deciding she would tell C-Note when he came home again.

⊙━◄►

JOHNNY STUDIED THE face of Larry, trying to read his mind. He had a frown of deep displeasure etched in his face, a wary look in his eyes. "Why'd you do it, Larry? Why? Jus' answer me that one fuckin' question."

Larry looked up from watching the television with a dazed look of triumph on his face. He took a few seconds to digest what Johnny had asked him, and telling by the hard look on his face, Larry knew he was in for an argument. His face looked blank for a moment, then it cleared.

"Why? Why *what?*" His voice was like iron, his face distorted into a grimace of hatred. "You always askin' me these stupid-ass questions like you some kind'a fuckin' therapist. Does it really matter to you how they died? They were gonna die regardless. I'm sick an' tired of you and that punk-ass cousin of ours always judging me. Y'all can keep your muthafuckin' comments to y'all muthafuckin' selves." His eyes were bright with conviction.

Johnny opened his mouth to argue, but the phone rang. Still looking at Larry stone-faced, he answered it. "Hello," he said with a spark of anger in his tone. The familiar voice of his cousin came on the line, slightly calming him down for a second. He listened intently as his cousin barked orders on what to do and what happened. Johnny could hear a note of panic in his cousin's voice, and the mere idea of it made his heart pound with fear.

He slammed down the phone, grabbed the remote to the TV, and began flipping through the channels until he came upon the news. Then he threw Larry a look of pure scorn. "Yo' dumbass is about to see why I'm always tryin' to figure out what's goin' on in that ant-sized brain of yours."

Larry sat up in the bed he was lying in. "Breaking News" flashed across the TV screen, and then the news reporter with his microphone in hand was standing in front of four burnt down houses. As Johnny looked closer, he could see the houses. They weren't burnt down—they were blown to smithereens. People were gathered behind the yellow barricade tape in fear and panic. A few people cried openly as the reporter told the grim story.

"Witnesses say they heard one enormous blast, followed by three more blasts of nearly the same magnitude. So far, firefighters have reported eight confirmed deaths in what appears to have been some type of gas leak. We'll have more for you in the later news. Reporting live for *Eyewitness News*, I'm Dionne Ashkins."

Johnny clicked off the remote and slowly turned to Larry, fighting an impulse to reach for his gun and begin shooting. For a moment, it seemed he'd lose control altogether. "Pack up your shit," Johnny said enraged. "We gotta get the fuck outta here. It's two plane tickets waitin' for us at LAX, so hurry up an' put a move on it!"

Larry aroused himself suddenly from his apparent state of meditation. Bitterness welled in him. "What's the big rush?" he asked, unfazed. "Nobody saw us, so no problem, right?"

Johnny's eyes flew wide open, completely caught off guard. His voice dropped to a whisper, as it always did when he was truly upset. "I ain't tellin' you no more, Larry. Either pack yo' shit or die right here. One of those houses you blew up was a fuckin' day care. An' when they find out it wasn't no fuckin' gas leak, they'll be coming for our asses. Now, if you wanna sit here an' play one hundred and one questions, I jus' can't let you do that. You'll be playin' with my freedom then."

Johnny's voice sent a coldness through him as Larry tried fighting a wave of dizziness that had come over him. His face and eyes became unreadable. He stood like a child wrestling with a difficult puzzle. A dull headache developed behind his eyes. He found himself paralyzed with fear.

"Please, Johnny, tell me I didn't hurt no kids." Tears slid down his cheeks.

Johnny knew from experience that fate played as cruelly with the innocent as well as the guilty. He knew if he told Larry that three out of the eight were children, he'd have to kill Larry on the spot to keep him from turning himself in. He hoped his quick, dark eyes hadn't revealed his entire soul.

"We got lucky this time," he said in his most convincing voice as he lied. "The owners of the day care took the kids on a field trip, so no kids was in the house at the time. But that still ain't gonna stop them from lookin' into it once them tied up bodies are found. So we gotta put wheels on it, Larry, an' roll out."

Hearing he had killed no children, Larry snapped back to his old self. He rushed around the hotel room, gathering his scattered underwear and clothes, stuffing them back into his travel bags.

A faint smirk curled the edges of Johnny's lips. For reasons he could not fathom, Larry always seem to buy whatever it was Johnny was selling. He was a convincing liar. There was never any doubt in Larry's mind, because Johnny's stories had the ring of truth to them. Johnny knew the steps of the charade, and he enjoyed it all. Like Larry, he began to quickly pack up the clothes that were strewn around. Johnny laughed to himself silently as he mused, thoughtfully, that Larry was so dumb he wouldn't be able to find his way out of a phone booth to save his life.

☞

SHEILA SAT ON the living-room sofa, waiting for her man's return home so she could replay what Diane had told her about Snake. The back door slamming brought her out of her deep state of thinking. "Baby, is that you?" she asked with a slight quiver in her voice.

"Who else would it fuckin' be comin' through my muthafuckin' back door at a time like this?" His voice held a mixture of sarcasm and menace.

She heard him quickly bolt up the kitchen stairs and, again, doubt began to plague her mind. She washed the doubt quickly away, though, and headed up the living-room stairs to their room. When she walked through the door, he had just finished dialing the last number on his private phone. Sheila grabbed the TV remote and muted the TV.

C-Note's head snapped up, his eyes glowering at her as if he cared nothing about hiding his disposition. "What is it now?" he barked while covering the mouthpiece of the phone with his free hand.

Sheila sat at the end of the bed. "Diane told me Snake has a new Cadillac truck, too. And that he came home with a bunch of money as well." She raised her hand and laid it on her breast. "I jus' thought you should—"

C-Note quickly cut her off. "Hold on, Sheila," he said pointing to the phone. He removed his hand from the mouthpiece.

"Honey Bee? Sorry about that, something just came up an' I'm going to have to call you back." He slammed down the phone, not caring if she had hung up or not. C-Note watched Sheila, trying to find something malicious in her gaze. A leaden stillness overcame the room. The expression on his face was dark, very wrathful.

"How long you been knowin' this?" he asked, disappointed but not surprised. He sat at the edge of their bed with his head in his hands. Somewhere behind his eyes, his head seemed to pound harder than it already was. Sheila flashed him a sympathetic nod of her head.

"Diane was tellin' me about it when you stormed out of the house. And I know you don't like talking over the phone, so I waited until you got back to tell you." She let out a worried breath, glad it was finally off her chest. He lifted his head from his hands as she continued. "And she said that they both won a lot of money, but he didn't tell her how much. But from the way she was runnin' her mouth, it supposed to be a grip."

Shelia sat next to C-Note, wrapping her arm around his back. She didn't know what to say, so she didn't say anything. She could see his face was marked with sorrow and confusion, because his face was showing more than its usual tic of agitation.

Just as she rested her head on his shoulder, she felt him tense up with rage. Quickly, she lifted her head to see him staring intensely at the muted television. "Where's the goddamn remote?" he yelled at the top of his lungs. His eyes were glued to the screen of blown-up houses with smoke still rising in the background as the reporter told of a story he couldn't hear. C-Note's hands searched frantically around the bed, finally finding the remote control. His finger hit the mute button.

"We haven't officially been told what caused this explosion, but from the looks of this destruction, it appears to have been some type of gas leak. We can confirm so far that eight people have been killed, and some of them were children at a daycare that operated out of one of the destroyed houses you see behind me. We'll have more on this breaking news later. I'm—"

C-Note hit the power button, devastated. Even though those homes were totally destroyed, he knew one of the blown houses was one of his dope houses. He rattled a frustrated sigh. Like a snake striking, Sheila snatched the TV remote.

"Did you see that?" she asked, quickly turning the sound back on.

"See what?" C-Note asked, mad because she had startled him, grabbing the remote.

Sheila flicked through the channels on the TV until she found the right one. "News stations always have other affiliate news stations." And sure enough, to C-Note's surprise, the same breaking news with the same reporter, saying the same thing, was just coming on the other channel. C-Note thought his composure might snap.

"Sheila, are you fuckin' crazy?" he said with a stricken look on his face. "I might be the person to blame for all those people dyin', and you want me to sit here and watch this shit again? Are you—?"

Sheila raised her hand in protest. "Fuck what the reporter is sayin'," she said, grabbing his arm and hunching closer to the TV to get a better look. "Check out that black Cadillac truck behind the reporter. That's what I want you to look at and tell me where you seen it before."

C-Note focused in just as the reporter was wrapping up the story. And to his amazement, there was no mistaking the truck or the light-skinned driver who had recently been to his house in the truck.

⌖

Honey Bee sat on her front porch reading the morning newspaper and drinking warm tea. A vibrating rumble began to shake her windows, causing her to look up from her paper just as a white SUV was stopping in front of her house. She set down her mug of tea on a stand next to the old rocking chair she sat on, leaned forward, squinting her eyes to try to get a better look at who was inside the SUV behind the dark, limousine-tinted windows. Just as she was about to get up and go see who it was, the passenger door opened. The driver's side window came down at the same time, and a wide smile spread across Honey Bee's face.

"I didn't know who the hell y'all were pullin' up in front of my house like that. I thought I was gonna have to get my gun out," she said jokingly.

"*Damn*, Honey! You still look like you in your early 20s."

Honey Bee held up her middle finger. "Snake, you still full of shit after all these years."

Snake's grin spread wide. "I still got yo' number programmed in my phone. When can I call you?"

Honey Bee laughed passionately, slapping her thick hip with one hand. "Snake, we always been cool. When you think you're ready for this, dial my number and we can get it cracking like we had it in '94. I ain't forgot."

The passenger door to Snake's truck closed. Snake rolled down the passenger window and spoke to the person who just got out of his vehicle. "Man! It ain't safe to be walkin' through different niggas' neighborhoods. You got me on chirp. I'll be around the corner at one of my broads' spots. You need a ride, jus' chirp a nig'." Then he rolled up his windows and hit the gas on his SUV and left.

Honey Bee opened the door, gesturing the man to come in. "C-Note called me earlier but forgot to call me back. I take it he sent your sexy ass over here to pick up the loot?"

He couldn't believe his ears. This was going to be easier than expected. "Yeah, I'm here for the ends," he said, stepping past her into the house. Honey Bee didn't try hiding the lascivious look on her face as he brushed past her.

"Have a seat wherever you please," she insisted as she turned the bolts on the door, locking them. "I'll be a few minutes countin' up the money gettin' it together. Can I get you something to eat or drink while you wait?" Honey Bee stood with her legs slightly parted and a hand on her hip. Her thick thighs could be seen partially through the slit in her robe. She smiled to herself inwardly. She could see the struggle he was having with himself as he tried his best not to stare so hard in between the slit of her robe.

After a long, awkward pause, she asked, "Well?"

Half-dazed, he finally moved his eyes up to her face. "Well, what?" he asked blankly, confused.

Honey Bee chuckled flirtatiously, liking the effect she was having on this man. She put her other hand on her shapely hips and spread her legs a bit wider. "Well, can I get you something to eat or drink?" she repeated in a more seductive voice.

His throat was as dry as the Mohave and Sahara deserts combined, and all he could manage to say was, "Jus' the money, H.B., jus' the money."

Honey Bee sighed irritably, shaking her head sadly. "You're just like C-Note. All business and no pleasure. It's no wonder why you two hang like you do. You two were made for each other. Let me grab the money for you."

Honey Bee turned on her heels and disappeared down the hallway. Moments later, she returned with a cordless phone to her ear and a backpack in her hand. "Jus' get the money together an' ready to be picked up when he gets there. So hurry up an' count the money and then call me back so I'll know how much it is." Honey Bee hung up the phone and tossed the backpack on the table.

"How much we workin' with?" he asked, smiling, while unzipping the zipper on the backpack.

"Forty-two gees," Honey said as she sat down on her reclining chair. She watched closely as he ruffled through the backpack. "It's all there," she said tartly while leaning back in the recliner, her legs crossed at the ankles. Uncrossing her legs, she brought one knee up as her foot rested under her, revealing the silky black hair in between her thighs. Honey Bee smiled as she watched his body language alter. She could see he was debating with himself.

Just then, the phone rang. Quickly, she reached for it and answered it, annoyed. "Hello!" she barked into the phone. Honey Bee could feel his appraising eyes lingering on her. She smiled seductively at him as she spoke into the phone. "I don't want him waitin' out there in front of the house, so be ready to run that money out there to him when he pulls up."

She paused, listening. Finally, she said, "Yeah!"

"It'll be the same people who was in that pretty-ass Cadillac truck that was in front of my house." Honey Bee rolled her eyes up in her head, now more annoyed. "Jus' have the damn money ready to go when they pull up."

She hung up the phone and resumed her same position as before with her leg cocked up. "That's Rock-Bottom's reason for sellin' dope," Honey Bee said offhandedly, "so he can buy himself a truck like Snake's." She watched the man sitting across from her, realizing he hadn't heard a word she was saying. Honey Bee took her hand and ran it between her creamy thick thighs.

"I hope you like what you see," she said, cocking up her other leg. The bulge she saw growing in his pants made her even hornier. Immediately, she started masturbating herself vigorously, moaning all the while.

He sat there stunned, hardly believing what his eyes saw in front of him. Unable to control himself any longer, he quickly unfastened his Rocawear jeans, pulled them down along with his Joe Boxer undershorts. Honey Bee reached out and grabbed his hard love muscle, drawing him to her. She wrapped her moist lips around his penis, and he nearly crooned aloud at the soft touch of her tongue playing gently on the tip. Violently, he shoved her back into the recliner and roughly parted her legs. He plunged his penis into her soft spot, and she squealed with glee. She pulled him down on top of her, digging her sharp fingernails into the small of his back.

Irate because of the stinging sensation in his back, he pushed up slightly with one arm and slapped her as hard as he could with his other hand. To his total surprise, this did the opposite of what he had expected. Honey Bee went into a frenzy. "Ohhh!" she moaned in ecstasy, while digging her nails deeper and deeper into his back. "Slap me harder," she pleaded in a low, hoarse voice.

The pain in his back was becoming unbearable. He repeatedly slapped her face, hoping it would stop her from digging into his flesh. When that didn't work, he wrapped his large hands around her throat and began to squeeze. The blood he felt trickling down his back only made him madder, causing him to squeeze tighter. Honey Bee smiled lovingly up at him. She couldn't believe that she had finally found a man that satisfied her. She was in total bliss. It was only until she was climaxing that she realized that her whole life was flashing before her eyes. Her last thought while her eyes closed was the regret that she wouldn't ever feel another orgasm that felt so good.

He stared down at Honey Bee's serene, smiling face and quickly pulled up his undershorts and pants. Once he was finished zipping them up, he reached into his pants pocket and brought out his Nextel cell phone and scrolled through the cell's phonebook until he found the number he was looking for. "Hey, Snake, I'm done wit' my business here. You can come scoop me up now, I'm waitin' on you."

chapter
10

The Infinity pulled into the alley behind the house. C-Note didn't want to see Sheila or Christian. He just wanted time to himself to sit and think. There was something eating at him, something he knew he had forgot to do, but he just couldn't put a finger on what it was. For reasons he could not understood, Cat-Daddy popped into his head. He realized he hadn't spoken with Cat since their argument. Like C-Note, Cat had not picked up a phone and called, let alone left a message. Now, C-Note started the Infinity and drove out of the alley. In the back of his mind, all he could do was think about all the time he had spent toiling in the ghetto streets to make it a little easier to live the game of life with a slight head start, not only for himself, but for his friends and family as well. And now, someone was ruining it.

A horn blared and the sound of screeching brakes brought him out of his reverie. He noticed he'd just run the stop sign on the corner street down the block from Cat's spot. His conscious took him there. Cat's Cadillac truck sat in the driveway. As he slowly passed the house, he noticed Snake's truck parked in front of a neighbor's house right across the street. C-Note went halfway down the block, busted a U-turn, and parked three houses down on the opposite side of the street. His windows were tinted, so he knew he couldn't be seen on the inside. He just hoped they didn't notice it was his car parked here. His alarm bells began to ring. Something was up, and he knew it.

Snake had made it his number one "don't do" on his list, and he always got on C-Note for doing it too. "C-Note, you gonna get yo' ass caught up in one of those dope houses if you stay there longer than you have to." C-Note remembered him saying it as clearly as if he were right next to him speaking it now. He continued to sit there, thinking, giving Snake the benefit of the doubt that he might have just got there only minutes before C-Note had arrived. Five minutes. Ten minutes. Twenty minutes had passed, and *still* Snake had not come out of the house.

Anxiety finally got the best of him. C-Note got out of the car, crossed the street, and walked the short distance to Cat's spot. He stood on the porch, hoping to hear something from inside the house. When he couldn't, he took out his keys as quietly as he could and opened the door. Unfortunately, the door made noise while being pushed open due to all the rain over the years and the house being as old as it was. As C-Note entered, Cat wheeled around with speed, pulling from his waistband a shiny chrome nine millimeter Smith & Wesson. He wore an astonished expression on his face.

"Nigga, you almost got yo' fuckin' head knocked off your shoulders creepin' up in here like that," Cat said ominously as he uncocked the gun and replaced it in his waistband. His eyes looked hard and cruel. "What the fuck you doin' over here?" he asked C-Note rather harshly, feeling no false need to disguise the venom in his voice.

C-Note was so shocked by the way Cat was acting towards him it took him a few seconds to recoup his thoughts. He became embittered by Cat's remarks. "What the fuck you mean, what am I doin' here? Either call me crazy, or better yet retarded, but I would'a sworn that this is my muthafuckin' spot!" C-Note's eyes moved over him coldly. The muscles in his throat tightened as the veins in his temples bulged. Now his eyes were charged with rage. "Nigga, I suggest you tell me what's goin' on here," C-Note snapped as he walked towards the kitchen door to where Cat was standing.

He felt a chill come over his limbs as he saw Snake sitting at the kitchen table with a pile of money in front of him and a miserable expression carved on his face. "What up, cousin?" Snake asked in a weak voice. He could see the fire burning in C-Note's eyes, and he quickly shifted his gaze to Cat.

"I told you, Cat, if it was gonna be a problem, I could jus' go through my own folks. I ain't here to start no problems nor be caught up in you two's bullshit. So if it's a problem, jus' let me know. I can pack up my loot an' be out."

Cat drew his lips in an evil smile, his expression on his face set for a scornful protest. "You all good, Snake! You ain't got shit to do with this." He then turned to C-Note with a look on his face that was wrathful and almost hideous. "Like I said at your joint when we last spoke, I ain't got to answer to you. You need to stop actin' like you're my momma or my daddy and worry about the shit that's got your head all fucked-up, 'cause I ain't gonna have you interrogatin' me like you're the fuckin' police."

C-Note snorted with resolve. He knew he was in the grip of suspicion, and there was nothing he could do. He and Cat locked stares. C-Note's brows furrowed in thought. He began to browse through his thoughts. He knew he had to play his cards close to his chest, because if not, surely he would lose.

"What's up with the money for those two byrds?" C-Note finally asked, still angry.

Cat tried to answer matter-of-factly. "It's in the same place where it's always been. In my room."

C-Note started towards the room but stopped at Cat's voice. "Only half of it is there. I ain't finished with the other half. But you can believe when I am done, I'm gonna hurry up an' blast you the rest of your money so I can be through with this bullshit. I got too much stressful shit to be worrin' about without you breathin' down my goddamn neck!"

C-Note stared into Cat's lifeless, cold eyes. He knew he couldn't let anger and rage cloud his judgment. Instead of coming back with a retort, he just decided to ignore Cat's last comment and go count up the money in Cat's room. He laughed to himself. Somehow, he'd managed to curb his own tongue.

While he sat on the bed counting the rubber-banded stacks of money, he could hear bits and pieces of Cat's and Snake's idle chatter. Cat boasted, "That nigga this, that nigga that. That nigga must be smokin' his own shit." Snake laughed hysterically in the background. C-Note began to put the stacks of money back into the bag. Then heard the sound of someone pounding on the door.

"Who is it?" he heard Cat yell from the kitchen, although he couldn't hear the reply. C-Note walked out of the room just as Cat was opening the door. Rico, his Mexican drug connection, came gliding through the door with a small box in hand.

"Hey, señor," Rico said with his Mexican accent, "I don't expect to see you here. How everything goes?"

C-Note smiled, thinking to himself, *What fucked-up English.* "Everything good, Rico, an' yourself?"

Rico looked at C-Note and then at Cat-Daddy. Like an animal, he could sniff the tension in the air. "It's all fine. Perfect. Perfecto," Rico answered hesitantly. He could tell something was up and he became visibly nervous. Cat could see this, too, and he quickly walked Rico to the kitchen so he could see the money on the table.

"It's all good, Rico," Cat said persuasively. "He's C-Note's cousin, too."

Snake stood up. "Here, have a seat and count up the money. It's all there to a T."

Rico sat down, a little more relaxed, and began to count the stacks of money. C-Note could tell he felt vaguely uneasy and tried to reassure him. At the same time, he was sending Cat and Snake a slight token of a hidden message. "You ain't got nothing to worry about Rico. Both these two clowns here are my first cousins, blood. Like that insurance company that comes on the TV all the time and says, 'You're in good hands.'"

Rico smiled broadly, now comfortable. C-Note walked to the front door, ready to make his exit as Cat followed close behind. On his face he wore a frown of deep displeasure. As they both stepped out onto the porch, Cat closed the door behind them. He met C-Note's gaze unflinchingly. "We ain't gonna pull no shit on Rico, if that's what you were tryin' to insinuate in there. You, of all people, should know I don't get down like that."

C-Note snorted sarcastically. "I don't know shit!"

A look of triumph crossed Cat's face, his eyes glittering. "Awhh, you jealous 'cause me an' Snake's been hangin' out? Is *that* it?" Cat burst into laughter, unable to control himself.

C-Note stood there, registering what Cat had said. He took a few seconds to digest that, and his eyes flashed anger. "Nigga, you must be crazy! Broads get jealous, *I* don't."

Cat stopped laughing when he heard the viciousness in C-Note's voice. They locked stares once again, neither saying anything. Finally, Cat shook his head from side to side. "You know, you got some real major issues goin' on in your head. I'm done arguing with you, 'cause no matter what I say, we'll end up arguing again. And I ain't tryin' to scare off Rico, the dope man. So if you want to get at me about what's pullin' on your dick so hard, holla' back at me when Rico's gone."

Before C-Note could open his mouth to say something in return, Cat turned and walked into the house, slamming the door behind him. C-Note stood there for a moment, trying to calm himself. It took all his strength and willpower for him not to go in there and start whooping on Cat's ass. After a few seconds, he regained control of his senses and began walking back to his car, telling himself all the while that he and Cat would have to bring the pent-up anger to a head eventually.

C-NOTE PARKED THE car in the driveway in front of his house. He could see Sheila walking in the living room through the sheer white curtains hanging in front of the big picture window. He never took notice of how easily you could see the image of a person inside the house at night when the lights were on the inside the house. He watched as Sheila walked over to the window, pushed the curtain aside, and peeked out at him.

As he got out of the car, he heard the locks of the front door being turned. Slowly he lumbered up the walkway with his mind somewhere else. He opened the screen door and then pushed open the wooden door. Sheila sat on the couch smiling happily as Christian climbed playfully on her back. He wasn't in the mood for her or the kid, but he put a fake smile on his face anyway.

"Da-Da," Christian cheered as he climbed off Sheila's back and ran to him.

C-Note scooped the kid up and planted a kiss on his forehead. "*Damn!*" he said smiling at Sheila with his fake grin spread across his face. "What are you feedin' this boy? His ass is gettin' heavy."

Sheila pursed her lips skeptically. "Now, you know you're the one who's always sneaking him food when I ain't lookin'."

C-Note's smile turned genuine. He knew what she said was true. Sheila was smiling from ear to ear, beaming with excitement, her eyes glowing. He put Christian on the floor and started for the stairs.

"Why don't you sit down?" Sheila coaxed in a sweet voice.

He could tell by the softness by which she was speaking that something was up. His head started to pound lightly. "I don't wanna sit down, Sheila, I wanna' go upstairs an' lay down on the bed and not be bothered for a while. Is that alright by you?" C-Note started for the stairs again, feeling guilty for being so harsh.

Sheila's face crumpled, her eyes threatening to explode. "Fine, then fuck it! Go upstairs an' rest all you want. But don't say shit to me about bein' the last person to know that I'm goin' to have another baby."

C-Note stopped dead in his tracks. He whirled around as if he'd just seen a ghost out of the corner of his eye. "You shitin' me?" he asked, flabbergasted, as a huge smile spread slowly across his face.

Sheila shook her head up and down with tears of joy streaming down her face. She was both mad and happy. Mad because of the way he had just been so rude to her. And happy because she could see how proud he was.

"What are you cryin' for?" he asked as he gently wiped away her tears.

Sheila looked up at him lovingly and said, "Because you always say the wrong shit at the right time. An' the way you were talking hurt my feelings."

C-Note smiled again and rubbed the back of her head. "Awwh, I'm sorry," he said in a baby's voice. "I forgot how sensitive women get when they are pregnant. I won't do it again, promise."

Sheila playfully slapped his thigh with her hand. "Stop talking to me like I'm a baby. You know how much I hate that." She reached out and wrapped her arms around his waist and pulled him to her. "I love you," she said resting her head against his stomach.

Christian climbed back up on the couch and jumped on Sheila's back again, chanting in his baby's voice, "Chit! Chit! Chit! Chit!"

Sheila looked at C-Note with big, excited eyes. "I hope you're ready for this all over again."

chapter

11

Leeway pulled his car on his front lawn and parked it. It was well past midnight, and he was tired and ready to jump into his king-size bed. He and Va-Voom had been out bowling since 9:00 o'clock with two women they had met together earlier that week. They had played seven games, a hundred dollars per game so that one of them had to lose. He had beat Va-Voom five games to two. As he got out of his car and walked to the door, he was already spending the money in his mind. He pulled his gun from under his shirt before sticking the key into the lock. He didn't want no jackers getting the jump on him opening the door. He walked in, noticing instantly he had left the hall light on.

"Shit!" Leeway said out loud, talking to himself. "That's the fuckin' reason my light bill is so damn high now." He laid his gun on the couch and moved to the hall and turned off the light. He then walked to his room, turned on the light, and sat on his bed taking off his shoes. Just as he began to toss his shoes in the closet, the closet door burst open.

"Lie on the fuckin' floor!" said the man who came out of the closet dressed in all black with a beanie and blue rag on his face. "You make a muthafuckin' sound an yo' ass is dead."

165

Leeway lay on the floor, not believing that this was happening to him.

"Who else is in here wit' you?" the gunman asked, keeping his voice down to a harsh whisper. "I heard you talking to someone else."

Leeway lifted his head up, trying to get a good peek at the man holding the gun. The intruder kicked Leeway viciously in the mouth, knocking out several teeth. "Keep yo' head to the fuckin' floor, dog, 'cause the next time you look up, nigga, you'll be catchin' a bullet to the head instead of my foot. Now who the fuck else is in the goddamn house?"

Leeway shook his head groggily. "Nobody! Ain't nobody in the house, dude."

The gunman slammed his shoe on the back of Leeway's neck. "Then who the fuck I hear you talkin' to about the light bill?" he asked as he pressed his shoe down hard on Leeway's neck.

He eased up a little so Leeway could speak. "I was talkin' to myself," Leeway strained through a bloody mouth.

The gunman untied three of the six pieces of rope he had around his waist and tied up Leeway's hands and feet. He then went back into the closet and came out with a roll of duct tape and then wrapped the tape around the rope to make it all the more stronger. When he finished tying Leeway, he dropped Leeway's back up against the bed. "I want you to listen, and listen close," the gunman said in a no-nonsense voice. He stood towering over the tied man to intimidate him even more. "If you scream or yell for help, I'll shoot you; if you don't tell me what I want to hear, I'll shoot you; if you think you can bullshit me, I'll shoot you. Now, it's up to you whether you live or die tonight, you got that?"

Through scared, bloodshot eyes, Leeway shook his head up and down slowly. He contemplated yelling, hoping his neighbors heard him. But for all he knew, they could have been the ones who had set him up.

"Where's the gun at?" the gunman asked brusquely. "Every nigga in L.A. selling dope out of their house keeps a gun somewhere."

Leeway thought about the gun on the on the couch and regretted that he had not brought it with him. "It's in the livin' room, on the couch."

The gunman left the room and was back in seconds. "Nice piece," he said admiringly as he took out the clip and stuck the gun and clip in his pocket. "Anymore straps laying around?"

Leeway thought about all the guns he had stashed around the house in various places. He knew what the man in front of him was there for, and it wasn't for the guns. He quickly decided not to tell him about the rest.

"That's the only one I've got." Leeway couldn't tell for sure, but to him, it looked like the gunman was smiling under the rag around his face.

"For your sake, I hope so." He grabbed Leeway by the ankles and dragged him to the living room in the middle of the floor. "Goddamn, you heavy," he said, breathing hard. Then he rolled Leeway on his stomach.

"I'm goin' to ask you this once, and once only. Like I said already, you can live or you can die. Now, where's the money an' dope you got from C-Note?"

Leeway could sense the seriousness of the man standing over him. But for some reason, he just couldn't see himself giving in so easily.

"C-Note? C-Note ain't gave me no damn money for as long as I can remember." His words sounded hollow, even to his own ears. Leeway tried to move his head just as the shoe caught him square on the jaw.

"Don't try an' be funny with me," the gunman snarled through clenched teeth. "I know he ain't gave you no money, asshole, but he did give you some dope to sell. An I want the money an' dope *right now!*" Leeway didn't think twice this time. He sounded hurt and defeated. "It's in the big gumbo pot next to the kitchen sink."

The masked gunman left the room and Leeway could hear him opening cabinets and rambling through pots and pans. He emerged from the kitchen with the silver pot in his hands. He set the pot right in front of Leeway's head and began to take out the bundles of money and dope.

"How much is here?" he asked in a cold, flat voice.

Leeway swallowed dryly, his hurt now turning to anger. In fact, his face blazed with anger. "How the fuck am I suppose to know? Look at how it's all bundled up. I ain't even counted it yet."

The gunman's eyes grew dark. He stood erect and swiftly whacked Leeway as hard as he could in the head with his foot. "Nigga, I'm runnin' this show. I ain't gonna take too much more of your smart mouthin'. If you wanna live to see tomorrow, I suggest you answer my question instead of trying to act like you're a badass. In case you ain't noticed, I ain't the one on my livin'-room floor all tied up."

Leeway's mind was spinning like the last cycle on a washing machine. His resentment burned hot, and it showed. "You got the money an dope, now go!" His voice faltered slightly. "That's it, an' that's all. I ain't got shit else."

The gunman's cold eyes flashed a skeptical expression, his eyebrows drawing together. "You really don't get it, do you?"

he asked, pacing back and forth in front of Leeway's head. "I ain't only here for your stash, but your boy's stash, too."

Leeway looked up at him strained and confused, clearly troubled. "And how you gonna do that?" he asked belligerently with a crooked grin spreading across his bloodied face.

The man stopped pacing and kneeled down in front of Leeway. He had a wicked twinkle in his eyes. "I ain't the one that's gonna do it," he replied wistfully. "*You are.*"

Leeway let his self-control crack, his eyes bright with conviction. "The hell I am!" he fumed through clenched teeth, "You might as well kill me now."

The intruder stood up and pulled the gun from out of his waist. He looked down at Leeway, who was looking up. "Alright, suit ya' self." He slammed the butt of his gun several times at the top of Leeway's head. Then he walked to the kitchen and came back with a box of Morton's salt. He opened it and poured half the box into the bleeding wounds on Leeway's head. The pain was so excruciating Leeway began to yell in pain. Another solid kick to the jaw shut him up instantly, breaking his jaw. Blood poured out of his mouth onto the floor.

The man smiled evilly behind the blue rag covering his face as Leeway groaned in pain on the floor. The attacker kneeled down once again. "Now, are you reconsiderin' what I asked you a few minutes ago?"

Leeway looked up at him with blood streaming down his face and one eye swollen shut. He thrashed around on the floor like a fish out of water.

"Life or death? I'm lettin' you choose your own fate." He stood up and kicked Leeway as hard as he could in the ribs. The pain was unbearable, and Leeway finally gave in.

"Okay! Okay! I'll do it. Whatever it is, I'll do it!"

The man bent over and rolled Leeway onto his back. He grabbed the gumbo pot, put all the drugs and money on the couch, and went into the kitchen. He filled the pot with cold water and returned. "This here should wake you up," he said, pouring the water over Leeway's bloodied head and face. "I need you to sound like your normal self when you call ya' boy up an' tell him C-Note's on his way over and he needs the two of you to have all the dope an' money ready, because he's got some people from out of town here an' he's tryin' to get them outta here on their scheduled plane at seven in the mornin'."

Leeway looked at the gunman as if he were crazy through his one good eye. "An' you think my boy is gonna fall for some sorry shit like that at this time of night?" Leeway asked wonderingly.

The gunman hunched his shoulders. "You better hope so; your life is the one dependin' on it." He chuckled coldly. "He's your boy. You know what to say to get him over here." He went into the bedroom and returned with Leeway's cellular phone.

"What name ya' boy go up under?" he asked Leeway, as he pushed buttons on the phone. "Vee," Leeway said, mad at himself for giving in. "Voom. Look for the name 'Voom.'"

The intruder looked up from the cell phone at Leeway. "What the fuck kind of name is Voom? Did the nigga like to play wit' toy cars or somethin' when he was a kid?" He laughed at his own joke, but Leeway didn't find it funny.

"He got the shit off of Felix the Cat. He's got a big mouth an' a loud voice, so he started callin' himself that when he was little."

The gunman shook his head in disbelief. "You serious?"

Leeway didn't respond to his question. He was just ready for this whole ordeal to be over with. "Did you find the number?" he asked dourly as if about to cry with his spirit sinking further. Disappointment lined his face. "What if he decides not to come an' says, 'Fuck C-Note'? You don't know Voom like I do. Sometimes he can be hardheaded and stubborn."

The gunman squatted once again, his eyes glittering like black jewels. "Like I said, you're the captain of your own fate. You got one time to get him over here, and one time only." He placed a sympathetic hand on Leeway's busted head.

Realizing it was a no-win situation, Leeway's eyes narrowed vindictively. "Dial the fuckin' number an' let me get this over with!" His eyes flashed undisguised anger.

The gunman smiled under the bandanna in a sly fashion. "Jus' make sure you tell him to come through the back door; it'll be open for him." He pressed the send button on the phone an' held the phone to Leeway's ear and mouth. The phone rang twice, and Va-Voom answered.

"What the fuck do you want now? You done already took my money bowlin'!"

Leeway chuckled casually, trying to sound as normal as he could. He stole a quick glance at the gunman's eyes and fear coursed through his veins. "I jus' got a call from C-Note, an' he needs us to do him a small favor."

Va-Voom sat on the other end of the phone, quiet.

"Hello? You still there?" Leeway asked, hoping he didn't sound so desperate.

"Yeah, I'm still here," Voom snapped irritably. "I go a hoe from Long Beach on her way over here, an' I ain't about to miss this pussy. What is it he wants us to do?"

Leeway exchanged conspiratorial looks with the gunman. "He needs us to get all the money an' work we got together so he can take care of some people he's got out here from out-of-town. He said they'll be leavin' in the wee hours of mornin', so he wants to do this tonight."

Va-Voom was wrestling with himself. All he had on his mind was the woman from Long Beach. "Can't this wait until tomorrow? It's too fuckin' late."

Leeway tried to suppress his sigh. He was on the edge of hysteria. A crafty look came over his face as he tried to think of something that would get Va-Voom to bring the money and dope. He knew this would be his last chance. His bowels tightened with fear, and his heart was in his mouth. "Listen, Voom, C-Note said it was real important to get this done tonight. The nigga always look out for us and take care of us. So we can't do'em like that when he asks us to do somethin' so simple as to givin' him his own money. If we don't come through, then we look bad."

Leeway paused, letting his words sink in Va-Voom's head. He knew Va-Voom well, and loyalty meant everything to Voom. "Jus' do this," Leeway said matter-of-factly, "bring the money an' work to me an' you can go on back to the house an' wait for your broad, an' I'll meet up with C-Note an' take care of everything."

Va-Voom jumped on this opportunity. He was hoping Leeway would find a way for him not to miss the big butt woman from Long Beach. "I'll be there in five minutes," Voom said and hung up the phone.

Leeway looked up at the gunman with pleading eyes. "Call him back," he said frantically. "He's on his way, but I didn't tell him to come through the back way." The gunman shook his head sadly, then pressed the send button. "Voom, I left the back door unlocked. Come through the back way."

Va-Voom's voice rose to a near shout. "Which way you think I was comin'? I damn sure ain't gonna drive around the fuckin' corner this late wit' dope and money when you live directly behind me. You know I ain't that fuckin' stupid!" He hung the phone up again before Leeway could respond.

The gunman grabbed Leeway around the ankles and dragged him back to the room. He grabbed the roll of duct tape, and suddenly, Leeway was seized by an urgent need to ask the man a question, his dark eyes filled with confusion. He looked up solemnly at the gunman, who held the tape in his hands.

"I need to know one thing," Leeway started brokenly, his voice stiff and formal. "How did you get into my house?" Leeway looked toward the windows. "None of the windows are broken, nor are the bars pulled off." He glared at the gunman, his eyes sparked with temper. "Did one of these hoes I fuck wit' sell me out? Or did one of them steal a key to the joint and give it to you?" Leeway paused for a second. "How?" he asked shaking his head. "I jus' need to know how you got in. Please, if you don't do nothin' else, jus' let me in on that."

The gunman saw the questioning look in Leeway's eyes. "Okay, I'll tell you," he said with a crooked grin spreading across his face under the bandanna. Leeway could tell he was becoming more and more absorbed with himself. "Listen, I gotta make this quick," he said in an almost polite but rushed voice. "Ya boy will be on his way in a few minutes, an' I don't wanna miss him." He began to wrap the tape around Leeway's eyes as he spoke.

"A few days ago, I sittin' out in my car scopin' out yo' pad, wonderin' how was I goin' to break in when I saw the mailman an' came up wit' my most smartest plan ever." He paused briefly, reliving the moment. "The mailman was three doors away and not payin' any attention to anything other than his job of delivering the mail. I saw this and used it against him. Now, he was two doors down 'n' gettin' closer to your spot. I started my car an'pulled into your driveway jus' as he was droppin' the neighbors' mail into their box. I parked my car as if I lived here, got out an' popped my trunk just as he was walkin' towards your door to deliver your mail. I grabbed the empty gym bag I carried, closed the trunk, an' met him right before he got to the porch.

"'How ya' doin'?' I said, catchin' him totally off guard. He barely even looked up, said, 'Hot as hell,' handed me your mail, an continued on to the next house."

Again he paused, basking with pride in his own story. He swallowed aloud, moistening his throat. "I then got your name an' address off your mail, went downtown to Alverado Street an' had a California driver's license made with your name, your address, and my picture. I then watched you tonight and followed you to the bowlin' alley. I called a locksmith right around the corner from your house an' told them I locked my keys inside my house. The locksmith came, I showed him my fake ID, an' here we are. The rest is history."

Leeway shook his head sadly, not wanting to believe the story he had just heard. He looked troubled but didn't comment. His flashing black eyes gave a skeptical expression. "An' the locksmith jus' let you in like that?"

The gunman nodded his head up and down slowly. "Jus' like that," he chimed, and began to wrap the duct tape around Leeway's mouth. Satisfied with the taping, he dragged Leeway to the closet and lay him face down. "Once I get the money an' work from ya' boy, I'll be on my merry way. Now, if you value ya' life, I suggest you lie here quiet an' wait for yo' boy to come and untie you. Don't get brave an' start kickin' the walls, makin' a bunch of noise, 'cause as you seen a while ago when

I asked you for the goods an' you lied, you made me have to show you I mean business. So believe me when I tell you this, I'll kill both of you without the slightest hesitation an' not feel shit about doin' it."

The gunman planted a hard kick to Leeway's ribs just to see if the tape was going to keep him quiet. Leeway's muffled moans could barely be heard. "I want you to shake your head up na' down if you get what I'm sayin.'"

Leeway did as he was told.

"Good!" the gunman said and closed the closet door. He turned off all the lights in the house except for a small lamp in the living room and then went to wait in the kitchen for Va-Voom to arrive.

The kitchen was almost pitch-black except for the eerie glow coming from the living-room lamp. The gunman opened a cabinet under the sink and squatted down on one knee, hiding himself as best as he could. He took the safety off his gun and waited patiently. Moments later, he heard the back gate being opened and then closed again. He readied himself as he heard the knob on the back door turn and the door open. Va-Voom stepped in, closing the door behind him.

"Leeway! What the fuck you got it so dark in here for?" Va-Voom started to walk toward the living room where the light was coming from. "Leeway! Is you cra—"

The gunman sprung up from behind the cabinet door with his gun aimed at Va-Voom. "Nigga, lie down on the muthafuckin' floor!"

Va-Voom stood there, stunned. "What the fuck is this? What in the hell's goin' on?" Va-Voom asked, surprised, while trying to get a better look at the gunman in the dark. "Where the fuck is Leeway? An' who the fuck is you?"

The gunman took a cautious step towards Va-Voom.

"Nigga, you jus' better get down on the floor an' leave the question-askin' to me."

Va-Voom locked eyes with the gunman, and a cold numbness came over him. Anger and fear gripped his heart. "I ain't gettin' on no damn floor!" Va-Voom stated indignantly. He held up the bag he was carrying so the gunman could see it. "Here's the cash an' dope. Take it an' be on your way. I ain't got no strap on me, so you ain't got nothin' to be worried about."

The gunman let out a bitter laugh. "From the way your talkin', I'd swear you were the one holdin' the gun." He took another step closer to Va-Voom, his eyes twinkling maliciously from the light of the lamp. "I'm not gonna tell you no more," he said, inching closer to Va-Voom with his gun only a foot away from his nose. "Get on the fuckin' floor!"

Va-Voom cast his eyes towards the living room, fear and anger running in his gut like an engine. He held the bag out towards the gunman and bent over as if he were about to get down on the floor. When the gunman reached to grab the bag, Va-Voom threw the bag at him as hard as he could and broke and ran for the living-room door with the gunman close on his heels. He twisted one of the many padlocks on the door, but that was as far as he got before the gunman brought the butt of his gun down on the back of Va-Voom's neck. He crumpled to the floor as the severe pain stole over his entire body.

The gunman dragged Va-Voom's limp body to the middle of the living-room floor, then rapidly tied and taped his hands, mouth, and feet. Once he had him securely taped, he then went into the room, opened the closet door, and grabbed Leeway by his tied ankles and dragged him into the living room next to Va-Voom. Standing over the two, he appeared to be considering whether or not he was going to let them live. Then, as if a decision were made, he laughed a cold, heartless, uncompassionate little laugh and took the bandanna off covering his face. His forehead was suddenly creased by a small expressive frown.

"Ya boy, here," the gunman said matter-of-factly as he kneeled down just above Va-Voom's bloodied head, "didn't cooperate as planned, so now there's a price you two got to pay." The gunman slammed his pistol down on top of Va-Voom's head. Blood spurted out of the open gash like a geyser onto the side of Leeway's face. The raw pain was almost unbearable, and Va-Voom could feel consciousness slipping away.

Leeway looked on with hurt-filled eyes, unable to do anything. He cast his pleading eyes at the gunman, who had an expression on his face that was almost too dreadful to behold. The gunman quickly stood up. "Who the fuck you think you eyeballin' like that? Instead of fear in your eyes, I see hatred. An' let me tell you, I don't like that shitty look in your eyes." With the tip of his shoe, the gunman drew back his leg and kicked Leeway as hard as he could right in the eye socket. Now it was Leeway's blood spurting over Va-Voom's already bloodied face. The gunman just laughed cruelly. To anyone watching the horrific scene, it was a monstrous humiliation mingled with sadistic torture. A change took place in the gunman's face that was slow and ominous.

"Now," he said, squatting back down to lean over the two beaten and bloodied men, "let me see that fear in your eyes." Leeway's eye socket had swollen to the size of a soft ball, with his eyeball hanging out of the socket by only veins and tissue. Va-Voom quickly turned his head as he watched the gunman reaching for Leeway's hanging eye. "You won't be seein' out this," he said mockingly as he pulled the eyeball loose from the hanging veins and tissues. The gunman roared with laughter as he watched Leeway squirm in indescribable pain on the floor.

The gunman cocked an amused eyebrow at Va-Voom, who had tears mixing with the blood running down his cheeks. He smiled to take some of the bitterness out of his tone. He looked at Va-Voom square in the eyes. "All this could've been avoided if you would have just listened. All you had to do was lie down on the floor." Va-Voom glanced up at him with red-rimmed eyes and an apologetic look on his face. "But no, you had to be a brave ass and make a run for the door." The gunman's smile was replaced by a dark scowl. "Thanks to you, your buddy here had to lose an eyeball due to your stupidity." He tossed the bloody eye in front of Va-Voom's face, just inches away. Va-Voom quickly turned his head, trying to avoid looking at the bloody eye, but the gunman reached down and twisted his head back violently so that he was face to face with it. His stomach went sour and his intestines clenched. The gunman smiled coldly as they exchanged silent looks.

Va-Voom's eyes charged with rage. "I bet you're wonderin,'" the gunman said as he let go of his head and stood back up, "what kind of human is capable of committing such extreme torture. Well, I'll tell you." He began to pace back and forth in front of the two tied up, bleeding men. Both there faces had gone horridly blank and chalk-white. "This really has nothing to do with the two of you. It has to do with that nigga you two are sellin' dope for. C-Note."

He paused, thinking, as the quiet stillness collected around them. His face went suddenly cold with menace. "That muthafucka has had the upper hand on me since I can remember. An' now it's my turn to one-up on him." Va-Voom shook his head in perplexity, his eyes glittering viciously. "Don't be mad at me because of what I'm doin', but be mad at yourselves 'cause of who you know."

He reached down and yanked the duct tape from Va-Voom's mouth. "You can thank your one-eyed friend here for not manning-up and keepin' you out of this. But he sold your soul as well as his own to the devil—which is me."

Leeway turned his head toward his best friend. Tears of sorrow ran out of his one good eye as the gunman brutally snatched the tape from his swollen lips. "I'm sorry," he mouthed, barely conscious as blood poured between his bloated lips. "I didn't know it was goin' to be like this."

Va-Voom tried to reason with his heart, but his heart refused all reason. "Why? Why me, dawg? After all the shit we been through, why did you set me up of all people for this?"

The gunman laughed raucously, his laughter echoing through the house menacingly. "What the fuck you think he did it for?" he asked sarcastically. "To save his own ass. How he was gonna do that, I don't know. But I'm quite sure you are hip to the laws of nature, aren't you? Save yourself before you save somebody else's ass. An' that's what it looks like he tried to do here, to save his own black ass." He laughed at his own sense of foul humor.

Leeway looked up at him with grave intensity on his face. "Fuck you," he said without emotion, and then turned back to his friend. He didn't try to hide his words or his anger. Tears were standing in his eye.

"You should've left me out of this Lee-baby. That way, I could've tracked this muthafucka down an' got revenge for you. I would've found his ass, even if it would've taken me my whole life."

Va-Voom moved his eyes back to the man standing over him. "I would'a hunted this son a bitch like the animal he is until he was dead an' skinned like he needs to be."

A devious smile spread across the gunman's face. "Awww, ain't that sweet. How sentimental." He again laughed at his own humor.

A spark of anger flared in Va-Voom that was like iron—cold and hard. "Don't get it in that fucked-up head of yours that you are gonna get away with this. I'm a street nigga, an' I'll go through every 'hood in California until I find out who you are. An' when I find out who you are, there's no place on God's green earth I won't come to get yo' ass."

The gunman's face went blank for a moment, then it cleared. "Ohhh, I'm shakin' with fear 'cause the big bad Va-Voom says he's gonna hunt me down, find me, kill me, and skin me like the animal I am." He paused for a brief second as he locked eyes with Va-Voom.

Va-Voom threw him a look of scorn. He knew the man standing over him was malicious and unscrupulous. He was hurt and outraged at the same time, but tried to reason. "You got what you came for, why not jus' leave? You got the money and the dope, what more do you want?" He stared at the gunman with sheer contempt, his fury bubbling inside.

The gunman folded his arms across his broad chest, then smiled evilly. "I sure like the way you make suggestions on what I should do. All right, then, give me a good suggestion on how I can make sure—no—guarantee—that you won't find me in the near future."

A puzzled look came across Va-Voom's face. He knew there was something demonic about the man standing over him. His eyes passed over him slowly, lingeringly. He knew in his mind that the gunman didn't understand the capacity for compassion in the human soul. His voice sharpened with distress. "What the fuck you want me to say? That I'll jus' forget about it an' go on livin' my life like this shit ain't never happened?"

There was undisguised hatred in his eyes. Finally, he lost all control over his feelings and tongue. A deep smoldering hate lit up his face as he spoke. "Unlike you, cocksmoker, I ain't gonna tell no lies. By the looks of things, I'm already a dead man. So believe me when I tell you this. You betta' hope the devil finds out you are dead before I do, an' if he does, that still won't save you. I can be in heaven with God Almighty, and I'll still trade places just to get to you."

The gunman watched in cold, unyielding amazement as he felt Va-Voom's anger moving through him as if it were a hot liquid. With all the force he could summon from his anger, he slammed his foot into Va-Voom's mouth. Blood and teeth particles sprayed across Leeway's face, with half a tooth landing in his empty eye socket. The intruder, a man surly possessed by Satan himself, bent down just above the two men's bleeding heads. "You did get one thing right, that's for sure. An' that is that you are a dead man already." He stood back up to his full size again with an evil smile playing across his mouth.

A dreadful and obvious thought came to Leeway's mind and the thought tormented him savagely. Through swollen lips, he began to plead. "Please don't kill us. I wasn't supposed to die like this. I can't die like this. *Pleeaasse!*" Tears dripped out of his one eye like a leaky faucet.

Va-Voom gave Leeway an undaunted look while boiling with rage. "Fuck this muthafucka, L-baby! Don't beg him for shit! If ya' got to beg to anybody, let it be God. But don't beg this piece-of-shit maggot." Va-Voom looked up to stare the gunman straight in the eyes before speaking to Leeway again. "I wouldn't give him the satisfaction of shit! I wouldn't piss down the filthy bitch's throat who had him if she was in hell an' needed a drink of piss to quench her thirst."

The gunman was frozen by rage. He was as frigid as a popsicle. Leeway went into an emotional frenzy, his voice faltering slightly. "We gave you everything we have. Please, don't listen to what the hell he's sayin'. He done went stark-ravin' mad. I don't wanna die right here or right now. Please, can't you jus' let us be an' go?"

Va-Voom cocked his head, looking at his one-eyed friend in total disgust. Disappointment lined his face. "I wouldn't be here if it wasn't for your bitch ass. And you wanna beg this same muthafucka who did this shit to you?" Va-Voom snorted disdainfully. "And to think, you said you'd die for me." Tears formed in his eyes as he shook his head sadly.

The gunman saw the faraway look in Va-Voom's eyes, and a scary chill stole over him. Somewhere, somewhere deep in his mind, something told him that if he didn't kill this man lying in front of him, the one they called Va-Voom, that one day he *would* find and kill him. He knew there was no point in toying with any ideas to the contrary. As hard as he could, he brought the butt of his gun down on Va-Voom's forehead. The first blow killed him, but as the gunman thought about Va-Voom's words of hunting him down and killing him, he repeatedly continued to smash the gun into Va-Voom's head until his body stopped twitching.

The gunman stood up half-shocked, half-amused by all the blood and tissue parts that seemed to be everywhere. "Shit!" he said with a crazed smile on his face, "I didn't think a head could hold that much blood." He looked around the bright crimson room, surveying his work, then down near his feet at what used to be a head. "I did him a good job," he said admirably, looking at Leeway with that same crazed smile on his face. "I guess I lost it there for a minute with him talking about my mother an' all. I jus' flipped. But who gives a fuck anyway? That's the shit that happens when you run your mouth the way he did. I couldn't take it no more, I had to shut him up one way or another."

He stuck the gun in the waistband of his pants. Blood dripped from his hands on to Leeway's face. "Now," he said casually as if none of this was taking place right in front of Leeway's face, "what are we gonna do with you?"

Leeway's voice had gone hoarse from screaming while the beating was happening. Through a strained voice, he pleaded one last time. "*Pleeaase!* Please don't kill me. Jus' don't kill me!"

The gunman rubbed his bloody hands together and chuckled sadistically. "With the way you're cryin', my two percent of compassion might cause my one percent of consciousness to fuck with me for the rest of my life. An' I don't wanna have to live with that one little annoying, tiny voice bothering me in my head, so consider yourself lucky. The big fish on the hook, the one that got away." He turned and went back into the kitchen.

Moments later, Leeway heard the water running and movement in the kitchen. What seemed like an eternity to him was only minutes. The killer came back into the living room, carrying the bag Leeway kept his money in. With his one good eye, he watched the gunman pick up the bag Va-Voom had brought and stuff it into the other bag with the money and dope. He started to walk past Leeway, then stopped. Leeway strained his neck to look up at the gunman.

"All this could'a been avoided," he began again, as looked around the blood-soaked living room, "but ya' boy had to be as hardheaded as you said he was. I was hope'n it didn't have to come to this, but it did." He bent down in front of Leeway.

"That small piece of my conscious I was tellin' you about, well, it done change its mind. I can't go through life worrying if this will come back an' bite me on the ass 'cause I showed some compassion." He reached his empty hand around his back and came forth with a ten-inch butcher knife that Leeway realized was from his own kitchen drawer.

"Please don't do this," he begged once more as he sobbed uncontrollably.

Again, the gunman laughed his evil little laugh. "I gotta do what my mind tells me to do," he smiled coldly at the begging man. "Look at it like this. You fucked ya' boy by callin' him over here. An' with all the extra bullshit he put me through, I guess you can say he fucked you right back. Sorry I can't let you live." The flash of the living-room lamp on the blade of the knife was all Leeway saw before he could close his one good eye. The gunman plunged the knife as hard as he could into the back of Leeway's neck. He twisted the handle of the knife several times until he felt the tip of the blade stick into the carpet, and then the wood beneath the carpet. Finished and satisfied with his handiwork, he stood and looked around the room, admiring his hard night's work. He wiped his bloody hands onto his pants as he stepped over the two dead bodies and headed to the front door near the living room.

chapter

12

C-Note woke up from his afternoon nap, startled, his face creased with anguish. The sun hung low in the sky, ready to make its exit for the day. He realized he had forgotten to call Leeway and Va-Voom two days ago and give them the heads-up that someone close to him, very close, possible even family, was knocking off his dope houses, as well as his people in them. Sheila had sidetracked his mind when he had come home two days ago with the news of having another baby. He cursed himself and quickly got out of bed and hurried to his private phone, where he hit the speed dial for Va-Voom's number. After the phone rang several times, he slammed it back in its cradle. He thought he had heard someone on the end answer the phone, but he had already hung up. He waited, knowing if Va-Voom did answer the phone, he'd see his number and call him right back. He waited for a little over a minute, and when his phone didn't ring, he dialed Leeway's number.

The phone rang twice and an unfamiliar voice answered the phone. "How may I help you?" C-Note removed the phone from his ear and looked at it as if it were a foreign object. He wondered what the hell was going on.

Stunned, he placed the phone back to his ear. "Who the fuck is this? An' what the hell you answerin' Leeway's phone for?"

The voice on the phone snapped back. "I got two cell phones an' two dead bodies here, an' you are callin' both of them pretty much back to back. So who is it the fuck I'm talkin' to?"

Shocked, C-Note rocked forward, catching himself on the stand where the phone sat. His legs felt like rubber. He pushed the phone to the floor and quickly sat on the stand to keep from falling. He played back in his head what the voice over the phone had just told him.

"Two dead bodies."

The voice yelling into the phone brought C-Note out of his horrified thoughts. "With whom am I speaking? I want to know your full name. We are going to trace all calls, and I will find out who you are."

C-Note gave his real name and then found out who it was answering Leeway's phone.

"I'm Detective Brooks with the Homicide Division for the Los Angeles Police Department. It's obvious you know the two victims, so I'd like to ask you a few questions."

C-Note sat quietly, stunned, on the other end of the line. He hoped his silence wouldn't look suspicious to the detective. "Question me about what?" C-Note asked nervously, wondering how much the detective knew about what was going on. "I ain't got shit to do with that, an' I don't know shit about it. So what kind of questions of importance can you possibly have to ask me?"

The detective let out a sigh over the phone. He was beginning to think the man on the other end of the line knew more than he was leading on about. "Look," the detective began, trying to sound persuasive, "you can make this easy or hard for both of us. You can come talk to me on your own free will, which would make things a lot easier. Or you could make me go to a judge, get a warrant signed, an' come pick you up." He paused briefly, letting C-Note think it over.

To speed up his thinking process, the detective continued, "Now, if I gotta go through all that paperwork just to talk to you, you can believe I'll keep you the seventy-two hours I can just to inconvenience you like you did me. An' that part I'll guarantee you."

C-Note sat there quietly, still thinking. He wondered if he should give his lawyer a call. "Do I need my attorney present while I'm being questioned?" he asked, giving in to the detective's request of making it easy for both of them.

The detective laughed skeptically. "That's your decision, totally up to you. But if you didn't do nothin' or had nothin' to do with it, like you said, then why would a smart man waste money on an attorney?"

C-Note thought about what the detective had said and realized it would look suspicious to pay money to a lawyer if he were innocent. So he dismissed the thought of the lawyer. "Where do you want to meet an' talk?"

The detective laughed again, sounding more sure of himself. "Smart man," he said. "I knew the moment we first started talking you had a brain in your head. Look, I'm still at the crime scene, and I'll be here a few more hours. If you want to, you can come to the scene and ask for me an' we can get this over with sooner than later. Or you could just meet me at the station when I'm done here. Which is it?"

C-Note took a deep breath and let it out. "It is Detective Brooks, right? I'll be over there within an hour." C-Note hung up the phone, got up, and went to the closet and slowly began to dress. Once finished, he stood there in edgy silence, thinking if he should tell the detective who he thought could be behind this.

The sun was sinking fast in the afternoon sky as C-Note drove his Infinity past Va-Voom's house. The four helicopters hovering in the sky told him all the commotion was on Leeway's street. He went to the end of Va-Voom's street and made a left turn. He cursed out loud when he saw the he couldn't make a left turn onto Leeway's street because of all the police and news vehicles parked every which way. So he turned the car around and parked it back on Va-Voom's street and walked around the block to meet with the detective.

As he walked, C-Note noticed how everyone had come out of their houses to be nosy and watch the spectacle that was going on in front of Leeway's house. He couldn't help but wonder where all these people were when all this bullshit was taking place. He shook his head in disgust as he made his way toward the yellow police caution tape seventy feet from Leeway's house.

As he approached the yellow tape and the two uniformed officers behind the tape, the strong smell of death caused him to pause as he wrestled the bile back down his throat that was threatening to erupt. It was now he knew why the nosy neighbors kept such a safe distance from the yellow tape.

As he came closer to the caution tape, one of the officers looked over at him with an irritated look on his face. C-Note gave the officer his own foul look. He wasn't going to take any bullshit from the officer or the detective he was coming to see. Seeing the irritated look on his partner's face, the other officer looked at C-Note with the same look as well.

"You can't come through here. You gotta go around the block an' come in from the other side where the sergeant is, that is, if you live in any one of the houses inside the barricade." He turned back to his partner and continued his conversation as if C-Note were not there. A moment after returning to his conversation with his partner, he noticed C-Note still standing there. His eyebrows drew together, and his face creased with lines of anger.

"What the fuck is your problem? Are you deaf or a retard? Or how about both?" Both officers laughed rudely at the cruel joke.

The expression on C-Note's face went from irritated to wrathful. His eyes were two pieces of pitch-black coal, revealing nothing except anger. "I'm guessin' you two dickheads must be rookies an' they ain't got shit else better for you to do other than to stand here runnin' ya' mouth about what you did last night and to make fucked-up jokes about handicapped people."

One of the officers took a hesitant step toward C-Note, but his partner put his hand out to hold him back. C-Note smiled defiantly as he looked both policemen in their eyes. "Now, if you would'a fuckin' asked me what I was here for, I would'a told you I'm here to see Detective Brooks. But instead of doing your job correctly, you wanna fuckin' make jokes about bein' retarded."

The face of the officer being held by his partner registered surprise. C-Note looked at his nameplate on his broad chest and realized it said Brooks. "Why didn't you jus' say that?" the officer named Brooks asked lamely. "That's my uncle. I'll go get him," he said turning and walking away quickly. C-Note smiled at the officer in a sly fashion just as he turned his back to him and pretended to be doing his job.

Two minutes later, he watched as the young Brooks and an older guy following behind him walked across Leeway's dirt lawn towards him. He noticed the strong resemblance of the two Brooks as they approached him.

The elder Brooks stuck out his hand. "Thank you for coming so soon. I'm Detective Brooks." His eyes quickly swept over all the people on their porches and lawns and the crowd that had gathered in the middle of the street. He lifted the yellow caution tape over his head and nodded for C-Note to come under it.

"This here is my nephew and his silly-ass partner Perkins," he said with another nod of his head.

C-Note smiled that sly smile again. "Yeah, I already met the two," he said unenthusiastically as he watched the officers keenly, both, of whom, were now pretending to do their jobs. C-Note had to stop himself from laughing out loud as the detective led him away.

They stopped at the front of Leeway's driveway, out of earshot of the officers inside the house as well as the nephew and his partner. Detective Brooks reached into his back pocket and brought out a little black leather notepad that C-Note assumed was issued because all of law enforcement had them. He watched the detective flip through several pages of paper before finding an empty sheet.

Detective Brooks looked up at C-Note. "Okay, what can you tell me about this?"

A wary look came over C-Note's face. He wondered if he should tell the detective standing in front of him that he believed wholeheartedly that there was a strong possibility that maybe some of his family members were behind this. Quickly, however, he decided not to. There were still some things he had to find out for sure.

"It ain't too much I can tell you," he said in a low, calm voice. "I knew both of them since school, an' we kept in touch on a regular basis." He covered his mouth and nose with his hands. A soft breeze had picked up and swept the foul smell of the bodies toward them, and it was overpowering.

The detective finished writing in the black book and looked up at C-Note with a suspicious look on his face. "Well, can you tell me how it is that you know there are two bodies in that house?"

C-Note laughed to himself. He had watched enough of the First 48 on the A&E channel to know the detective was trying to trip him up with his story. He looked at the detective with a mixture of coolness and contempt. "First of all, when I called an' asked who you were answering my folks' phone, you said you had two dead bodies here an' who was I callin' on both phones. An second, like I said, I knew these two since school, an' they were closer than brothers to each other. What one did, the other did."

Detective Brooks smiled wisely and then quickly jotted something else down in his black notebook. C-Note's cell phone began to ring. He pulled it out of his pocket and looked at the unfamiliar number. "You ain't gonna answer your phone?" Detective Brooks asked with a sly grin spreading across his face. "It could be important," he added, never taking his eyes off his black notebook as he continued to write.

Before the phone could ring for the third time, C-Note pressed the power button and turned the phone off. He didn't know who it was calling, and he was certainly not in the position to be talking his business in front of a detective. He put the cell phone back in his pocket and grinned slyly back at the detective as he closed his black notebook.

"Ain't nothin' more important, Detective, than findin' the person or persons who did this."

Detective Brooks shook his head slightly, his grin erased from his face. "You need to knock off the bullshit and come clean with what you know. I been doin' this for over twenty years, and I can tell when I'm being bullshitted." He paused for a brief second and took a step closer to C-Note. "I can see it in your eyes. You know something you ain't tellin' me." Again, he paused for more emphasis, his eyes glittering with rage. "If I find out there is something you know about this case an' you didn't tell me, you can bet your last little dollar I'm comin' for you. An' when I come get you, you're goin *down*! Down *hard*!"

C-Note took a step back to get Detective Brooks out of his face. The threats of the detective washed away his sly grin, and his anger boiled through his voice. "I came here on my own free will, as you called it, an' now you're talkin' to me like I'm juvenile and petty. I ain't gotta take yo' shit or anybody else's shit." He paused to catch his breath and gave Detective Brooks his I-Don't-Give-A-Fuck stare.

"You had your turn to say what you wanted to say, now it's my turn." He fixed his ill-tempered eyes coldly on the detective. "I came here to answer questions you said you had to ask me, not to be talked to like some little bitch who's scared of the police. You threaten me with goin' down hard, and I don't take kindly to threats from the police or anybody. So take this, just like how you wanted me to take your words about me goin' down hard. Don't think for one second just because you're the police that you can't go down even harder."

C-Note paused to smile grimly. "What'cha think high-powered assault rifles are used for?"

Detective Brooks' eyebrows scrunched together. "Boy, you threatenin' the police?" He quickly put his notebook in his back pocket, moving his police jacket slightly so C-Note could see he had a holster on his side. He smiled deviously at C-Note. "Are you mystified by the question I asked you? Or is it the gun?" Detective Brooks rested his hand on the butt of his gun, still staring at C-Note with that crazed look.

"Again, I'm gonna ask you this one more time. Are you threatenin' the police?"

C-Note snorted sarcastically, shaking his head side-to-side. It took every once of strength in him to hold himself back from reaching over and slapping the detective across the face. He really wanted to see if Detective Brooks had the balls to use the gun he had his hand on. They locked stares, neither one saying a word.

Just then, a young, white plainclothes officer stepped out of the door of Leeway's house onto the porch. He looked around and spotted the back of Detective Brooks. "Excuse me, Detective," he said loudly enough for all to hear who stood around watching the show. "I think we found something here you're gonna wanna look at." In his gloved hand he held up a Triple-Beam Scale as if it were a trophy he had just won.

C-Note snorted again, this time in disgust. He knew the white cop was only doing this to show everyone outside looking that this scene was drug-related.

Detective Brooks turned back to C-Note with that devilish grin spreading across his lips again. "You know anything about *that?*" he asked accusingly.

Nodding his head towards the porch, C-Note's face contorted in a wince of anger. "I already said I don't know shit! An' if I did know somethin', I could be dyin', and if I was told I could live if I told you, I'd be one dead muthafucka." C-Note smiled openly at the crumbling smile on the detective's face.

Detective Brooks shook his head sadly. "I'm tired of riding on this merry-go-around with you, an' I can see you feel the same way. I want you to look at it from my point of view. All I'm tryin' to do is my job. Don't you want the son of a bitch who did this to your friends be caught?" He looked into C-

Note's eyes and could tell there was more to him than the average hustler-around-town type. He had tried to back the man in front of him into a corner with his police intimidation, and man standing in front of him nicknamed C-Note had come out of that corner swinging, tooth and nail. Detective Brook secretly admired C-Note's toughness, and he tried not to think bitterly about his weaknesses.

"Enough of the bullshit on both our ends," the detective said earnestly as his face softened a tad bit. "I got a few more questions to ask you, and you can be on your way. To let both of us cool off and get our minds straight, I'm gonna go in there an' see what it is they want me to see."

C-Note stood stock–still, eyeballing the detective as Brooks shifted his gaze to the officer on the porch, unable to hold C-Note's stare any longer. "Give me fifteen minutes and I'll have you on your way." Detective Brooks stuck out his hand, and C-Note took a few seconds longer than necessary to clasp it.

"Let bygones be bygones and don't take it personal," Brooks said mildly, as if they hadn't been at each other's throat at all. "I was just doing my job," the detective said ruefully as he turned and headed quickly back into the house.

chapter
13

Sheila breathed a sigh of relief as she put the last load of laundry into the dryer. The sun was sinking and now all she wanted to do was relax and enjoy the rest of the evening in peace and by herself. As if on cue, she heard a loud crash coming from the living room. She looked around the laundry room and noticed Christian had managed to sneak off. "Shit!" she cursed out loud as she stormed off to the living room.

When she entered the living room from the hall, she saw Christian standing over an expensive lamp she had bought and didn't tell C-Note about. He looked up at Sheila and smiled at her with the lamp cord still in his tiny hand. "You better hope you didn't break my lamp," Sheila said as she picked it up off the floor and put it back on the small end table.

She scooped Christian up in her arms and nuzzled her nose into the side of his neck, causing him to squirm and giggle. "If your daddy knew how much I paid for that lamp, he'd be kickin' both our asses." With Christian still in her arms, Sheila went into the kitchen. She set the kid down in his own chair at the table and went to the refrigerator, where she grabbed a Capri-Sun, ripped the straw off the back, punched it through the hole in front, and handed it to Christian.

"Now it's Mommy's turn for a drink," she said with false cheer in her voice as she grabbed a highball glass out of C-Note's bar cabinet. Sheila glanced over all the expensive bottles of liquor before she realized that only two of the bottles had been opened. Camus XO and Remy Martin XO. She rarely drank cognac, never heard of Camus XO, and decided to stick with the Remy Martin. She filled her glass half full before sticking the bottle back in the cabinet just the way she found it.

"Your daddy would have a goddamn fit if he knew I was drinkin' his exquisite cognac." She laughed out loud as she sat down across the table from Christian and began to talk aimlessly to the child. "I wish your daddy was here so he could watch after you, and I could go out an' pamper myself. I ain't been to the nail shop in three weeks."

Sheila took a big swig of the cognac and quickly spit it out all over the table. Her eyes bulged at the taste as Christian laughed at the funny faces she was making. "Fine cognac, my ass," she said derisively as Christian continued to giggle at the look on her face. "This shi—" Sheila quickly caught herself, remembering Christian only seemed to pick up on the curse words spoken. "This stuff tastes terrible." She wiped her mouth with the back of her hand and then grabbed a dish towel from the sink. "I better hurry an' clean this up. Wit' my luck, your daddy'll come walkin' through that door and the crap will hit the fan if he see's his alcohol spilled out across the table." Sheila wrung out the dish towel and put it back on the sink, then she went to the refrigerator and opened it.

"Let's see what we got to mix this with ..." Sheila grabbed the half-gallon carton of Donald Duck Orange Juice and went back to her seat at the kitchen table, where she filled the rest of the glass with orange juice and took a small sip. She looked up at Christian with a smile spreading across her lips. "Ahhh ... Now that tastes a whole lot better."

Christian tossed his empty Capri-Sun pouch on to the table. Sheila cocked her eyebrows in a playful manner and then took a nice drink from her glass. "Is throwin' that juice pouch supposed to mean I'm to get you another juice?" She stood up, shaking her head. "You gonna be worse than that damn daddy of yours." She grabbed him another juice, opened it, and handed it to him. Before she sat down again, she grabbed three cookies out of the cookie jar next to the microwave. "This should keep you busy," she said, handing him the cookies and sitting back down.

She picked up her drink and took another hard hit of the alcohol, then she noticed a slight burning sensation in her belly and remembered she was pregnant. She got up and went back to the sink, taking one final swallow before pouring the alcohol down the drain. As she did so, she turned to look at Christian, who was smiling at her.

"If your daddy walked through that door right now, he'd be kickin' my butt three times." She turned on the hot water, rinsed out her glass, then went back to the table and sat down, still smiling. Sheila was talking to her child as if he understood everything she was saying.

"First of all, he'd be pissed 'cause I was drinkin'. Then he'd have a serious attitude because I was drinkin' his so-called good stuff." She reached across the table and tickled Christian on the belly. "An' the one thing he'd be really mad about is pourin' his 'exquisite' liquor down the drain." Sheila laughed sarcastically out loud as she tried her best to mimic C-Note's voice. "God-damn-it, woman, what's wrong wit' you pourin' out that drank like that? That's jus' like you, always pourin' money down the drain."

Christian snickered at the funny voice she was talking in. Sheila smiled pensively. "I see you know when I'm talkin' about your cheap daddy, huh?" The twinkle she saw in her son's eyes when she talked about his father overwhelmed her with joy. As she sat across the table watching the happiness on her son's face, she realized how good her life had become. She had no worries. All the bills were paid. Money was in the bank. She had a nice car to drive and a comfortable home to live in. But most of all, she realized that she had that love she'd craved all of her life.

Sheila stood up, then quickly sat back down, feeling lightheaded. It was hard for her to believe that she had got drunk so fast and so easily in such a small amount of time with such a small amount of liquor. "I guess I underestimated that alcohol your daddy keeps in that cabinet," Sheila half-slurred, putting her head down on the cool table. "That is some strong shit!"

As if on cue, Christian began to chant the only word he truly understood. "Chit! Chit! Chit! Chit! Chit!"

Sheila groaned and for a moment seemed incapable of speech. "Christian!" She almost yelled just as the doorbell rang. Her head whipped up from the cool table, and she caught herself before she could curse. "I wonder who the heck is this comin' by at this time of night?" she said with an inscrutable expression on her face as she put Christian down, who was immediately on her heels. She had locked the screen door and the wooden door was open, so she knew whoever it was could hear her.

"Who is it?" she asked, becoming more irate as she got to the door. Christian came and stood beside her. A mad look took hold of Sheila as a small flash of bitter memory came back to her. She flicked on the porch light so she could see better.

"C-Note is not here. So what are you doin' at my door?" Her brown eyes flashed a coldness.

"I was supposed to meet him here to pay him the rest of his money," the man said, digging into his two front pockets and pulling out wads of cash. He held the money up high for her to see it, and anybody else who might be looking. She quickly turned the porch light back off.

"Well, he ain't told me shit about you comin' over here an' droppin' off no money."

A short silence ensued. "Well, why would he tell you I was supposed to be droppin' off money here when I was supposed to be meetin' him here, not you. Fuck it, then! Tell 'em I came by to pay 'em his money an' he wasn't here. I'm goin' O-T tonight, an' I'll get back to him in a week or so when I return." He turned to leave, but Sheila stopped him. She didn't want C-Note mad at her for not collecting the money or for not letting him wait on C-Note. She unlocked the screen door.

"Put that money back in your pockets. I don't want my nosy-ass neighbors seein' nothin' outta the ordinary."

Smiling, he stuffed the cash back in his pockets. Sheila pushed the screen door open and stepped to the side, letting him in. Christian stood next to his mother, smiling. As the man came through the door, he scooped Christian up in his arms playfully. "My God, little man, every time your uncle sees you, you're gettin' bigger. How old are you now?"

Christian, loving the attention, held up four fingers.

"Boy, you startin' off jus' like your daddy lyin', 'cause you're only three," Sheila said, walking past the two to the sofa. She sat down on the sofa, feeling ill at ease and unable to hide her unhappiness. She didn't like the man in her living room, and she never would. His words caught her utterly unprepared.

"Look, I know you don't like me, I can see all over your face. An' to be honest with you, I don't like you either. But business is business, so let's take care of business." He put Christian down and pulled out one of the wads of money.

"We gonna both count this right here so it won't be no discrepancies when C-Note gets it." He sat down on the sofa next to Sheila, putting the money on the table in front of them. He was looking at Sheila in a sly and strange way.

Sheila stood up quickly, too uncomfortable. Something was up, her street senses told her. But she just wanted to get this whole money ordeal out of the way so he could be gone. "Can I get you somethin' to drink while you count out the money?" Sheila asked tentatively, wanting to get out from under his fiendish glare.

Suddenly his tone became different, dark and cold. "Yeah, get me a beer and a shot of what C-Note drinks on a regular."

Sheila hurried to the kitchen with her mind in a frenzy, racing this way and that way. She quickly poured half a glass of Remy Martin and grabbed a beer out of the refrigerator, trying to restrain her thoughts as well as her impulses. Then she went back into the living room wearing a fake smile that died immediately when she saw Christian sitting on his lap.

"Boy, get down an' go play up in your room," Sheila said in a stern but controlled voice. She set the beer and glass on the table in front of him and reached for her son, feeling an eerie sense of trepidation.

He moved Christian away from Sheila's outstretched arms. "It's cool! I got'em! Can't you see he's playin' with his uncle he ain't seen in a long time?" He grabbed the glass of cognac and in one swallow, downed the amber liquid. Satisfied, he gave a little martyred sigh and wiped his mouth with the back of his hand.

Sheila could feel the bile rising in her throat, but she kept her lips pressed together, trying not to show her annoyance.

"If you gonna jus' stand there lookin' retarded, make ya' self useful an' open my beer." He wrapped his arm around Christian's belly and smiled coldly at Sheila. Something in her brain reacted sharply as his words ricocheted through her head. Her forehead furrowed in an annoyed perplexity, and her voice went unnaturally low.

"I don't know who the fuck it is you think you're talkin' too, but you got me fucked up! I ain't one of those stupid bitches you fuck wit'. Open your own damn beer an' hand me my child."

He stood up slowly, holding onto the child more firmly, still smiling coldly. He didn't like receiving hidden threats without a clear understanding of what it might cost him later. "An' if I don't give you your fuckin' brat, what you gonna do about it?"

Sheila's stomach soured, and her face went through a quick transition of expressions: anger, hatred, sorrow, surprise, and suspicion. They exchanged silent looks of dislike for one another for a moment. Sheila was feeling an itchy distress, and then she felt a murderous rage. She reached down and quickly grabbed the bottle of beer off the table. "If you don't give me my muthafuckin' son, I'll cut yo' ass so many times you'd swear I was a butcher. Now put my goddamn son down. *Now!*" Holding the beer bottle by the neck, she slammed the fat part of the bottle over the edge of the table, and then brought the neck of the bottle up with it sharp shards for him to see.

Sensing his mother's anger, Christian began to kick and scream while trying to squirm from out under the man's arm. The man, in turn, tightened his hold on the kid as he stepped back and away from Sheila. He reached under his shirt into the back pocket of his pants and brought out a .380 Beretta handgun, smiled again, this time his cold features registering nothing but listlessness. He put the gun up to Christian's tiny head. Sheila stood frozen like a snowman.

"Now, drop that bottle, bitch, or else you'll have a dead baby to deal wit!"

Shocked by the gun to her child's head, she let the broken bottle drop to the floor. A look of pure terror covered her face. Her world had just taken a sudden turn for the worse. "Please! Jus' move that gun away from my son's head. I'll …" She stopped midsentence and just for a split second, her whole body threatened to crumble.

"I'll do whatever it is you want! Jus' don't hurt my baby!" Sheila stood there motionless, looking submissive with tears standing in her eyes, her stomach doing somersaults and wanting to throw up.

He removed the gun from Christian's head with an ominous smile curling on his lips and his black eyes glaring like two pieces of cold steel. "Now that I see I got your attention an' understandin', maybe we can get down to the nitty-gritty of why I'm really here." He gave Sheila a false solicitous expression. "Where does C-Note keep the real money at? I know it has to be here somewhere. Them dope houses of his I knocked off were only partial payments. Now, I'm here for the final an' full payment."

Sheila felt the blackest dread drop down on her like a suffocating blanket and smother her heart as it all now began to make sense to her. All the robberies and murders that had been going on at C-Note's dope houses were caused by the man standing in front of her holding a gun on her with her son in his arms. She had always had bad dreams somewhat similar to this, but not always this vivid and graphic. A stark cold rage enveloped her entire body. Her eyes turned cold, vindictive, and glittered with hate. She stared at him as if he were some unknown vile creature in the woods. Sheila stood so still and mad, she seemed almost dead. Only her lips moved.

"How can you be doin' this? C-Note considered you as a brother to him. You two grew up an' were together since you were kids on tricycles. An' even after all he's done for you, you come into his house an' put a gun to his son's head? This is your nephew, for Christ's sake." Sheila struggled in her mind to regain clarity and strength. She spoke to him with a mixture off coolness and contempt.

"You've done all this bullshit over money? Or is it just jealousy an' envy?" She shook her head sadly side to side with a bewildered look on her face. "Of all the people in the world, you had to do this to someone who treated you better than family."

"Shut the fuck up!" he said, crinkling his forehead, his face contorted in fury, suffused with anger. His rage was so sudden it caught Sheila off guard. The gun slammed in the bridge of her nose, reeling her back to the couch half-conscious. Blood leaked from her broken nose and both her eyes began to swell instantly. At the sight of seeing his mother's blood, an expression of utter panic appeared on Christian's face and he began to kick and scream, nearly slipping from his uncle's arm. However, the man regained hold of the child's left arm and snatched him violently up in the air by his one arm. "You need to shut the fuck up!" he said brutally, shaking the child like a rag doll.

With Christian still hanging in midair by one arm, he hurried over to the door, quickly looked outside through the screen, and then slammed it shut. He turned back to Sheila, who was trying to stop the blood from running out of her nose with her hand.

"Go in the fuckin' kitchen an' grab a towel or somethin' to wipe your fuckin' face wit'. An' don't get brave, bitch. Remember, I got this little bastard right here in front of me." He held Christian up by his one arm.

Sheila struggled to get off the couch and stumbled into the kitchen. She came back out with an oven towel pressed to her swollen face and sat back down on the couch. She had thought about grabbing the biggest knife in the kitchen but remembered he was holding her son hostage. And she was too weak to attempt vengeance in either words or action.

Looking into his cold, shameless, glistening eyes, she said, "Whatever it is you want, I'll give it to you. Jus' let my son go. You're hurtin' him."

His forehead was suddenly creased by a small expressive frown, and he laughed in a cold uncompassionate way. "Awww ... Look at the high an' mighty Sheila," he said in a mocking voice. "All tears an' blood now. The slut that was suppose to be mine, but instead, got wit' my best friend who was more of a brother to me. Now she has finally climbed down off her pedestal."

His eyes moved over Sheila coldly. The muscles in his throat tightened, and the veins in his temples bulged. "I bet you thought you were gettin' the best bargain in the deal when you hooked up wit' C-Note instead of me. You wouldn't be sittin' here now if you'd chosen the real go-getter. But you chose the 'now' back then over 'later.' An' look at where 'now' got you sittin': wit' *me*, 'later.' You're still here wit' me later, but on the wrong side of the fence."

He laughed triumphantly at his own crude joke and then made a dramatic sigh. "I've been waitin' for the day to pay both you muthafuckas back. An' *today* is that day. You chose C-Note over me. An' he chose you over me."

Sheila watched him with amazed, swollen eyes as he began trembling with uncharacteristic rage. His face was hideously blank, and she was stunned by his revealed resentments.

"Frankly, I think you two were made for each other. Two weaklings. Two conceited assholes. An' two, too-smart muthafuckas for your own good. Yea, the two of you, an' look where it got you now." Now his face displayed no human emotion. His eyes were cruel, hard. Then there seemed an awful calm in him, an unhappy and grim calm.

"Everything was perfect until you came around. Me an' C-Note hardly argued. We were together on a daily basis. We made money together. We fucked hoes together. We beat an' shot niggas up together. We did everything together. That is, until *you* came around an' started to change him."

Sheila felt no false need to disguise her anger and grief. Her soul was too hurt. Inside her lurked a dreadful anger and an unreasonable hate. She removed the bloodied towel from her face so she could speak, her expression a mask of suppressed rage.

"You really are a nutcase," she said nervously, her voice low and serious.

He laughed at her again, a chilling, merciless laughter. She turned swollen, bloodshot eyes on him and took a deep breath for courage. "So all these years you been harborin' these fucked-up resentments, jus' waitin' for the opportunity to do somethin' like this to the one person you knew who really loved an' cared for you?" Sheila shook her head in a gesture halfway between amazement and disgust. The look she leveled at him was pure hated. "An' to think," she said reluctantly, "all the times I tried to warn him about how fucked-up in the head you were he told me to keep my mouth shut an' my thoughts to myself. He said I didn't know you like he did. He said sooner or later you'd get your shit together an' y'all would go back to bein' the brothers y'all once were."

He cocked an amused eyebrow at Sheila with feigned interest and a wistful look on his face. "I wish our lives could be like one of those soap opera shows you watch all day while that dummy C-Note is out there in them streets, puttin' his life on the line. But the truth of it all is that this ain't no goddamn TV show, an' it ain't always no good endin.'"

He looked at her as if she were dense. "Jus' so you'll know, this ain't got nothin' to do wit' you or him. It's all about the money, the green. It's the evil that makes people like me do whatever it takes to acquire it. It don't matter who you are. It don't matter the friendship or relationship. When it comes to money, it jus' don't matter. If you got it an' I want it, I'm takin' it. It been that way long before I was thought of, an' it's gonna be that way when I'm gone. So while I'm here on this earth, I'm takin' my fair share of it."

Sheila sat there listening with unhearing ears. She realized that plenty of sleepless nights of planning and longing had gone into his strategy of robbing C-Note. She was willing to bet there were a lot of miserably envious, greedy, unhappy people in the world, and he was one of them.

He looked at her wildly with a smug smile on his face. "So don't take it personally. It really has nothin' to do wit' you. Bitches come an' go, but that money—that money will always be out there waitin' for me to get my hands on it."

At that point, he set Christian on the floor, but still held on tightly to his arm. He glowered at her, as if he cared nothing about hiding his disposition. "Where do C-Note keep the money stashed at?"

A quiet stillness collected around the living room, and Sheila tried to focus her mind, clearing it utterly of all preconceptions or fear. She stared forward at nothing, as if she were about to go mad.

"Bitch, I said, where's the money at? If you care about that money more than your son's life, then you jus' sit there lookin' crazy an' see if I don't put a bullet in his head. He'll be the first to get it if you don't start talkin'!"

Christian began to cry brokenheartedly, which brought Sheila out of her shocked trance. She looked at her crying son and saw the stricken look on his face. The tightening in her chest was unbearable and before she knew it, she was on her feet, clawing like a madwoman at the man's face with her fingernails. She went into a frenzy, hearing and seeing nothing until the blast of the gunshot echoed through the room. She stopped fighting instantly and looked down at her son, who was sprawled out on the floor. Sheila bent down to pick up her son and was rocked by a pain exploding in her mouth. It sent her reeling backwards and crashing headfirst into the table in front of the couch, barely conscious. Through a dazed fog, Sheila looked up at C-Note's once-upon-a-time best friend.

"My baby! You killed my baby!"

He quickly walked over to Sheila and kicked her as hard as he could in the stomach. His scratched, bloody face was pure cold menace. "Bitch, you are a real fuckin' nuisance! One

more damn stunt like that an' I *will* shoot your fuckin' baby."
He reached down and snatched Christian up by the same
one arm as before. The loud shot from the gun blast had
traumatized and rendered the child quiet. He held the child
out by the arm for Sheila to see that he was alright. A sadistic
smile spread across his lips.

"If I would'a known that's all it took to finally shut this
little bastard up, I would'a shot a hole in the fuckin' wall
before now."

Sheila struggled up from the broken table back onto
the couch. The pain she felt when she thought her son was
shot somehow overrode the physical pain in her head and
mouth. Her nerves betrayed her, and she began to shake
uncontrollably. All she wanted was this whole episode to be
over with and her son back safe in her own arms.

Finally, Sheila was willing to accept defeat. She reached for
the bloodied towel and spit blood and broken teeth fragments
into it. Her voice was a strangled whisper. "It's a safe upstairs,
but I swear I don't know the combination. He wouldn't give it
to me because he said he didn't want me blowin' hard-earned
money on useless or unnecessary things."

Sheila thought about the thousand dollars C-Note had
given her two days ago to pay the bills for the week. Plus,
she had saved up thirteen hundred dollars from the previous
weeks she had paid the bills and still had some leftover money
which C-Note had never asked for. Her once-pretty face
now looked like she had been in a plane accident and barely
survived. Her swollen eyes looked like slots on a video-game
machine. She tried to mask the fear in heart, but her heart
kept skipping beats.

"I got twenty-three hundred dollars put away. You can
take that. All of it!"

He stood there in edgy silence, smiling coldly with a confident look on his face. He studied Sheila for what seemed an interminable duration. Finally, he laughed raucously, and his laughter echoed menacingly.

"Bitch, you think I done came here an' gone through all this trouble for twenty-three hundred lousy fuckin' dollars?" He laughed again, his eyes steely. "I hope I ain't kicked you too hard in the face that I done rattled your brain loose. I want the *real* money. An' you know what the real money is."

Sheila sighed then shook her head sadly, giving him an evaluating stare. She saw a dark glow of cunningness flash in his eyes. She knew she had to focus on what she could do to get her son away from the madman holding him hostage and not on what she was powerless to change. Her voice held reason, devoid of all emotions.

"What is it you want me to do? I ain't got the combination to the safe, an' if I did, what if there wasn't no money in there? What then? You jus' kill me and my son?" She was uneasy, filled with misgivings and bad thoughts. He drew his lips in a clown's grin and smiled at her enticingly, looking coldly amused. Christian just hung there by one arm, still shocked into silence.

"Get on the phone an' call C-Note."

He walked over to the end table and picked up the cordless phone and tossed it next to her on the couch. "Don't try an' call 911, 'cause I don't think they can make it here in the time it takes for me to squeeze the trigger. By the time they get here, both you an' the kid will be dead an' I'll be halfway across California makin' my escape. You know, jus' like I do, how long it takes 911 to respond when niggas are callin'." He laughed at his own joke again, and Sheila winced inwardly at how true his words were.

She grabbed the phone next to her off the couch with a sheepish look on her face. She couldn't help but think about that very moment when she unlocked the screen door and let him in. Her street sense had warned her, and now she regretted not listening. She turned hurt, bloodshot eyes on him.

"What do you want me to tell him?" she asked solemnly, wiping blood from her mouth.

He stared at her grimly, mystified by her remark. "How the fuck do I know what to tell him? You're his bitch. You should know what to say." He glanced down at the limp kid he was holding and then back at Sheila. "Make up some kind of story about the kid an' you need him here ASAP." He gave her a sly wink and went on remorselessly. "Tell him the kid fell an' you think he broke his leg. You went to start the truck, an' the truck didn't start, an you want him to come home so he can take you to the hospital."

Sheila shook her head dismally.

"What the fuck's your problem?" he asked truculently as he tightened his grip on Christian's arm. His eyes narrowed dangerously low, and Sheila, again, felt her heart doing step aerobics in her chest.

"I don't think he's gonna believe that story. He's gonna ask me why I didn't call an ambulance. Or why didn't I go next door for help. C-Note's not as stupid as you think he is. He's gonna ask questions, you know?"

His face went stiff as stone as his eyes moved coldly over her. "I don't give a mad fuckwhat you think he's not gonna believe. If you value your son's life, then you'll get him here." A crazed look of triumph illuminated his face, exposing the evil. "If you ain't gonna try an' get him here, this gun goes back up to Christian's head.

"I have about had it wit' your bullshit, Sheila! It's either you an' the kid take bullets, or you better get to callin'. I been here too goddamn long, an' the little patience I did have ran out."

Sheila's hurt face showed her thoughts. She began to feel pangs of regret. But she knew the basic facts of life: sides change, and now she was willing to do whatever it took to get her son out of harm's way. She dialed C-Note's cell phone number as she looked up at the cruel face near her.

The answering machine service on the phone came on immediately, and she quickly hung up the cordless. "For some reason, his phone is off, an' he never turns his phone off. Somethin' jus' ain't right. He wouldn't jus' turn off his phone."

The intruder walked over to Sheila and slammed the butt of his gun into the side of her head, opening up another gash there. "You get back on that phone an' leave a message about his son's broken leg, an' he'll be callin' back soon enough." He smiled wolfishly at her. "I want you to sound jus' as you are now, scared an' hurt when you leave the message, so he'll know you're not bullshittin'. An' that'll get his ass into gear, an' he'll come runnin' home in a hurry." He laughed sadistically at his own words, which somehow he found to be funny.

Sheila picked up the phone off the floor that she had dropped when he hit her and left a crying message on C-Note's cell phone. Then she set the cordless next to her on the couch and tended to the bleeding wounds on her beaten up face. She watched the assailant closely as he walked over to the other couch and sat down. To her, the situation was surreal. It was so strange that she began to wonder if she were dreaming. She touched the new gash in her head and winced in pain.

Again he laughed crudely. "Dumb bitch, it's a cut; it's supposed to hurt." He brought his wrist up in front of his face and looked at his watch. "I'm givin' C-Note thirty minutes. If he ain't called by then ... oh well." His expression went from sarcastic to serious. "I can't take the chance sittin' here half the goddamn night waitin' on him. So you better hope somethin' ain't wrong an' he hurries up an' calls back." He smiled again, cruel and wolfish.

Sheila tried to clear her head. She knew something was tapping at her consciousness like moths at a light, but she couldn't quite put her finger on it. There was something sad around her swollen eyes, cuts there that marked her vision of her own impending tragedy. She felt the breath of death breathing on her heavily and lustily, and suddenly her memory came marching through her mind like soldiers preparing to go to war. Sheila realized her time was limited. She used her mind like a prostitute uses sex. She feign surprised, moving the bloodied towel away from her mouth.

"I know where he's at!" Sheila exclaimed, trying to sound as excited as possible. "He was supposed to pick up tickets for the Katt Williams Comedy Show at my sister's house." She paused, hoping she sounded sincere. "You know my sister is married to a sheriff's deputy an' him an' C-Note don't get along too well." Again, Sheila paused for effect, while her brain felt as if it were doing flips in her head. "Every time we go over there, C-Note turns his phone off. He ain't as stupid as you think he is. He's gonna ask questions, you know?

"With all this new technology, C-Note don't want his phone bein' tapped or for them to put a tracer on so they can follow him around. That's why he's always adamant about turnin' off his phone."

Sheila picked up the cordless phone, and the man sprang up off the couch onto his feet. He pointed the gun at her. "Hold on, bitch! Let's get some thangs straight before you start makin' that call." He hoisted Christian up by one arm and wrapped his forearm around the child's belly, with Christian's back was to his chest. Sheila placed the phone back on the couch, and he smiled coldly at her.

"First of all, how do I know you ain't lyin' about him bein' over there? An' second, how do I know you won't try an' pull a fast one?"

Sheila fixed her swollen, bloodshot eyes on his eyes. She pointed to her beat-up, battered face, then she spoke quietly. "You think I went through all this, gettin' my ass kicked over nothin'? Well, you're wrong, muthafucka!" She hesitated briefly, shaking uncontrollably. "My face looks like this 'cause I want my child back. Back an' safe an' away from you." Sheila wiped the blood and tears out of the corner of her eyes and continued to roll on.

"You got my son wit' a gun to his head, an' you think I'll jeopardize his safety by sayin' somethin' stupid over the phone?" She shook her head sadly. "I know you might think I'm dumb or stupid or whatever. But jus' like you know, I know if I do say somethin' over the phone that can get my son hurt, not the police or nobody can make it here in the time it'll take you to squeeze that trigger. So believe me when I tell you I wouldn't do nothin' to endanger my son's life."

He sat back down on the couch once more and placed Christian on his leg. "I don't want no funny shit out of you. You call over there, ask to speak to C-Note, an' tell 'em to get his ass home 'cause the kid got a broken leg. If he starts to ask a bunch of questions, jus' yell at him to get his ass home an' hang up the phone in his face. An' if he tries to call back, you won't answer it. That'll really get his ass to hurry'n up."

Sheila reached for the phone again, dialed her sister's number, and prayed silently that she'd answered. The phone rang three times, and, finally, her sister answered. "Hey, Janice, did C-Note come by an' pick up those tickets yet?" Not giving her sister time to even ask her what she was talking about, Sheila quickly rushed on. "When C-Note gets there, tell him it real important that he calls me or comes straight home. His phone is off an' the only time he turns it off is when we are over there. You know how leery he is about your husband. But jus' make sure C-Note gets this message, Janice. Right now, I'm kinda' pushed for time, so I'll call you later an' we'll talk then." Sheila hung up the phone. In the back of her mind, she hoped her sister had remembered what they had previously discussed and planned in case of an emergency.

For a brief moment, Christian's scared eyes locked with hers and she had to turn away. She was beginning to abandon all hope and she started preparing herself for battle. Sheila looked over at the man holding her terrified son in his arms and knew right then and there that tonight, one of them was going to die.

Janice stood there with the phone still in her hand and a puzzled look on her face. Something definitely was up, she told herself. She thought back to the conversation she and Sheila had just yesterday. They hadn't talked about any tickets. And then an alarm bell went off in her head. She tried to remember how many times Sheila had mentioned her boyfriend's name. Three. Three times Sheila had mentioned his name. Janice thought about the call she just received, and then quickly called her husband. She explained to him the call she just got from her sister and told him that something wasn't right. Janice's husband told her he'd send a sheriff's deputy over to Sheila's address and he'd call her back when he heard something.

chapter
14

Janice hung up the phone. She felt half-relieved but apprehension still tugged at the back of her head like a drunken hangover. She picked up the phone again and dialed C-Note's cell number and cursed under her breath when the answering service came on. She left a message, telling him to call her or Sheila as soon as possible and hung up. Her husband didn't know she was an alcoholic. Janice went to the linen closet and grabbed her hidden bottle of vodka. "I might as well have me a few Apple Martinis to knock this edge off while I wait for someone to call me back," Janice said merrily, opening a new bottle of apple puckers.

C-Note cursed to himself as he got into his car. Detective Brooks had said fifteen minutes more and he would be through with his questions. C-Note looked at his watch and realized the detective had taken more like an hour and fifteen minutes. "And for what?" he asked himself as he started the car and began to drive. He was highly pissed at the detective because he had asked him the same damn questions, only in ten different ways. He recognize immediately that Detective Brooks was trying his damnedest to get him to contradict himself. C-Note just laughed. He thought about the look on

Brook's face when Brook asked him a question he had already asked, only reworded.

"You already asked me that question, Detective, but you used different words an' different sayin's. So look back through your notes an' use that same answer for this same question you keep askin' me," he told Detective Brooks without missing a beat. C-Note noticed how the detective eyeballed him coldly, but never said anything about it. Detective Brooks, he figured, was tryin' to maintain his composure an' keep it professional.

C-Note looked up at the half moon and noticed there wasn't a cloud or star in the sky. He wondered to himself why you couldn't see the stars in Los Angeles like you could in Bakersfield on a clear night like this. Then he heard his stomach growl and realized he was hungry. Quickly, he took his eyes off the road and looked in the passenger seat where he usually kept his phone.

"Aww, shit!" he said aloud, fumbling with the seat belt. He dug in his pocket and grabbed the phone, only to get the antenna stuck in his pocket and his elbow stuck in the seat belt. The phone fell between the seat and door, and he swerved slightly, trying to catch it before it hit the floor. The phone went somewhere under the seat, and he cursed again as he pulled the car over.

"Today jus' ain't my day," he said, looking around, checking out his surroundings. Perturbed, he got out of the car and began to look under the seat for the phone. "It'll be jus' my luck some young punk tryin' to earn some street stripes walks up an' shoots me for nothin.'" He finally found the phone and quickly jumped back in the driver's seat and drove off. When he flipped the phone open, he cursed again because he saw that the phone was off.

"Goddamn police," he said spitefully, turning the phone on. "They'll do any an' everything to catch a muthafucka like me." He looked at his phone and saw he had messages. He called his message center and was surprised when he heard Sheila's sister's message. And then he listened to Sheila's message, and his mind went haywire. He dialed up his house number and got no answer. He then dialed Janice's number, and she answered on the first ring.

"Where are you? My sister has been tryin' to get in touch with you for the longest." C-Note could hear the slur in her voice and knew she had been drinking again. It wasn't the first time he had heard her drunk. Janice had gotten into the habit of getting drunk, and then she would call Sheila and ramble on drunkenly about her husband and her other problems. Plenty of nights, Sheila would insist that he get on the other phone and listen. So he knew when she was drunk, and she was drunk right now.

C-Note tried to keep the worried concern out of his voice. "I was busy takin' care of some business I had. What's it got to do wit' you?"

Janice made a sarcastic sigh, and C-Note could hear her contempt through the phone. "What kinda business is too busy for your family? The Drug Business?" Janice grunted accusingly. "Or was it one of those drug dealer-lovin' hoes y'all keep on the side." She laughed drunkenly at her own remarks.

C-Note fumed, but managed to keep his temper under control. He pulled into a gas station and put the car in park. He needed to clear his head. Janice's drunkenness, Detective Brook's questioning, and his son being hurt were too overwhelming. He took a few deep breaths to calm down. Janice was still on the phone, rambling aimlessly.

"Listen, Janice," he said, cutting off her drunken chatter, "what hospital did Sheila take Christian to?"

This time, Janice snorted sarcastically. "*Hospital?* She ain't at no damn hospital. Her sorry ass is where she always is. At that drug-bought house of y'alls. Why's she gonna be at the goddamn hospital for?" Janice paused for a brief second, and C-Note could see her in his mind's eye taking another drink from a glass. He looked around the gas station to make sure his surroundings were safe. Janice's drunken words brought him out of his daze.

"Her ass ain't call her about no damn hospital. She called here talkin' crazy 'bout some damn tickets you were supposed to pick up. Now what tickets? I don't know. Jus' like this hospital shit you talkin' 'bout, I don't know that either." Janice snorted again. Then her voice became serious. "You ain't beat'n on my sister, are you?"

C-Note didn't say anything; he knew Janice was blitzed.

"You hear me talkin' to you! Answer me right this second. You probably on that shit you sell'n. I'ma call my husband an' tell'em—"

C-Note hung the phone up on her. He'd listened to all he could take. Once again, he tried his house phone and got no answer. He put the car in drive and sped out of the gas station. His day was already bad and something in the back of his mind told him it was only to get badder.

❦

SHEILA SAT ON the couch across from C-Note's best friend feeling worn down and weary. Rage was etched on her face, and her voice sounded thin and vunerable. "Why didn't you let me answer the phone? I told you it was him callin'. His number showed up on the Caller ID." There was a lot of bitterness in her voice as she cut her swollen eyes at him.

He shot her a look of poisonous fury, and Sheila heard that "don't argue with me" note in his voice. "We're doin' this *my* way, an' my way only. I wanna be the one doin' all the surprisin' when he shows up here. I don't want him to have the slightest clue that I'm here." He smiled at her again, his cold face creased with sadistic pleasure. "I can't wait to see the look on that nigga's face when he walks through the door an' sees his son in my arms, an' his bitch all fucked-up. Then he'll finally realize that the ball's been in my court all along. If he's smart, he'll un-ass the money an' I *might* let the kid live. But if he's his usual stubborn self an' makes me go through a bunch of bullshit, I guarantee I won't let any one of you live." Sheila knew the end was nearing. What she didn't know was if her son would be alright. She put the bloodied towel back to her face and sobbed uncontrollably.

C-Note maneuvered the car onto his street and slowed down not draw attention to himself. A couple of houses from his home, he could see the living-room light in his house was on. Something in his bones tingled, and he cruised slowly past his house. Through the sheer white curtains hanging in front of the big picture window, he thought he could see two shadowed figures sitting in his living room right where his couches would be at. Three houses from his home, he pulled his car into Rodney's driveway. He had known Rodney ever since he had moved into that neighborhood. Rodney had wanted to make a little money on the side of having a job and had become a client of his. Everything was running smoothly until Rodney claimed he had taken a loss. That had been seven months ago, and Rodney still owed him six hundred dollars.

C-Note called his house again and still got no answer. Something was definitely up, and he was about to get to the bottom of it. He got out of the car and went to Rodney's front porch. Before he could even knock, Rodney opened the door.

"Look, C-Note, I know I still owe you, but I'm in between jobs right now an' I'm—"

C-Note cut him off abruptly, waving a hand in the air. "I need you to do me a favor," he said matter-of-factly. Rodney looked at C-Note with skeptical eyes. He didn't know the man standing on his front porch well enough to be doing favors.

"I can't right now. I got my three kids I'm watchin', an' I can't leave them home by themselves at night."

C-Note wanted to reach through the screen and grab Rodney by his neck and literally choke the shit right out of him. But instead, he tried another tact. "Listen to me, Rodney. This don't call for no dangerous situation, nor can you get in trouble. I jus' need you to walk down to my house an' knock on the door an' ask for me. That's all there is to it."

He watched Rodney's eyes lower in suspicion behind the screen door. Then a knowing look popped into his eyes and a slight smile spread across his lips. "What you tryin' to do, catch ya' girl cheatin'?" Rodney asked with a leering grin, wanting to know why C-Note wanted him to knock on his door.

C-Note seized the moment to capitalize off Rodney's nosiness. He smiled slyly at Rodney. "Damn, Rod, you hit the nail on the head wit' the hammer this time. How you figure that out so quick? You been seein' somebody sneakin' by my house when I'm not there? Or you done heard about her fuckin' around on me in the streets?" C-Note watched Rodney soak up what he was saying like a sponge.

His ego got bigger. He knew gossip about every neighbor on the street except C-Note. And now he knew his, too. "I don't like gettin' in the middle of people's personal problems. Can't you get one of your buddies to do it? I still gotta live here when it's all said an' done. An' I don't want nobody comin' after my family for some bullshit like this."

C-Note shook his sadly. He was trying his damnedest to hold his temper under control. "Look, Rodney, I need your help. If you do this for me, let's call it even on that six hundred you owe me." C-Note watched him as greed took hold of his body. Rodney's eyes flashed with an excited twinkle. He moistened his lips and looked back over his shoulder.

"Let me get my oldest to watch out for the two little ones. I'll be right back."

C-Note watched Rodney disappear inside the house, and thought about the power of money. He knew that if it weren't for money—his money—that Rodney wouldn't come back to the door and step out onto the porch with C-Note.

Underneath the veneer of concern in Rodney's eyes, there was that greedy twinkle registered there. "Now let's get one thing straight, C-Note, before I do this." Rodney looked up and down the street as if he were expecting someone to materialize. "In no way do I want to be caught in the middle of your family affairs. Me an' my family got to live here for the next twenty years." He looked up the street again, nervous. "If my wife knew I was doin' this, she'd kill me first, an' then throw me out. She don't like no one in our business, an' she damn sure wouldn't condone me in yours. She's real anal about shit like that. An I don't need her find'n out I did this for you by some third party, 'cause she most definitely will throw my ass out of the house then." He looked at C-Note with shifty eyes to make sure he was getting his point across.

"I'm in between jobs right now, an' she's payin' all the bills, so she's lookin' for a good excuse to get rid of my ass once an' for all."

C-Note shook his head coldly. His eyes glimmered in the night like a hot flame. He had heard enough of Rodney's strict demands. "Listen here, cocksmoker! All you're doin' is knockin' on my muthafuckin' door. You ain't helpin' me do no bank robbery or no murder, so stop wit' all your worry'n. You're gettin' paid six hundred dollar to knock on a goddamn door an' ask for me. Tell me, where're you gonna make money like that for two fuckin' minutes of your lousy time?" C-Note looked at him appraisingly, and he saw the enlightenment dawn on Rodney's face.

"Let's get this show on the road," C-Note said, and they both started off towards his house. They made it to the house and stood on the other side of the garage so that they couldn't be seen from the front of the house. C-Note walked down the concrete path on the side of his house and unlocked the gate leading to the back of his home. He quietly pushed the gate open and went back to where Rodney stood nervously.

Rodney glared at C-Note impatiently as he looked up and down the street again. "I hope the nosy-ass neighbors don't think we're burglars an' call the law, thinking we're try'n to break in," he said, trying to hide the nervous twitch in his voice. He looked back at C-Note. "What it is you want me to exactly do?"

C-Note smiled at Rodney. He was somewhat glad to see the man so nervous and visibly shaking. Now he felt he was getting his money's worth. C-Note lowered his voice to a conspiratorial whisper. "Go to the door an' knock. And when Sheila answers the door, ask if I'm at home. I want you to look inside the house an' see if you can see anything out of the ordinary." Rodney heaved a courageous sigh and walked around the garage up to the front porch. He banged hard three times on the screen door and waited impatiently for someone to answer.

Sheila nearly jumped out of her skin when she heard the three loud knocks on her screen door. She wanted to scream, but thought twice about it when the gun shot up to her son's head. She looked at the man holding her son. "What do you want me to do?" she asked him in a voice so low she wasn't sure he had heard her.

He brought the gun up to his lips and whispered in the same low voice, "*Shhh.* They'll go away."

Sheila looked at her son's scared little face and began to cry again ever so quietly.

Rodney walked back around the garage to where C-Note stood hidden from the front porch. The sweat glistened on his forehead in the cool of the evening. "She didn't answer, man. Are you sure she's in there?"

C-Note looked at Rodney with a hostile glare. "Yeah, I'm sure she's in there. I want you to go back an' keep knockin'. An' if she don't answer this time, call out her name. Tell her you know she's in there an' you need to talk to her about me an' it's important." C-Note paused and thought for a few seconds. He could see Rodney was ready to protest, so he hurried on, not giving him the chance. "Tell her I was in a fender bender an' I'm alright, and I'll be home in twenty minutes or so. Tell her I tried callin' the house an' I got no answer, so I sent you to deliver the message."

Rodney stared at C-Note as if he were looking at a ghost. "I'll do it this last time. But that's it, an' that's all. I gotta get back home to my kids, I ain't got all night to be dick'n around wit' you an' this bullshit." Just as C-Note was about to go off on Rodney, he turned and walked off, back to the front porch.

Sheila's head whipped up like a snake about to strike when she heard the pounding on the door again. She heard her name being called this time as the knocking continuously persisted. She looked over at the man holding her child and could see the annoyance creasing his face. She lowered her voice to a barely audible whisper. "It's C-Note's friend from down the street. What do you want me to do?"

Sheila paused for a few seconds, thinking. "I can tell by the way he's beatin' on the door he knows I'm in here. He ain't gonna jus' leave if I don't answer the door." She watched him closely with keen, swollen eyes as he wrestled with what she had just said. Her words had done what she had wanted them to do—create doubt.

She watched as he moved next to the door out of eyesight from anyone if the door were opened. He still held Christian tightly around the waist and hugged to his chest. Well positioned, he waved at her with his gun, and she walked to the front of the door. He put his lips so close to her ear, she could the moistness of them brush her ear occasionally when he spoke. "Barely crack the door so he can't see your fuckin' face. Tell him whatever you have to in order to get his ass away from here." He stepped back away from her and hid himself next to the door again.

"Open the door," he mouthed so quietly that no sound came from his moving lips. Sheila took a deep breath and let it out. Her voice had gone hoarse from all the crying, so she sounded already like she just woke up.

She cracked the door an inch and a half and saw Rodney, who lived just a few houses down, standing there with sweat glistening on his face. "C-Note's not home right now, Rodney;

come back later on," she croaked and started to shut the door. But his words stopped her instantly.

"I know. He called me an' asked me to come down here an' tell you that he was in a fender bender an' he'll be here in twenty or thirty minutes." Rodney paused and looked back over his shoulder and then turned back to her. "He said he's been callin' an you didn't answer the phone. Is everything alright?"

Sheila gave the best little laugh she could. "Everything is good, Rodney. I jus' had a few too many drinks an' fell asleep. I'm sorry you had to walk down here, but thank you anyway for bringin' me the news. I really do appreciate it."

She closed the door and went back to the couch where she had been sitting. "Now we know why it's been takin' him so long to get here," Sheila said miserably, sitting down. She looked at the man holding her son with pleading eyes. "Can I have my son now? He'll be here, an' I jus' want my son back in my arms."

The intruder looked at her coldly and the laughed cryptically. "Oh, you'll get your son back sooner or later. But for now, he's my bargainin' chip. Whether you get him back dead or alive remains up to that stubborn, cheap nigga of yours. When he gets here, then we'll see who he loves more— his bitch or kid. Or his secret stash of money." He laughed again, this time more ominously.

"If you know him like I do, which I don't think you do," he looked Sheila squarely in the eyes, "I think you an' the kid here may be seein' your last day on earth. You of all people should know, Sheila, how C-Note is when it comes to his money. You jus' better pray that his love for money don't get you two killed tonight."

chapter

15

Rodney stepped off the porch and went back around to the side of the garage. C-Note had disappeared. He whispered C-Note's name as loud as he could without alarming the next-door neighbors. He thought about going to the back of the house where he'd seen C-Note unlock the gate but then quickly changed his mind. He knew if he saw C-Note, he'd probably want him to do something else for the six hundred dollars he owed him. As far as he was concerned, they were even. And plus, he had to get back home to his children.

He started walking down the sidewalk towards his home. Halfway there, the headlights of a car lit up the street with its beam. Rodney wanted to break and run the rest of the short distance to his house, but just quickened his pace instead. When he reached the driveway of his house, he turned around to see where the headlights had gone. He almost peed in his pants when he saw the sheriff's car pull to the curb facing the wrong way for that side of the street and turned his headlights off. The car was parked catty-corner, almost in front of C-Note's house. Rodney cursed out loud, and then thanked his lucky stars. If the sheriffs had arrived a minute earlier, he'd be in the back of a police car. Then he'd have to tell them that his kids were home alone, and then the shit would really hit the fan. His wife would find out, and he knew that would be the last straw.

"Thank you, God!" He said out loud as he threw his hands in the air with praise and walked quickly into his house.

Officer Sheena Moore pulled the sheriff's car in front of the address the dispatcher had given her and turned off the lights. She surveyed the surroundings of the middle-class neighborhood and began to wonder if she was at the correct address. When she had first pulled up, she noticed a man standing in the driveway several houses down. He did something odd with his hands and then walked into the house he was in front of. Officer Moore looked at the computer in her car again, and then back to the numbers next to the door on the house. Tonight was training night, and she was on duty with a rookie who had just got out of working the jails, and it was his first night working street patrol. He was a twenty-three-year old white boy name Billy.

Officer Moore muttered a curse word under her breath. "Billy, punch in the address to dispatch an' make sure we got the right house." She knew this would take him a while. He hadn't quite learned how to use the computer yet. Plus, she wanted some extra time to see if the serene scene would change. She knew firsthand what went on behind the doors of houses like this. Before she had become Deputy Sheena Moore, she had been Sheena Henry, abused wife of Darion Henry. Eight years she had suffered his abuse, which finally ended in a divorce and her joining the sheriff's department. Her only real desire was to combat domestic violence, so three years ago, she signed up for the department's DVU,

Domestic Violence Unit, and with a few arrests under her belt, she'd make sergeant.

She watched closely as Billy fumbled with the computer. "I would do it," Officer Moore said smiling, "but you really need to know how to work that thang. It could save your life one day."

Billy looked up from the computer at her and smiled back. "Dead as it is around here, I guarantee you, Moore, today's not that day." They both laughed openly as Billy went back to fumbling with the computer.

As soon as Rodney went back to the door, C-Note made his move. He slipped off his shoes and opened the bottom-floor bathroom window screen and climbed in through the window. Silently, he stood there in the tub and listened for a moment to make sure no one had heard him. After that, he slipped out of the bathroom to the right and went down the short hallway towards the kitchen. He started up the kitchen stairs and stopped dead in his tracks on the fourth step. His best friend's voice floated to his ears.

"You of all people should know, Sheila, how C-Note is when it comes to his money," he heard Scrappy saying. He couldn't believe what he was hearing. *Sheila and his best friend making plans about his money?!* C-Note went down to the bottom step so he could hear better. Scrappy's cold voice sent chills down his spine. "You jus' better pray that his love for money don't get you two killed tonight."

C-Note stood there, stock-still and confused. *What was Scrappy talkin' about? The two of them dyin'? How he was about his money?* Finally, he made a decision to sneak a peek around the stairwell through the kitchen and into the living room. He stuck his head out just enough to see around the banister on the bottom step. His face crumpled, and he reeled back into the wall, not wanting to believe what he saw. He put his palms over his eyes and shook his head, trying to dislodge the confusing thoughts and vision. He wanted to see again and hoped that it would be different this time.

Cautiously he peeked around the banister again—and, again—yanked his head back in shock. "This ain't no dream," he told himself. It was his *best friend* holding a gun to his only son's head. He saw the bloodied towel on the couch next to Sheila and goose bumps erupted down his body. He knew what he had to do, and had little time to do it.

He ran up the stairs as quickly and quietly as possible. Rushing through his bedroom door like a bolt of lightning, he went straight to his closet. Off the top shelf, he grabbed the .45 Ruger with the infrared and the silencer he had bought from Leeway. Quietly, he cocked the slide back and loaded a round into the chamber. He pointed the gun at the wall and the infrared beam lit up in a deadly looking red. Taking a deep breath and saying a silent prayer, he walked out of his room, went down hallway, and stopped where the wall ended and another banister started. Peeking around the corner of the wall, he could see the whole living room spread out. He took another deep breath.

One chance, and only one chance did he had to save his son, he told himself over and over again. Slowly, he let out his deep breath and inched his head to the corner of the wall.

Sheila saw the headlights of a car go out in between her house and the neighbor's house. She told herself it was C-Note and once he came through the door everything would be all right. Scrappy, too, saw the headlights and stood up from the couch where he had been sitting. He secured his arm firmly around Christian's midsection and smiled deviously at Sheila.

"I can't wait to see the look on the nigga's face when he walks through that door." He turned, facing the door, and Sheila's head did the same. They both waited in anticipation for the front door to come flying open and C-Note to come walking through. But the seconds turned to minutes, and Scrappy became restless.

"What the fuck's takin' him so long?" he asked Sheila, as if she knew.

Sheila hunched her shoulders, her expression deadpan. "I don't know, an' I don't care. I jus' want my baby back."

Scrappy shot her a scolding look. "Listen, bitch! Don't get tough 'cause C-Note's here. Remember who's holdin' the gun here." Anticipation got the best of him. Scrappy walked over to the window, flattened his back against the wall, and with his gun hand, moved the sheer white curtains and peeked out. He froze for a moment, then he slowly turned his head towards Sheila.

"It's the muthafuckin' police!!" He turned and looked out the window once more. "They're jus' sittin' there." He looked back over to Sheila. "I hope you wasn't dumb enough to call the police, 'cause if you did, you an' this kid is good as dead." He turned his head and peeked back out the window. Sheila saw his body go rigid. Then he quickly twisted his head towards her with a shocked look on his face. "I can't believe this bullshit!" he said in a nervous, high-pitched voice. "They're gettin' outta the fuckin' car!"

Deputy Moore knew Billy would be another few minutes on the computer. Her legs were cramping from riding in the car all day. Plus, Billy's cheap cologne was overpowering. "I'm steppin' out the car to stretch my legs an' get some fresh air. An' next time you're puttin' on cologne, don't put so damn much on. That shit is givin' me a headache."

Billy looked up from the computer, smiling at her. She opened the door and began to get out. "Don't be lookin' at me with that shit-faced grin. You need to be concentrating on that computer so we can get the hell outta here."

C-Note stood at the top of the stairs, peeking around the wall at Scrappy, who, in turn, was peeking out of the picture window. Everything was all quiet except his own voice in his head, and it kept repeating over and over again: "One chance only." C-Note knew what "one chance only" meant, and he didn't need his brain to keep reminding him. His kid's life was at stake, and that's all he wanted to concentrate on.

Everything seemed to be happening in slow motion. He watched Scrappy turn and say something to Sheila and then turn back to peek out of the window. He raised the .45 caliber and put the infrared beam on Scrappy's hand holding the gun. He took one last deep breath, and squeezed the trigger on the .45 three times.

Deputy Moore had just finished stretching when the window to the house the dispatcher had sent her to shattered in a thousand tiny shards of glass. Something powerful hit the hood of the police car, and she quickly jumped behind a tree.

"Take cover!" Deputy Moore yelled at Billy as she removed her service weapon from the holster on her hip. Billy jumped out of the car and ducked behind the back passenger door of the sheriff's car. He began to shake uncontrollably.

"What do you want me to do?" he yelled at Officer Moore from the other side of the vehicle.

Officer Moore could hear the panic in the rookie's voice

and hoped like hell he wouldn't fall to pieces. "Remember procedures, Billy," she yelled back to him. "Get on your radio an' call it in. 'Shots fired at officer.' An' give them the location. An' tell'm to hurry up an' send backup."

She heard Billy doing as he was told and took a deep breath herself. For some strange reason, she noticed she wasn't nervous or scared. But she sure as hell was excited. Her vagina began to moisten, and she really liked the feeling. "Tonight," Deputy Moore told herself with a grim smile, "I'm getting my first kill."

It all happened so fast that Sheila didn't have time to think about what she had to do in order to protect her child. At first she couldn't comprehend what happened. The gun in Scrappy's hand mysteriously exploded into pieces. Then the picture window shattered, raining glass everywhere. And then she saw Christian on the floor, lying next to Scrappy just out of reach and finally freed from his arms. Sheila didn't hesitate. She sprang from the couch and grabbed her son, then ran to the door and twisted the locks.

Just as she was running out the door, she caught a glimpse of C-Note in the corner of her eyes coming down the stairs with a gun in his hand. But fear told her to run—*run* while she had her son in her arms. Sheila never looked back. She ran through the front door like a sprinter headed for the finish line, like Rachel Alexandra, the only filly in 85 years to recently win the Preakness Stakes horse race, leaving all those male horses behind her, eating her dust.

Deputy Moore had her gun ready. She could hear the locks being turned on the door of the house where the window had just shattered. She raised her gun and took aim at the door. Tightening her finger on the trigger, she exhaled a deep breath and watched as the door hastily swung open.

Sheila hit the front porch like a lightning bolt. She knew Rodney was at home up the street, but saw the sheriff's car parked in between hers and the neighbor's house. Then she saw the officer behind a tree with a gun pointed at her. She was so scared of being shot by the police that all she could do was start screaming, "He's got a gun! He's try'n to kill me an' my baby!"

Deputy Moore silently thanked God that she hadn't pulled the trigger. She had three pounds of the four pounds of pressure needed to pull the trigger on her gun aimed at the woman and child. Sheila saw Deputy Moore standing behind the tree. Deputy Moore thought of all the training she'd been through and took charge of the situation immediately.

She screamed frantically, "Billy, take the woman and kid to safety behind that parked car across the street." Billy nervously came out from his hiding place as Deputy Moore took aim again at the door. "I got you covered, Billy, hurry the fuck up!"

Billy grabbed Sheila by the arm and quickly rushed her and the child across the street behind the parked car. Deputy Moore became excited again. From the looks of the beaten woman's face, she knew she was dealing with a madman. The sensitive area between her legs began to moisten once more, and it took her every once of willpower she had not to rub herself. Her past thoughts came flooding into her mind of her ex-husband's daily abuse. "This muthafucka's gonna pay with his life," she vowed to herself, "for all the abused women in the world." She quickly stole a look to make sure Billy had the victims safe and to make sure Billy couldn't see her. She wanted to keep him occupied, so when it came time for her to tell her story, only she would be able to tell it.

"Billy, get on your radio an' request an ambulance. An' while you're at it, contact dispatch and see where the hell backup is. Someone should've been here by now." She trained her eyes back on the house and reached down to feel the throwaway gun strapped to her ankle. Her whole body was numb except for that sweet, aroused sensation between her legs. All she had to do is wait, she told herself, because once she had the shot, she was taking it.

C-Note came down the stairs slowly, in a daze. He still had his gun aimed on his once-upon-a-time best friend. He'd seen Sheila grab Christian and run out the front door.

Scrappy lay sprawled on the floor in front of the picture window, bleeding from his hand and hip. The first bullet had hit him in his gun hand. The second bullet went through the window shattering it. The third bullet lodged itself in the side of the fatty tissues on his hip.

Scrappy looked up and saw C-Note coming down the steps. He could see the look on C-Note's face was far more of disappointment than anger. Also, he could tell by the look on what was once his best friend's face that his soul was torn, just as his heart was. Scrappy tossed his head back and laughed hysterically. Unconsciously, he rubbed his bleeding hand across his face, making himself look even crazier than he was.

"I can't believe this shit," Scrappy said, shaking his head. "Here I am, worryin' about the goddamn sheriffs outside, an' you fuckin' shoot me from behind. What a fuckin' movie this would make! You think we got a shot at a movie deal?" He laughed again wildly.

C-Note paused on the last step, trying to clear his eyes as well as his head. The shock was so great it took him a few seconds to fill his lungs with air. The world went deaf to his ears, and he seemed incapable of speech. A small flash of bitter memory came back to him of the fight he and Scrappy had as kids. C-Note seemed perturbed, and then his face hardened. He felt he was entitled to an explanation.

"After all these years we've been like brothers to one another. What would make you put a gun to my child's head?"

Scrappy's black eyes flashed a chilling coldness, and a mad look plastered itself across his face. "We stopped bein' brothers when that bitch of yours came into the picture."

C-Note stepped off the last step with his gun still pointed at Scrappy. A long silence ensued, and then Scrappy continued. "We were like brothers. But that bitch, Sheila, changed you. We use to hang out all day an' every day. We use to get money together in these streets. We fucked broads together." Scrappy paused briefly, shaking his head side to side. "We use to beat up niggas an' shoot up fools together—*that's* the C-Note I once knew. Not this sorry muthafucka standin' in front of me pointin' a gun. I don't know who he *is*." Scrappy wiped the sweat off his forehead with his bleeding hand and smeared more blood across his face.

C-Note could see Scrappy wanted to say more, so he just let him roll on. "It's really not about the bitch, Sheila, it's about *you*." He looked C-Note squarely in the eyes. "All our lives I tried to convince myself that we were the same. I really wanted to believe we were. But when Sheila started comin' around, that's when I knew we weren't. I tried over an' over again to fix it so that we were one. We thought alike, did the same things alike, liked the same things. But that jus' wasn't true. An' when Sheila came around, it only confirmed the thought I was try'n' to hide.

"You weren't like me, dedicated to the streets. You weren't loyal to our neighborhood an' willin' to die for it. The first chance you got, you moved up outta the 'hood an' only came back to drain it for its cash." Scrappy had a disgusted look on his face.

"You can make money in the 'hood, but you can't live in the hood. That's total bullshit!" Scrappy couldn't disguise his emotions. He smiled sourly at C-Note. "All the money you made in the 'hood really ain't yours. It stopped bein' yours when you moved over here. So rightfully, that money belongs to *me* an' *I'm* takin' what's mine."

C-Note couldn't believe what he was hearing coming out of his best friend's mouth. He looked at Scrappy incredulously. There was more, and in his heart he knew it. Scrappy's face showed more than its usual tic of agitation—the expression on his face was dark and wrathful.

C-Note sensed his resentment. "You done all this murder'n and mayhem jus' because I moved outta the 'hood? Because I didn't want my family in the middle of a war zone?" C-Note paused, as tangled images and memories of misery flooded his thoughts. The change in his face was slow and ominous.

"If it was me you wanted to ruin, why do that to all them people? Some of them were mutual friends, from the same 'hood we're from."

Scrappy threw his head back and laughed inhumanly. "WHY? Is *that* your prize question?" Scrappy shook his head sadly, and then focused his cold eyes spewing hate on C-Note. "You're askin' me why I did what I did? You need to be questioning yourself. Here it is, you have all these people out pushin' your poison for you, sellin' it to our mothers an' fathers, to our brothers an' sisters. An' why? So you can get up outta the ghetto an' leave everybody else behind. You tell me, C-Note, how ironic is that?" Scrappy saw the look on his best friend's face and continued.

"Look at all the people you're killin'. I did society a favor." He paused and lifted himself up on one elbow, and then rolled on again. "Think about what I did. I ended the lives of all those you had sellin' dope, an' that, in turn, saves the lives of those who use it. You were my next victim, an' then I was goin' after that muthafucka who sells you the shit, Rico."

Scrappy looked at C-Note with triumph in his eyes. "I listened when Cat and Snake talked about you retirin' from the dope game. But I want you to think about it. All those stupid niggas you had sellin' dope wasn't goin' to stop jus' because you did. I doubt that. They were your protégés; they looked up to you. They all would've continued to sell dope until they reached your status. Then think of how fucked-up our street would be and how many people would be dyin' of the drugs."

C-Note almost laughed but didn't. Some of what Scrappy said he found to be true. He seemed repulsed for a brief moment, his anguish was apparent. He looked at Scrappy lying on the floor, cocked up on one elbow, smiling wolfishly. Then he stepped toward his friend on the floor. "You took it upon yourself to play God wit' so many people's lives, now I'm about to play God with yours."

Scrappy tossed his head back and howled with insane laughter. He looked at the gun in C-Note's hand and then at his dark face. "Whatcha' gonna do, kill me? You can't. The sheriffs are outside." Scrappy nodded his head towards the window. "Go on, look. They're out there. Go on an' ruin your fuckin' life some more. You're not the original C-Note I once knew. Ohhh nooo! You're the new an' improved version. The smart one who only loves money—not the one I grew up wit."

C-Note edged closer, and suddenly, he felt transported out of reality and into a dream. His ears heard no sound, and his head teemed with images of his childhood. He saw himself and Scrappy riding bikes; standing on the curb waiting for the ice-cream truck; walking to the bus stop in the early morning, fighting with bullies and rival gang members; joy riding in rented cars from crackheads; ditching school and losing their virginity. He recalled the first time they were shot at. And the first time they had shot at someone. C-Note's memory hung on to these images like a pit bull. He couldn't conceal his emotions any longer and tears ran from the corner of his eyes.

"Me an' you weren't only best friends, we were family. You were closer to me than my own two cousins. Than Sheila. You were there for me when they wasn't. Women come an' go, you an' I know that. But what I was doin' was for my son." C-Note tried to hide the hurt and disappointment in his voice but couldn't.

"I didn't want my son growin' up the way we did. Nor did I want him to have to see it. You can remember the cold nights when our parents would go on crack sprees an' we wouldn't have nothin' to eat. I know you can remember the lights bein' cut off every other month and not havin' no hot water or heat." C-Note wiped the tears running down his cheeks. "You can't forget how we stole candy an' chips an' then had to save them because we didn't know if we would eat that night. An' then we got smart when the store owners got hip to our stealin' candy and chips, so we started stealin' lunch meat and Top Ramen."

He looked at Scrappy's heartless and indifferent face, still wearing a cold smirk. "I still remember your words from twenty years ago. It was the smartest thing you ever said, an' I kept it always in my head. It made the most sense to me at a time when we were most desperate." C-Note paused, and Scrappy looked at him with puzzled eyes.

"An' what was that?" Scrappy snorted, not hiding his resentment.

C-Note wiped his tears again. By now, he had finalized in his mind what he had to do. "We were eatin' the food we had stole, an' I guess it jus' popped in your mind. You said, 'Why are we stealin' this petty shit? We might as well go for the gusto. Either way, we're gonna get the same amount of time. If we steal from the corner store an' get caught, why can't we steal from the grocery stores? If we're goin' to do somethin' like that, we might as well do it right. From now on, everythin' we do, we do it to the fullest.'"

C-Note's face changed, and so did Scrappy's. "Everything I did, I always tried to take it to its max." C-Note's voice hardened, and he frowned cruelly. "Sellin' dope and gang bangin', I became the best at it. But I guess you were right when you said I changed, because now I realize I did. I figured out gang bangin' wasn't payin' the bills, an' dope was. I guess the sayin' is true about money, it does change you after a while. I seen gang bangin' was limiting me from makin' money outside the 'hood, so I gave it up an' recognized shootin' a nigga like me from another neighborhood was senseless. They were just like me, wanting a better life for themselves an' their families."

C-Note took a deep breath and let it out. "An' here you come along an' ruin everybody an' everything I had goin'." C-Note leveled the gun to Scrappy's face. "Because I considered you my brother an' me my brother's keeper, I'm now givin' you yo' chance to make amends with God."

240

Scrappy threw his head back and laughed hysterically. "This ain't no fuckin' movie, C-Note. An' the shit don't always have a fairytale endin.'" He paused and licked his lips. "I got all your money stashed. An' when the sheriffs come in here an' get us, I'll do six months to a year for kickin' your bitch's ass, an' then I'll be back on the streets—spendin' your hard-earned dough. So 'make amends' my ass. Fuck you! An' fuck God! You ain't got the heart to shoot me wit' the sheriff right outside. Think about your family you love so much. You shoot me, you're goin' to jail. An' I guarantee that bitch, Sheila, will have another man. An' that son you love so much will be callin' *him* daddy." Scrappy threw his head back again, and boasted proudly. "You really ain't the same nigga I grew up wit' twenty years ago."

chapter
16

Deputy Moore stood behind the tree with her gun aimed at the house. The light from the living room made it easy to see through the sheer white curtains. Out of nowhere, the shadow of a man emerged and he seemed to be walking towards the broken picture window. She could see clearly that the shadow of the man had something long in his hand. A few neighbors stood on their porches watching the drama unfold. Deputy Moore knew she had to make it look good.

"Billy, you got the woman an' kid safe?" she yelled over her shoulder loud enough for all who stood watching to hear. "I got the suspect in sight. You jus' make sure they're safe." She heard Billy's nervous voice yell they were safe, and she concentrated on the shadow in the window. She remembered the procedures she was taught in the academy. She relaxed her shoulders, closed one eye, and took aim.

"Drop what's in your hands an' come out with your hands in the air. I repeat, drop what's in your hands an' come out with your hands in the air." Deputy Moore looked around her. She wanted to be satisfied that all who watched from their porches and driveways heard her attempt to get the suspect to drop the weapon. She repeated it one more time, even louder than the first two times. Then she aimed her gun at the shadow's head and smiled to herself. She saw her abusive ex-husband's face on the shadow where the face would be. All the years of abuse she'd been through came spinning through her head like a top. She tightened her finger on the trigger and exhaled a breath to relax more.

"Jus' one more step, Darion, an' your ass is dead!" she said whisper to herself. Deputy Moore was in such a trance, she hadn't realized she said her abusive ex-husband's name.

<hr />

C-NOTE STOOD THERE in front of the picture window with Scrappy on one elbow sprawled on the floor. He was furious he'd got caught in such a sucker's situation. Tears threatened his eyeballs again, but he refused them the privilege of running down his face. He looked at the laughing madman who was once his best friend, and more thoughts of their past flashed through his head. The good times and the bad times.

Somewhere in his mind, C-Note heard a woman's voice, but he didn't comprehend what she saying. He didn't *want* to comprehend. He just wanted to stop the reign of madness caused by the psychotic, crazed man in front of him. He aimed his gun at Scrappy's face, who stopped laughing abruptly. Scrappy looked in C-Note's eyes and saw what he knew was there all along. Fear seized his whole body, and he began to shake uncontrollably. Just then, Scrappy realized he'd pushed C-Note to the point of no return. He opened his mouth to scream, but it was too late.

C-Note squeezed the trigger twice on the .45 caliber. He watched as flames jumped out of the suppressor and the first bullet tore through Scrappy's eye socket and blew out the back of his brains. Just like his victims, C-Note wanted Scrappy's funeral closed casket. The second bullet ripped off his chin and went into his neck.

He stood there watching the blood spout like a fountain when he heard three pops like a firecracker. Now, he felt something hit him in the shoulder hard, and then another searing pain in his neck. His brain told his body to run, but his legs gave out from under him. C-Note looked up at the white ceiling and smiled. Heaven was pure white he told himself. *Stop the pain* his brain told him, and he tried to reach for the wound at his neck, but his arms wouldn't move. He felt God tugging at his soul and closed his mind and eyes to give up what he could not control. Everything went black, and finally, he felt peace.

chapter

Epilogue

TWENTY-THREE MONTHS LATER ...
"It's chow time, chow time, chow time," came the correction officer's voice over the PA system. "You have thirty minutes before chow, so wake up an' get dressed and be ready for chow when the gates rack."

C-Note stayed in bed while his cellmate, Carl, jumped off his top bunk and took a piss. Carl was mentally handicapped, but other than that, he was fine. Carl grabbed his washcloth from the homemade clothesline they had made from old sheets. Then he put his washcloth in the sink and walked over to C-Note's bottom bunk. He reached under C-Note's bunk and pulled out the paraplegic wheelchair, then shook C-Note's shoulder.

"Wake up! Wake up! It's time to eat, C-Nose." Because of his mental disability, he couldn't pronounce C-Note's name correctly. He put his big hands under C-Note's armpits and began to lift him out of the bed.

Enough of try'n to play asleep, C-Note thought to himself. He opened his eyes, and he and Carl were face to face. "Put me the fuck down! I told you I can get up on my own."

Carl laid C-Note back down with a crushed look on his face. C-Note felt bad. All Carl was trying to do was help him.

"Listen, Carl," he said apologetically, lifting himself up on both elbows, "I know you're tryin' to be helpful, but let me get up on my own. You seen me do it plenty of times, so let me do it by myself." C-Note looked at Carl's still-hurt face. "You gotta let me do it myself, Carl, 'cause one day they might move you an' I'll be here all alone. An' if I can't get up by myself, then I'll lie here an' die. You know, like I know, those CO's ain't gonna help my black ass."

Carl's sad face turned into a smile. "I'm sorry, C-Nose. I won't do it ever, ever, ever again. I promise."

C-Note smiled at Carl. "I heard that yesterday. An' the day before that. An' the day before. An' the day—"

Carl waved his big hand in the air. "All right! All right! You're confusin' me." Carl brushed his teeth and washed his face. "The sink's all yours," he said looking through the bars of the cell. "I'm all finished."

C-Note lay back down. Once or twice a week he found himself in a bad mood. "I ain't goin' to chow today, Carl. You go on wit'out me."

Carl's head whipped around like a snake. "If you don't eat breakfast, C-Nose, you don't get no lunch, too."

C-Note pointed to a half-full bag filled with prison commissary food next to his head on his bunk. "I got enough food to last me two weeks, Carl. You go on without me."

The bar door on the cell slowly opened, and Carl stepped out. "I'll see ya' later on, C-Nose. I got special school today."

C-Note waved a hand. "Later, Carl," he said candidly, smiling to himself. "Don't come back too soon, ya' hear."

The bar door started to close, and C-Note rolled on his side, facing the wall. He lay there thinking how drastically his life changed because of money. It really was the root to all evil, he mused to himself. He thought about a book he had read years ago called Street Poison. He remembered what the writer had said would eventually happen if you sold drugs. Three things, he said, would happen. "You either wind up dead, broke, or in jail." C-Note couldn't help but think that two and three-quarters of those three things had happened to him. He rolled over and pulled his wheelchair close to his bed, climbed in it, and pushed himself up to the three-inch window in his cell. The sun was coming up behind the mountains. He loved the beautiful sight.

How ironic, he thought to himself, *of all the simple things you could love, watching the sun rise over the mountain is certainly one of them.* The mountains and the sun couldn't hurt him like people did. Tears came to his eyes and slid down both cheeks. He thought about all the lives he had ruined, and even his own. Sheila had left him his first year in jail. She sent Christian to live somewhere down South with her mother. She claimed she had had a miscarriage, but Cat had written him a letter. C-Note reached under the thin mat and grabbed the letter. Every time he was in this bad mood, he read the letter to remind himself that some people were in worse shape than he was. He opened the letter and began to read.

What's up, Cousin, what it do?
By the time this letter reaches your fingertips, I hope you're in good spirits, because what I have to tell you ain't so good. First of all, I sent you a postal money order for three grand. I know it's not all I told you, but I have my reasons why I didn't send it all. I'll get to that later.

I hear Christian is doing fine down South with Sheila's mother. But that Sheila, she's a piece of work. Take if from me right here and now—forget about her, cousin. I, like you, thought she would at least stay down, even if she wasn't loyal or faithful. But the bitch ain't shit! I know she's the mother of your child, but I got to call it like I see it.

A few months after you went to the clinker, she met up with a fast-talkin' Jamaican dude who had a little money. The dude was staying two or three nights a week at first. An' then he just moved on in. Well, to make a long story short, 'cause I ain't the writing type, I do enough of that in school. The Jamaican dude got her hooked on heroin and crack. Once she got that monkey on her back, he conned her into sighing over the house to him for fifteen thousand funky-ass dollars. I'm sorry I didn't get to her before he did. I know you didn't owe much on the house, 'cause I remember you saying something about payin' it off before you moved to the new one you were planning to buy. But the house is long gone, jus' like she is. Last I heard, she was turnin' tricks to support her habit. I know you think you got problems now, so that's why I told you so she won't be one of those problems.

Now, cousin, on to some more wild shit. You ain't gonna believe this shit, but I'm gonna tell you anyway 'cause it's been all over the news. Your boy you killed, Scrappy, as it turns out, had two cousins from Louisiana, Johnny and Larry. Well, from the story the news is tellin', Scrappy sent for the two imbeciles to come down here and rob dope houses. You know whose houses they were. But anyway, they came down here, robbed the houses, and went back to Louisiana.

Larry took the money they had robbed and bought a small house and a couple of acres. Johnny, on the other hand, took his money and blew it on drugs, women, and booze. Johnny got broke quick and broke into Larry's house and stole what money Larry had left. Larry knew it was Johnny who broke in his house, because Johnny was the only person Larry had showed where he had stashed his money. Larry caught Johnny at a strip club spendin' his money and killed him in front of everybody there.

So, they sent Larry to prison for life in one of those famous prisons they're known for making you work all day no matter what the weather was like. Larry, being half-witted and all, came up with a plan that he thought was ingenuous. He got in touch with detectives down here and told them about the murders he and Johnny had done. His dumb-ass went all the way and signed a confession letter as long as the detectives promised him he didn't have to do his time in Louisiana. Well, the detectives did just that for him. They got Larry back to California and charged him with so many murders, I think even he lost track of how many it was.

You do remember the day care, too, that blew up with one of the houses? It didn't take a jury long with that signed confession. They gave Larry the death penalty, and he's up in San Quentin goin' crazy. That's good. I hope he gets what he deserves. Well, I'm about to end this letter, but before I do, let me fill you in on what's goin' on with me. I took the money I made with you and took my ass back to college. I had to. The game an' shit all around me was coming down fast. First you and what you went through, and then some shit with Snake. The Feds picked Snake up and hit him with the RICO Act. They're tryin' to give him twenty-five years unless he snitches!

I don't know what he's gonna do, so I cleaned up my shit. I took what I needed out of the game, and now, I'm living a productive life. Thank you for helping me keep my head on straight and not letting me get blinded by the money we were making. When your thirteen years are up, I'll repay you then by making your life as comfortable as possible with the millions I've made while you were gone. It's the least I can do for a Black brother who always stayed as true as you!

Your relative,
The Cat

C-Note folded the letter and put it back in its envelope and under his bed mat. The sun was halfway up over the mountains, and everything in its wake seemed to be the color of burnt orange. He sat there and thought about how money had come into his life at an early age and how it had ruined him and his family and his friends, and then took leave so easily, leaving all in its path devastated and destroyed. He thought about how quickly his life had collapsed—five years for the manslaughter of his best friend and eight years from the Feds for not telling who and where he had gotten the gun and the silencer from.

He realized he had caused enough grief and didn't want anyone else to feel the pain he was feeling. The money Leeway's folks were making from the gun sales would catch up to them soon enough, just as it did to C-Note. He didn't want any part in telling the Feds where the gun came from, because ultimately, he knew that money would be the reason, and as usual, it would be playing a major part as it always does. C-Note thought about what money did to him, the loss of his son, the loss of his future wife, the loss of friends and their lives, the loss of him ever walking again, and the loss of his freedom.

He smiled as the sun finally made it up over the mountains and bitterly thought to himself, *Money does bring drama, and it really is the ROOT OF ALL EVIL.*

THE END

STREET ENTERTAINMENT WRITING ETC

PROUDLY ANNOUNCES

STREET POISNED II
"I Lied! I Returned To The Game"

Christopher Buchanan

Coming in Paperback from

STREET ENTERTAINMENT WRITING ETC

The following is a preview from

STREET POISNED II

Prologue

THE YEAR IS 1999, and we are coming into a new millennium. To tell this story is somewhat difficult, yet, it really is easy. I consider it a tale and in some sense, it's the truth, *reality*. I must tell it like I honestly know how, and that is the way it happened. Better yet, the way it's still goin' down.

Like a whirlpool, I was snagged and pulled back into the game. I thought when I was released from prison the first time, I had it down pat. I was the mastermind of the game of life. But in all actuality, I was an ignoramus—gullible, weak-minded, dim-witted, and a whole buncha more adjectives that you can probably think of. Needless to say—but I'm going to anyway—I ended up back where I said I'd never return. On top of that, I lost my broad and my young family because of me being dishonest with myself while out there. I never thought about the seriousness of the bullshit I returned to. My iron will continue to feed me misleading thoughts, thoughts that I believed were stored in my past. But as I adjusted back in society, those thoughts and ways of my past resurfaced, landing me in the joint back through the revolving door.

My foolish pride is rebelling against me telling the story of my irrational and unwise mishaps. Self-pity, I feel none. I, again, reaped what I **had** sown. The price I'm paying is the loss of everything that is of real value to me. Money can't buy it back either. Out the window has gone my family. Vanished is my freedom. My erratic sense of thinking foiled me for the umpteenth time. Again, the wicked streets outmatched me. Now I'm back on the sideline, watching instead of participating. Besides all that, the endless conflicts I'm experiencing in trying to find myself and my position in life is a struggle that I can't seem to endure. I'm stuck in a timeless void, unable to advance or grow. I have to detach myself from old friends and the so-called *hood*. Regardless of my disgrace, I have to tone my ethics and correct my living habits; not only for me, but, also, for my children. Women come and go, but children are there forever.

Street Poisoned II is charged with vitality written straight from the soul, as well as the streets. It's a page-flipping story that is convicting and fascinating, engrossingly hypnotic and hard-hitting. I could continue with the dazzling adjectives and the creative tongue, but instead, I'll end it and let you lose yourself and find out what it feels like to be caught up in the game...

Chris

chapter one
My Day Upon Arrival

IT WAS THE BEGINNING OF MARCH, and I was eager to leave the place. I'd been there for nine months, since mid-June, and was happy to finally be leaving. My dress-outs were fancy, and I quickly put them on. My girlfriend at the time, or you could have called her my common-law wife due to the longevity of our relationship, had plugged me up with some fresh Fubu. White, red, and black shirt with black Fubu pants to match. Shoes were Jordan, the same colors as the shirt. I was close to a thousand miles away from L.A. To get home required a bus ride, an airplane ride, and a car ride. When the doors to prison opened, I finally felt free after fourteen months and twenty days. I almost ran before I caught myself. Where was I going in the desert of Susanville?

The bus finally came after five cigarettes and a Pepsi. Smoking cigarettes was another bad habit I had picked up in the joint. But like usual, I told myself I would stop. The bus ride was a pleasant thirty minutes into Reno, Nevada, and I sat back and absorbed the view with uncuffed hands for a change. The now-freed inmates who also rode the bus (they were picked up from other prisons before they had got to me) chatted idly about what they were going to do once they got home. All their clamor flew over my head and out the window with the breeze. I didn't say anything, solely occupied with my own thoughts.

The bus ride ended at the airport for me. I couldn't see myself taking any transportation other than a plane. A Greyhound would've taken seventeen hours and Amtrak just a slight bit under half that. I chose a plane because of my impatience. My children were the most important things pounding in my head at the time. I was truly in agony, wanting to see and hold them in my arms. I wanted to kiss them, play with them, and talk to them. I needed to ask their forgiveness for my sudden abandonment of them. I had to let them know I truly loved them. My mind reeled on the plane at the thought of my son meeting me at the airport. I had been gone, in jail and in prison for half of his life and I felt apprehensive about meeting him now. I had a reason for feeling this way, or did I?

The plane landed smoothly and that's when the butterflies began to flutter in my stomach. I knew that my woman wouldn't be late because she had been anticipating my arrival for fourteen months. I exited the plane and slowly strolled through the terminal, savoring my freedom. I tried hard not to think of the place I had just left. But the thought rested freshly in the back of my mind. As I tried to erase the thoughts of prison, my mind was conjuring up what would be the first thing I'd do when I saw my child and girl. So many thoughts crowded together in so little time that I just decided to take it in stride. You know, go with the flow and ride the wave in.

It seemed no time to cover the distance of half the airport. I had only my novels, a few pictures, and some school papers for a computer class I had taken, showing me how to work Windows '95. I didn't have to wait for any luggage. I stepped from the terminal doors and immediately saw my girl's black Mazda parked in the green loading zone. I could see the other side of her face as she peered through the other door, expecting me to come through it. I slid up smoothly to the back door and opened it. She jumped, a little startled. "Stupid ass," she said to me as I slid in the backseat next to my son's car seat.

It took my son several seconds to register who I was before his face broke into a broad grin. "Daa Daa!!" he exclaimed, trying to get loose from the restraints of the car seat. I tickled his stomach and undid the safety lock on the car seat. Instantly, he jumped into my lap, showering me with kisses and hugs.

I wrapped an arm around his waist as he stood up in my lap and his mother put the car in drive and pulled away from the curb. Then I reached to the front and ruffled my girl's freshly done hair with my other hand. "Long time no see," I said sarcastically.

With a fake pout, she said, "Don't start acting an ass already. I did my share of comin' to visit you." I didn't reply to that. She was right.

I sat my son back in his car seat and leaned up between the seats and gave her the wettest kiss on her tender cheek. She knew I was glad to see her, just like I knew she was delighted to see me.

In a voice barely audible and choked, I said, "Thanks. Thanks for everything—for bein' there, for comin' to see me all those miles, for the money, the packages you sent, and the letters and phone conversations. Thanks for everything."

I saw her look at me in the rearview mirror; my eyes were clouded with tears. She quickly put her eyes back on the road.

With a cracked voice and tears filling her eyes, she said, "Let's just hope you're here to stay with us this time."

I had no answer to that, so I went back to playing with my son. I reached over and pulled him out of his safety seat and kissed him affectionately with a slobbery kiss.

"Uhhhg!" he said, wiping his cheek where I had just kissed. I laughed and put him back in his seat, buckling up the straps as we were getting on the 105 Freeway.

"How was your trip home on the plane?" Dink asked as she moved the car swiftly into the carpool lane.

"Same as all my other trips on planes," I answered, looking at the Xerox Building on my right side. Before I had gone to prison, I had partied at a club called The Golden Tail in that same building. Friends who had been writing me told me that the club had closed.

"Shit," I almost cursed aloud. Now some of the false promises I had made to several women came to me. I quickly put those thoughts somewhere in the farthest part in the back of my mind. Actually, I had a few days before I needed to deal with some of those things. I'd been released on the 10th of March, but everyone believed me to be coming home on the 14th. Dink saw the look on my face through the rearview mirror. She had been observing me closely, and I hadn't been paying attention. Now she caught me a little off-guard.

"Unless you done went crazy or somethin', you sure are actin' weird."

I moved uneasily under her stare in the rearview mirror.

"Disgraced!" I said, shaking my head in the negative. "I feel worthless."

She said nothing to this. I did feel worthless. Here I was, riding home with the woman I felt I really wanted to spend the rest of my life with and I'm thinking about the different women who had been writing me. It was scandalous, downright scandalous. Shamefaced, I said, "There are a lot of issues I must deal with, secretly as well as openly."

Her face twisted as I said this. She was clearly surprised by this statement. "I see you still haven't learned to live with guilt," she said dryly.

My throat swelled so tightly, I was barely able to swallow. She gave me a sly look. Her demeanor changed slightly. It was as if she could read my thoughts, and I honestly believed she could because she then said almost coolly, "You don't owe me nothin'. If it ain't to be, please let me know right now."

I knew she was a devoted woman at heart, even though my misguided thinking wanted me to believe something else. I wanted to believe she had been faithful for fourteen months, but street instinct wouldn't allow me to believe that. "Keep it real," I said, smirking with a devious grin. It was like me to think I was being clever. "You can tell me how many niggas you screwed while I was gone."

She was staring at me with distaste. Her startled eyes went cold as ice when she replied, "As many dicks as you took while you were in there."

I was a little hurt and shocked at first. I smiled a sad smile, trying to cover my embarrassment. I'll never forget her face when she said this. That was a phrase I would always remember. It shattered some of my illusions about her. Her hardness was still there.

"Don't say things like that around my son," I said with the utmost seriousness. She just stared at me for a brief moment, her eyes hard and calculating. I went back to playing with Kamal without anymore harsh words.

www.ingramcontent.com/pod-product-compliance
Lightning Source LLC
Chambersburg PA
CBHW032025240626
47154CB00003B/788